TERENCE BAILEY

SMALL JUSTICE

THE SARA JONES CYCLE BOOK THREE

Published by Accent Press Ltd 2019
Octavo House
West Bute Street
Cardiff
CF10 5LJ

www.accentpress.co.uk

The story contained within this book is a work of fiction. Names and characters are the product of the author's imagination and any resemblance to actual persons, living or dead, is entirely coincidental.

ISBN 9781786153814
eISBN 9781786153807

Printed and bound in Great Britain by Clays Ltd, Elcograf S.p.A

For Julian

ACKNOWLEDGEMENTS

Thanks to Greg Rees and Katrin Lloyd at Accent Press. Dr David W. Grossman and Inspector Alun Samuel have been invaluable, as ever. Thanks also to Mandy Samuel for all her help.

PROLOGUE

Long before sunrise, two young women emerged from a house in the Elm Park area of Hornchurch, Essex. The younger one shivered and plunged her hands into the pockets of her black leather jacket. The older, already a couple years into her twenties, smiled reassuringly and said, 'Cold?'

'It was toasty inside,' the younger woman replied. 'Like we were in…' She half-shut her eyes – it made the light from the streetlamp all streaky – and tried to think of somewhere famous for being sunny. In her mind's eye she saw palm trees, and a beach, and teddy bears in swimsuits. But that wasn't a real place. It was something she'd seen in a book, a long time ago. She sighed. On any other day, she could have listed a lot of real places. Right now, though, she couldn't recall a single one. Finally, she shook her head and settled for, 'Like we were in a hot country,'

'You'll be warm when we get going,' the other woman promised. 'Anyway, it's not so cold. It's early April.'

The girl shrugged. She couldn't remember how cold April was supposed to be, either.

The block-paved driveway was nearly twice as wide as its neighbour's, because this was an end-of-terrace house. That was why it could hold two cars side-by-side. One was a twenty-year-old Fiesta. It was rusty and dented, but true Essex royalty nonetheless. It had been built just down the road in Dagenham, back when the plant still made complete automobiles. The other car was foreign and newer – but not much newer. The young women headed for the Fiesta.

Inside, the girl in the thin leather jacket said, 'Brrr! It's just as cold in here.'

'Give it a moment,' replied the other, and started the engine.

By the time they'd reached the Dartford Crossing, the Fiesta was warmer. The window on the passenger side didn't roll quite to the top anymore, and that meant a thin breeze whistled constantly through the car – but still, it was a big step up from their frigid start.

The driver snuck a glance at her travelling companion.

‘You remember Joe?’ she asked abruptly.

‘Who?’

‘Joe.’

The girl pondered this. ‘Uh-uh,’ she said finally.

‘Think hard, now… Nothing at all?’

The girl scrunched up her face and thought as hard as she could. ‘Nope,’ she said. ‘Not a sausage.’

The woman nodded; the tips of her afro brushed against the roof. ‘How about Bournemouth? You ever been anywhere near there?’

‘No.’

The woman grinned. ‘I know for a fact you have. You don’t remember a whole helluva lot, do you?’

‘That’s the thing,’ the girl said. ‘I don’t. I mean, I remember some stuff. I thought of a book I read once. And feeding chickens – I remember doing that. But those memories are like…’ She held a finger to the slit at the top of the passenger window. ‘Like this tiny sliver of wind. Everything else is on the other side of the glass. I don’t even know why I’m here.’ She shifted in her seat until she looked full-on at the woman driving. ‘And I sure don’t know where I met you,’ she concluded.

The woman laughed merrily. ‘I know you don’t, babe,’

she said. ‘But you’ve got to trust me when I tell you this – not knowing any of that stuff is a very good thing.’

ONE

Sara Jones walked up Harley Street, trying to keep four pizza boxes level in her arms. Overnight there had been cold late January rain, then the temperature had dropped. Now the ground was icy. Each time Sara passed one of the pear trees that lined Harley Street's pavements she would steady herself with a forearm pressed against its cold bark. This, and an exaggerated gait, kept her moving and her pizzas intact.

As Sara crossed Queen Anne Street, she heard faint music – the opening of a song by Take That. Her ringtone. Instinctively, she tensed. On the northern side of Queen Anne, Sara scanned for a place to set down the warm, slightly soggy boxes. The marble steps of a private clinic were the best surface she could find. Fumbling in her handbag, she glanced at her iPhone's screen. Sara did not recognise the number. She answered with trepidation.

'Hello?'

'Dr Sara Jones?' a voice said. 'This is Detective Sergeant Adeela Mir from the Metropolitan Police.'

Sara caught her breath.

'Are you alright to talk?'

Sara could feel a warm surge behind her ears. *What I'm feeling there,* she thought, *is pulsatile tinnitus. My blood pressure's just gone mad.* For months, the sight of a panda car had also set her pulse racing. Even the sound of her ringtone could make her feel queasy. 'Actually, I'm running errands at the moment,' she said.

Sara had often rehearsed what to say if questioned by the police. She kept the number of a high-priced law firm ready in her contacts list. Dr Sara Jones – psychiatrist, police consultant, and all-round respectable citizen – had been dreading a call like this ever since she'd committed murder.

'Dr Jones, are you still there?'

'Oh, yes,' Sara said. 'Sorry – distracted.'

An elderly couple emerged from the hospital and stepped over her pizzas with disdain. Sara grimaced apologetically. 'May I ask what this relates to?' she said.

'I'd rather discuss it in person,' Detective Sergeant Mir replied. 'Is there a place we can meet?'

'Not really,' Sara told her. 'I'm in the process of moving house.'

'Oh… you're not living in Brixton anymore?'

The day's chill sank deeper into Sara's bones. This woman had already researched her. 'No… I mean, not always,' she stammered. 'At the moment, I'm in Marylebone. It's where my new house – well, my house and office – will be.'

'Then you're close!' Mir said. 'Give me the address and I'll pop right over.'

Sara closed her eyes. She touched the cold bark of a pear tree to steady herself. Her muscles sagged in a sign of subconscious surrender. 'That would be fine,' she sighed. 'You can join us for pizza.'

On the corner of a cobbled mews just off Harley Street sat an eighteenth-century stable block. Until the previous year, it had housed the offices of a European investments firm. When the business owners relocated from London to Frankfurt, Sara had taken on the lease. Soon, the place would become her home, as well as the office of her new psychiatric practice. As Sara approached, pizza boxes level, she could hear the whine of a circular saw. To make the needed renovations, she'd been forced to scale a mountain of local bureaucracy. The new building was in one of Westminster's conservation areas; Sara had needed separate permissions for every single alteration.

At least the process had helped keep her thoughts away from darker things.

The door to the newly-added entranceway was open. This had been installed so Sara's partner Jamie could get upstairs without trudging past her clients. When Sara entered, she noticed her oldest friend facing away from her. Ceri Lloyd was clothed in worn jeans and an oversized man's shirt. She had dressed for construction – or, at least, for supervising those actually building something. Right now, Ceri squinted at the ceiling, hands on hips. Although Sara could not detect it over the shrieking of the saw, she knew her friend was clucking softly, tongue against molars. It was something Ceri did when deep in thought. Finally, Ceri called out: 'Where are the ceiling joists?'

A builder cupped his ear. 'What?'

Ceri grimaced at the worker with the saw. He cut the power.

'The ceiling joists,' she repeated over the dying din.

The builder slackened his jaw in understanding.

'Perpendicular to the new wall.'

Ceri nodded, satisfied. 'Are you anchoring the floor joists, too?'

'We weren't planning to.'

'Why the hell not?' Ceri demanded. 'They'll be firmer that way.'

The builder looked helplessly to his foreman, who glanced towards Sara.

Ceri followed his gaze and noticed Sara standing in the doorway behind her. 'Aha!' she said, 'pizza's here!' As an afterthought she added, 'You should anchor your floor joists, *fach*.'

Sara looked upwards with a blank gaze. 'Yes, I suppose I should.'

Ceri smiled victoriously at the builder. The floor joists would be anchored. 'Take five, gentlemen,' she called with a clap of her hands.

Sara set the pizza boxes on a work table. Numbly, she watched the builders converge. She was all-too-aware that soon, one of Ceri's fellow officers would arrive to question her about the poisoning of a young man named Tim Wilson. It was an outcome Sara had been dreading for months. She would have to admit to knowing the man; it was certain Wilson's partner had mentioned Sara to the police. Still, she planned to claim total ignorance of Wilson's death. She was ready for her first reaction upon hearing the terrible news: a face tightening into shock and confusion. Perhaps, in her eyes, a sheen of sorrow for a life lost so young. Sara had been working on that expression for months, and could now throw it on like a worn jacket. What she would never do was try to explain anything. Sara knew that innocent people rarely justified themselves in an interrogation – they simply restated their innocence. That's what Sara planned to do now. If there were any evidence against her, such intransigence would force Detective Sergeant Mir to disclose it.

Still chewing, Ceri wiped her mouth with the back of her hand. 'The only thing that could make this pizza better,' she said, 'would be a stuffed crust.'

Distractedly, Sara said, 'This place doesn't do them.'

Ceri took another large bite. 'It's bloody Oxford Street,' she rebutted, her words thick with mozzarella. 'Someone must.'

Sara watched her friend's jaw churning. Ceri had always been protective of her. If she were to hear DS Mir's accusations against Sara, she would be outraged. And when indignant, Ceri acted like a Rottweiler with a bone – she tore at the evidence until she'd laid it bare. On this occasion, that habit might end up uncovering Sara's guilt.

'Have some pizza,' Ceri urged.

Sara grimaced dismissively. 'Not hungry,' she said.

'Hello?' a voice sounded from the open second doorway. 'Dr Jones?'

Sara looked over to see a woman in her early thirties, dressed in a blue suit and a white, open-necked shirt. She carried a brocaded cloth handbag that seemed too fancy for the rest of her attire. Sara wondered what that said about the sergeant's personality. Noticing the silence, she realised she was staring. She shook herself into action. 'Yes, I'm Sara,' she said. 'Please come in.'

Ceri eyed the new visitor with heavy lids as she stepped into the room. 'Well, well,' she muttered. 'You didn't tell me we were expecting company.'

Adeela Mir cast her eyes over Sara's dusty ground floor. It was still all bare timber, wiring and cement. The builders had finished their pizza and were drifting back to their tasks. 'This is your new home?' she asked.

'Upstairs, mostly,' Sara said. 'Downstairs will double as

my office. I'm a psychiatrist.'

'Oh – you're returning to professional practice?' the detective sergeant asked. 'You haven't done that since you moved to Wales.' She thought for a moment. 'That was roughly four years ago, wasn't it?'

With a pleasant vagueness, Sara replied, 'Maybe it's time to get back in the saddle.'

Ceri stepped forward and extended her hand. '*Bore da*,' she said. 'I'm Ceri. You are?'

'Err – hello.' The detective turned to take Ceri's hand. 'I'm DS Mir from the Metropolitan Police.'

In the corner, a worker positioned a two-by-four and picked up the circular saw. For the second time in minutes, the saw's whine filled the room. Ceri bared her teeth at him once more. This time, he ignored her.

Glancing back to Sara, Mir spoke loudly. 'Is there somewhere we can talk privately?'

'You said DS,' Ceri mused over the din. 'So, you're a copper?'

Mir nodded politely.

'Well then, let me re-introduce myself,' Ceri said loudly. 'I'm Inspector Lloyd from the Dyfed-Powys Police.'

Mir's lips parted in recognition. 'Of course!' she said. 'Ceri Lloyd. I read about you in the papers. You investigated those awful murders in Aberystwyth. The *Daily Mail* loved you!'

'You have a good memory,' Sara said flatly.

'Not really,' Mir admitted to Sara. 'I looked you up this morning. The papers had a lot to say about both of you.' She turned back to Ceri. 'Are you visiting?'

'Taking a bit of leave,' Ceri said, angling her head at Sara. 'Couldn't trust this one alone with builders.' She swept her arm towards the work crew. As the sound of the circular saw died, Ceri said, 'These slick bastards would cheat the poor girl blind.'

In the hollow silence, Sara smiled at the crew awkwardly.

'If you two need a place to talk,' Ceri continued, 'how about my room?'

She gestured up the stairs. Although the first-floor flat was in an almost-finished state, Sara and Jamie had yet to move in. They'd decided to wait until the rest of the house was less of a construction site. The shambles hadn't bothered Ceri, though. Rather than sleep on their sofa in Brixton, Ceri had chosen to stay here in Central London.

This had required Sara to buy a new bed and linens, but also had kept Ceri a full five miles away from Sara's domestic life. It was a solution that made everyone happy.

But right now, using the space Ceri thought of as hers suggested she would also be present. That was something Sara was anxious to avoid. 'You don't need to hold my hand,' Sara said to Ceri. 'Stay here with the builders. I'll be fine.'

'Wouldn't dream of leaving you alone,' Ceri said.

Sara's chest sank heavily.

Ceri turned to Mir. 'I'm her oldest friend,' she explained. 'She'll feel safer if I'm there.'

'That's perfectly fine,' Mir said. 'Lead the way.'

Ceri grinned and turned to the builders. 'And I was just kidding, folks,' she told them. 'Not all of you are criminals.'

The upstairs part of the stables consisted of a reasonably sized sitting room, a bathroom, and a large double bedroom with an en suite. At the moment, the new bed was the room's only furniture. Sara apologised as all three women perched on the mattress. Mir laughed.

'It makes a change,' she said. 'I don't usually conduct

my business on a king-sized bed.'

Ceri smiled. 'It's the best place to do it,' she said.

Sara tried to look at ease. Her friend would have found out what the sergeant was doing here, eventually – but Sara had counted on a chance to spin the story later. That wouldn't be an option now.

'Right,' Mir said. 'I just want to ask you a couple of questions.' She reached into her handbag and produced a sheet of paper. 'Do you recognise this?'

Sara tried to keep her hand from shaking. As she accepted the paper, images of what damning evidence it might contain flashed through her mind. An enlargement of her fingerprints, taken from the scene of the crime? Impossible, she thought – she'd worn gloves. Some personal item she'd dropped in Tim Wilson's flat? Unlikely – she'd been careful. An image from a security camera she hadn't noticed?

That was more likely.

Sara looked down. On the page was a colour photocopy of an illustration contained within rectangular borders. Overall, it was slightly larger than a playing card. The drawing was of a muscular grey creature spitting blood from its lips.

Sara's brow creased. 'What am I looking at?'

'I was hoping you could tell me,' Mir said. 'It was found lying next to a murder victim in West Kensington. At first, I thought it might be some sort of tarot card, but it's not.'

Sara stared at the woman blankly. *West Kensington? Tarot card?*

In the melee of Sara's thoughts, the pieces connected. Detective Sergeant Mir was not here to accuse Sara of murder. Instead, she knew about Sara's professional reputation as an expert on the occult, and was hoping for a consultation. This realisation made Sara's breath grow rapid and shallow. Suddenly, she felt giddy with relief.

She also wanted to be a million miles away from this detective, now that she knew it was possible.

'That's the actual size of the card,' Mir said.

'Well, it's definitely not tarot,' Sara heard herself replying. 'It's possible it's from some other divinatory system.'

Mir offered an uncertain shrug. 'As far as we can tell, it's not from any deck of mystical cards available commercially.'

Sara looked at the horrific creature on the card and

wondered how to extract herself from this conversation. 'It might be the image has no occult significance at all. It could come from a fantasy trading card game. There are a lot of those out there.'

Just as Sara was about to hand back the paper and bid the detective a fond *hwyl*, Ceri piped up. 'D'you have a copy of the back of the card?' she asked.

Mir blinked. 'No. Sorry.'

'If it's from a fantasy game,' Ceri went on, 'it would have the manufacturer's logo on the back.'

Sara's nerves all screamed out at once: *For heaven's sake, Ceri, just let the woman leave!*

'That's true,' Mir conceded. 'The reverse side is just solid grey.'

'There you go,' Ceri said to Sara. 'So, it's not from a game. But it's got to be from somewhere. Does the card tell you anything else?'

Sara shook her head. In truth, what the illustration reminded her of most was a Roman Catholic prayer card. The artwork used the same highly-saturated colours, and was framed by a similar ornate border. The only difference was, the artist had replaced the image of a saint with a blood-drooling demon. Sara tried to return the sheet to DS

Mir. 'Sorry,' she said decisively, 'There's just not enough to go on.'

Mir held up her hands. 'Would you mind keeping it?' she asked. 'If anything occurs to you, I'd like to know.'

'Good idea,' Ceri said quickly. She produced her phone. 'Give me your number.' Ceri angled her head towards Sara. 'If this one has any sort of brainwave, I'll let you know.'

As the women exchanged mobile numbers, Sara stood pointedly and positioned herself near the door. Eventually, Ceri and Mir rose as well. 'Actually, Sara,' Mir ventured, 'I came here hoping you might get even more involved with the investigation.'

'I'm sorry?' Sara said.

'I'm asking you to do more than just look at the card,' Mir explained. 'From what I hear, you're the Met's best when it comes to this kind of thing. I'm sure you have a lot to offer us.'

'The Met's best?' Sara repeated. She felt a prickle of irritation. 'I'm not the Met's *anything*.' She shook her head in exasperation. 'Forgive me, Detective Sergeant, but I've got a lot going on in my life right now.' She gestured down the stairs. 'As you can see. I really don't need to get involved in a murder investigation.'

'Sara!' Ceri admonished.

Mir tried to mask her disappointment. 'It's OK,' she said, laying a hand on Ceri's forearm. 'I understand.'

Sara realised how she must have sounded. 'I don't want to be rude,' she said, 'but it's been a few years. And frankly, my last investigation was rather upsetting.'

If Mir had researched Sara's past, she must have known the toll the Aberystwyth murders had taken on her personally. For one thing, they had led to her brother's death.

'No need to explain,' Mir said. She accepted the paper from Sara. 'I'm sorry to have bothered you.'

Ceri glowered at Sara and took the officer by the elbow. 'Let me show you out,' she said.

Sara stood at the top of the stairs and watched them descend. They lingered near the front door. Sara could not make out their hushed conversation, but fancied she heard Ceri whisper, 'Don't worry – I'll talk to her.'

'I think it's high time you went back on your medication,' Ceri said to Sara.

They walked along New Cavendish Street, towards a

coffee shop on Portland Place. Sara glanced sideways at her friend. 'You know something?' she said. 'You've become awfully sanctimonious since you quit smoking.'

Ceri cackled. 'I was sanctimonious long before that.' Her breath billowed into the frigid air. Wistfully, she added, 'But I do miss my Marlboros.'

'You've lost weight, too,' Sara noted. 'Who gives up cigarettes and loses weight?'

'Every day, in every way, I'm getting better and better,' Ceri said.

'Anyway,' Sara said, 'Your advice comes too late. I'm already taking SSRIs again.'

'You're back on anti-depressants?' Ceri asked. 'That's wonderful! Are you seeing Dr Shapiro, too?'

'I was,' Sara admitted. 'But only to get the prescription.'

In fact, Sara had started seeing her old psychiatrist not long after poisoning Tim Wilson. The meds Dr Shapiro prescribed had helped balance her in the wake of that horrible event. The therapy itself, however, had proved less successful. There were simply too many things Sara could not admit to the doctor - like the way her mind would constantly replay one late-spring evening's act of murder.

Repeatedly, Sara would visualise herself opening Tim Wilson's window. Easing her way through his dark flat. Watching his sleeping form. Creeping to the kitchenette. Pouring thallium into his drink. What unsettled Sara most was that, each time, her main question to herself was, *what could I have done better?*

It turned out Sara Jones was a perfectionist even when it came to murder. How could she have explained that to Dr Shapiro?

'You don't need analysis?'

Unconsciously, Sara edged away from her friend. 'I'm fine.'

'Then why were you so rude to the sergeant?' Ceri asked.

'I wasn't. I simply don't want to be part of an investigation. That's in my past.'

Sara hoped her denials rang true. The real truth was more complicated. If Sara could assist police the way she used to – innocently, a dispassionate expert – she might enjoy the challenge. But that was not what was on offer. She would have to work cheek-by-jowl with people who could arrest her in a heartbeat – and the project itself would constantly remind her of her own guilt. There would always be a voice whispering *there's no turning back the clock*.

'What did you say?' Ceri asked.

'Sorry?'

'You said, "There's no turning back the clock."'

Sara flinched, then swallowed. 'Well, there isn't.' She frowned. 'Besides, you used to tell me I should leave all this investigation nonsense behind. Why have you changed?'

'I haven't changed,' Ceri insisted. 'You have.'

Driving home her point, Ceri waved towards Portland Place, its stately buildings housing embassies, corporate headquarters, and independent schools. A world of privilege and wealth. Here was the summit Sara had been climbing towards four years ago, before she had lost her nerve and run home. A disastrous decision, as things transpired. Sara had once justified her work with the Met as a way to give back – something worthwhile, after she'd put in her hours listening to privileged people tell her about their First World problems. Maybe Ceri was trying to remind Sara she'd already turned back the clock – but without reclaiming the worthwhile part of her past.

'You're back on your medication,' Ceri continued.

'You're starting a new practice. You're stronger now.'

If she only knew, Sara thought.

Then again, maybe she was being silly. If the police had anything on her, it wouldn't matter whether Sara was consulting for them or just cowering in a corner of her posh new home. They'd arrest her anyway. Maybe she'd feel better working for justice in a less-morally-complex way than her psychic mentor, Eldon Carson, had taught her. Maybe working with the Met might even serve as a diversion. If they had hard evidence they would still arrest her, of course. But if there was only suspicion… well, it's harder to suspect someone you work with and trust.

'OK – maybe,' she said finally.

Ceri snapped her gaze onto Sara, suddenly hyper-alert. 'Maybe you're stronger now, or maybe you'll do it?'

Sara snorted grimly. Why was Ceri so insistent she join this investigation? 'Maybe both,' she acknowledged.

'Excellent decision,' Ceri said.

'I said *maybe*,' Sara replied.

They had reached the coffee shop. Ceri silenced her with a raised finger and peered through the glass doors. 'Good,' she said, 'it's not crowded, and it's noisy as hell out here. Let's go inside before I make the call.'

‘The call?’ Sara said. ‘Hang on a minute, I haven’t said I’d–’

But Ceri wasn’t listening. She was already stepping inside the café and pulling out her mobile phone.

TWO

Their meeting had been set for a couple mornings later at the West End Central police station. In the corner of an office, Adeela Mir clicked through a series of photos on a laptop. She had angled the screen towards Sara, to offer her the best view. Each image caused Sara's stomach to lurch. This surprised her: she had seen photos of countless murder victims, many as grisly as these. What had changed since she'd last been in this situation?

What has changed, Sara told herself, *is that you've killed someone*.

The pictures were of the body of a heavyset man in an open dressing gown, sprawled on a double bed. The handle of a pair of heavy scissors protruded from his left eye socket.

'Mr Gregory Blackadar,' said Adeela Mir.

'Deceased,' Ceri added jauntily.

Ceri was sitting away from Sara, on Mir's other side.

She had no reason to be there, other than boredom and curiosity. An inspector from Dyfed-Powys had no official status in London. Ceri was here only as Sara's friend – emotional support that Sara did not need. Ceri reached across the police sergeant and tugged at the corner of the laptop to get a better look. The photo on screen was a tight shot of Mr Blackadar's face.

'Ouch,' Ceri drawled.

Sara sat at the end of the meeting-room table, a Moleskine notebook in front of her. She looked over at her friend and frowned pointedly. Ceri gave her a look of faux-innocence. It was as though she were trying to draw attention to herself. Her sly behaviour reminded Sara of a neglected kid showing off for teacher. In Aberystwyth, Ceri had always frowned upon the kind of gallows humour police officers might use to get through the day. Her staff knew better than to let loose any dark jokes in Inspector Lloyd's presence. Yet here Ceri was, yukking it up like a club comic.

A lot had changed since Ceri's heart attack.

'Mr Blackadar was a forty-nine-year-old businessman from Dorset,' Mir continued, 'with interests in a number of enterprises.' She glanced at her notes. 'He owned a poultry farm, three caravan sites, and a handful of houses in Bournemouth. Student slums, basically – black mould, peeling linoleum. His main residence was on the farm, but he also spent time here' – she gestured towards the screen – 'in his flat near the Queen's Club.'

'Next of kin?' Sara asked.

'Long-divorced.' Mir replied, 'No children, either. Dorset Police are speaking to staff at the farm.'

Sara toyed with her Mont Blanc fountain pen. She forced herself to look once again at the screen and swallowed bile. 'What do we know about his death?'

Ceri offered her a heavy-lidded stare. Blandly, she said, 'We have reason to believe he was stabbed in the eye.'

Mir suppressed a grin. 'We know he'd been in London for less than a day,' she said. 'And that he'd recently had intercourse.' She paused. 'Vaginal.'

Sara nodded and wrote the word *sex* in her book.

Ceri shrugged as if the solution were all-too-easy. 'So the fellow arrives in town and he's had a long drive, so he dials up a call girl,' she said.

'Let's not jump to conclusions,' Sara advised, wishing she hadn't given in to Ceri's pleas to come.

'Forensics are on the DNA,' Mir informed them. 'The

building has a porter, but he didn't see anything. There were no signs of forced entry, so we have to assume Mr Blackadar let in his killer voluntarily.'

'What about security cameras?' Sara asked.

Mir shook her head.

'Ten-to-one the hooker did it,' Ceri said. 'She was on top, right? Riding him like a bronco, and then, pop. One in the eye.'

Sara felt the corner of her own eye twitch. She looked down at her notebook and began doodling spirals. The smooth flow of ink was soothing. After a breath she admitted, 'You may be right about the timing. The angle and depth of the scissors suggests the murderer was on top of Blackadar.' She twitched a hand. 'The killing and sex could have been separate, I suppose, but it's certainly possible that Mr Blackadar –'

'Died shagging,' Ceri said, and Mir grinned.

There were things about this killing Sara did not know for certain, but rather sensed. Sara felt certain Gregory Blackadar had known his killer intimately - and in a way that was not purely sexual. Sara could not claim this insight as a psychic flash; Jamie, an experienced profiler, would have said the same thing. The grotesque intimacy of the violence the offender had perpetrated – choosing scissors as a weapon, and going for the eye – suggested unchecked emotion. Assaults on the face often pointed to some personal grudge. What was less easy to defend in profiling terms was Sara's sense that another person had been in the room at the time of the victim's death. There was nothing evidential to suggest two killers, or that Blackadar had other visitors. Sara simply sensed it was true – someone else had been there.

Sara, Ceri, and Mir were interrupted by a rapping at the door. Before Mir could answer, a high-ranking police officer leaned in. He made meaningful eye contact with her. Mir half-rose. 'Superintendent,' she said.

'Are we interrupting?' the superintendent asked.

'Not at all,' Mir said. 'Please come in.'

The superintendent stepped into the room. As soon as he had, a man in his mid-fifties entered and squeezed past him. This second man wore a well-tailored blue suit. His hair was a luxuriant shade of brown – a youthful hue that did not match his face. Men could dye their hair, Sara reflected, but they couldn't iron out those wrinkles. Not without surgery. Through the open door, she saw two young aides waiting in the hallway.

'Oh – Minister,' Mir said.

'Sergeant,' the man replied.

Mir introduced him to Sara and Ceri as the Right Honourable Joseph Bennett, Minister for Policing. It seemed Bennett had attended the investigation's morning briefing. Bennett shook Sara's hand with little curiosity, instead noticing the image on the computer. He bent and peered at the screen with a wince. 'Any developments since this morning?' he asked Mir.

'Nothing,' she said.

Bennett clicked through the grisly photos. He landed on images of the cards. 'Ah, yes,' he said. 'The angels.'

'More like one angel and one demon,' Mir noted.

'Dr Jones,' the superintendent told Bennett, 'is the expert we mentioned in the briefing.'

'Aha,' Bennett said, showing a sudden, increased interest in Sara. 'Then you're the one who knows all about these images, then.'

'I wouldn't say that,' Sara told him. 'They're a bit of a puzzle, aren't they?'

Bennett nodded. 'Sergeant Mir updated us on the current thinking this morning,' he said. 'Not a tarot card and not from a game. Not even commercially produced.'

'It's early days,' Sara said. 'We'll keep on it.'

'I'd like to be kept informed,' Bennett said.

'Of course, Minister,' the superintendent said. 'You will be. We're putting everything we know onto the HOLMES system, and–'

'And I'll keep up with all the details,' Bennett said. 'But it's rare to get to talk to an expert such as Dr Jones.' Bennett glanced at Sara. 'Would you be willing to meet me sometime soon?' he asked her. 'I'm fascinated to hear all about what you do.'

'Yes,' Sara blurted. 'Yes, of course.'

'I'll tell one of my young lads to get your number from Sergeant Mir,' he said. 'Expect a call.'

Righting himself, he said his goodbyes. Sara smiled politely and shook his hand, wondering what she could possibly tell Bennett to justify his interest. Certainly, she could not reveal her unsubstantiated notions to him.

The door closed, leaving Sara alone once again with Ceri and Mir. She couldn't reveal her hunches to them, either. Sara didn't really understand what she was feeling herself. Sara noticed the image Bennett had left on the screen was a close-up of the drooling demon. Mir saw her looking at it. 'This card,' she said, 'is the reason I came to you in the first place. I suppose if you'd had any new thoughts, you would have shared them with Bennett?'

'Nothing yet,' Sara said, 'but I'll work on it. Can you send me that photo?'

Ceri raised her hand. 'Text it to me,' she told Mir. 'I'll make sure she gets a copy.'

At the flat in Brixton, Sara sat at the dining room table, the photo of the mystery card saved as wallpaper on her computer screen. It wasn't any creature she could name. It seemed more like a generic hell-image, as though someone had copied a detail from Hieronymus Bosch. Sara had tried a reverse image search online and come up blank. She was about to email some old colleagues for help when she heard keys jangle on the opposite side of the door.

Jamie entered, bringing with him a waft of cold air. 'Classes over?' Sara asked.

'None today.' Sara's partner crossed to the table and tried to kiss her on the cheek. Sara recoiled from his unshaved chin. Jamie shrugged off his brown suede coat, and said, 'I was in the library.' He dropped the coat and it landed on the sofa with a heavy thud. After a quick rub of his stubbly face, Jamie chose to kiss the better-insulated top of Sara's head. That was when he noticed the screen. 'Aha,' he said. 'Looks like Adeela's caught up with you.'

'Yesterday,' Sara said absently, then started. 'You know her?'

'Old friends in common,' Jamie said. 'Why didn't you tell me about her last night?'

'Guess I forgot,' Sara said. 'It's not all that important.'

Jamie snorted. 'You're working for the police again and think it's unimportant?' he said. 'I'll tell you, it's a lot more interesting than my days.' He moved into the galley kitchen and pulled a beer from the fridge. 'I thought you'd be more excited than this.'

'Why?'

'Why else?' he cried in mock exasperation. 'You're looking at a mysterious card with an ugly demon on it. That's like Christmas for you.'

Sara turned in her chair. 'You knew about this,' she said accusingly. 'Did you suggest me to DS Mir?'

'Nope,' Jamie said. 'She just rang here first. I gave her your mobile number.'

'Did you also tell how to get background on me? She seemed to know quite a bit.'

Jamie raised his hands like a man surrendering. 'Don't shoot,' he said. The sudden gesture made foam gush from the mouth of the bottle. He stepped over the beery puddle and slid into a chair, taking a pull on his drink. 'Adeela had already looked you up,' he told Sara. 'You've still got a solid reputation at the Met. People talk to one another. Frankly, they're lucky to have you back.'

'I'm not back,' Sara muttered, 'I'm just helping with this.'

She reminded herself not to get too moody with her partner. 'But thank you,' she added, 'for thinking of me.'

Last summer had been so traumatic for Sara, she needed to work hard to remember how awful it had been for Jamie, too. He'd had to deal with his employer at Thorndike Aerospace pressuring him to kill a business associate, and then watch that same man murdered before his eyes. Jamie had given a statement that evening with a packet of deadly poison in his jacket pocket. Sometime soon, he would also have to testify at the murder trial of his boss's killer, Levi Rootenberg. Currently, Rootenberg was on remand in prison, speculating wildly to anyone who would listen. Even under oath, Jamie would have to be careful about which parts of the story he told.

‘You know what?’ Sara said to Jamie. ‘I’ve been thinking we should get a kitten.’

Jamie blinked. ‘You want to–’

‘Get a kitten, yes.’

He grimaced. ‘Is that wise?’

‘I want one.’

Jamie set down his bottle. ‘I know you miss Ego,’ he said, ‘but soon we’ll be moving to Central London.’

‘That’s why we need a kitten,’ Sara insisted. ‘At my old practice, Ego always came with me. The clients loved him.’

‘He lived his life indoors,’ Jamie said. ‘He got old and fat before his time. This one would, too. It’d be cruel.’

Sara did not look at him. ‘You hate cats.’

Jamie opened his mouth, closed it again, and then smiled feebly. He and Ego had built an uneasy truce over the years, but he couldn’t deny Sara’s point. It amazed Sara that they could share so normal a conversation after the time they’d been through. She knew it was due to Jamie’s good nature.

‘I’ll *consider* a kitten,’ he said.

After the events of last summer, Sara had tried to get Jamie to open up to her. She’d done it for herself as well as for him. In the aftermath of killing Tim Wilson, Sara would have found it reassuring to focus on her partner's problems rather than her own. Jamie had always changed the topic.

Now, he stared at the screen of her MacBook. 'So what are you doing about that blood-vomiting monster?'

'I'm going to send some emails,' she said.

'To who?'

'I have old friends, too,' Sara reminded him. 'And one of them might just know more than I do.'

THREE

Twenty miles north of London, in rural Hertfordshire, a middle-aged man lay naked in the early February chill of his garden shed. His skin was a terrain of gooseflesh. His wrists were fixed to the shed's grimy floorboards by three-and-a-half inch nails; each rested in its own pool of congealing blood. The man tried to focus on the young woman who stood above, straddling him. 'Please,' he breathed. 'I won't call the police. Just go now. You can take whatever you want.'

The woman – her name was Morven – twirled her dark orange hair thoughtfully. Its strands were so matted they looked like dreadlocks. 'Whatever I want,' she repeated slowly. 'Now, what would I want from you?'

The man took a moment to grasp it was actually a question. 'My car,' he said urgently. 'Take my car.'

'I have a car,' she replied. 'It's better than yours.'

'Then I'll give you money.'

'I have money, too.'

The man released a frustrated cry and kicked out. Then he yelped as the jolt to his wrists shot pain up his arms.

'That was silly,' Morven said. She cocked her head and held still, as though listening to an unseen conspirator.

'What are you doing?' he asked.

'Shhh,' she said. 'I'm listening.' She nodded slowly, like someone taking directions. Finally, she looked back at the man. 'He suggested I break your knees.'

'Who?' he asked, then added, 'Wait... break my knees?'

'Says you won't kick then.'

'Who wants to break my knees?'

Morven pursed her lips. From her parka, she produced a thin deck of cards. She selected one. Squatting over him, she held it close to his face. The card showed an illustration of a beautiful-but-stern young man with flowing hair and dark wings. In his right hand, he carried a whip. It was on fire, or perhaps made entirely of flames. 'That's Kushiel, the Rigid One of God,' Morven told him. 'He's been guiding me in your particular case.'

'My case?' the man asked.

'He's an angel – the one who thinks I should... you

know.' She mimed a karate chop to his legs. 'You should memorise his face,' she advised the man. 'Then you'll know who to look for when you make your passage into the underworld. He'll guide you.'

'You said *my case*,' he gasped. 'Have there been others? Other people you've–'

'Just one so far,' she acknowledged. 'Different angel, though. An *arch*angel, actually – his name is Af. But I don't have any more of his cards.' She patted her pocket. 'I'm going to get more soon. I may need him again.'

'Listen,' the man said. 'I'm sure this angel–'

'Af?'

'No – my angel!'

'Kushiel.'

'I'm sure Kushiel would want you to let me go.'

The young woman frowned sceptically. 'You know a lot about the Celestial Kingdom, do you?'

'I know angels are merciful,' he ventured.

She released a delighted laugh. 'Some are, yes,' she said. 'But not mine.' She bent towards the gas-powered nail gun next to the prone man. 'My angels can be right bastards.'

With unusual strength for someone so slight, Morven

hoisted the weighty tool and placed it against her victim's left knee. Its spurs bit into his flesh. He whimpered.

'Dropped through darkness they may be,' she added, 'still they toil in service to the Light.'

When she pulled the trigger, he screamed.

'It all comes from the same place. Light and darkness, peace and evil. All angels work to one divine end.' Abruptly, she cocked her head. 'Hang on… did you just hear something?' she asked.

He continued to moan. 'Your angel?'

She held up a finger. 'Shhh.' Her tone hardened. 'Shut up for a minute.'

The man clenched his teeth. Finally, only his jagged breathing remained.

'Hear that?'

He grunted *no*.

'Well, I do. And it's not an angel this time.'

Morven raised the nail gun, stepped over the man and nudged the shed door with her foot. 'Wait here.' she said, as if he had a choice. 'There's something I've got to take care of.'

Morven kept the nail gun raised, scanning the property like

a squaddie on patrol. She moved stealthily across the patchy grass and onto a wide gravelled driveway. An hour ago, when she had frog-marched the man to his shed, Morven had left the patio door open a fraction. That had been careless, she thought. She hadn't considered draughts blowing through the house. With the nail gun's muzzle, she pushed the sliding panel. Inside, a baby squalled over the popping and honking of children's television.

'Cherub?' Morven called.

She set down the gun on the dining room table and passed into the open living-room-kitchen. On an upholstered chair, Cherub was fussing in his car seat.

'Who's a sad baby?' she asked in a mushy tone. 'Is Cherub hungry or just ever-so-bored?' She glanced at swirls of colour and noise on the TV. 'Ah,' she said. 'This show always kind of sucks.'

The baby calmed at his mother's voice. Reached out.

'Fraid not, little one,' she said. 'You've got to stay in there a teensy bit longer. When Mummy's all done, I'll give you a bottle.'

Morven filled the man's kettle and switched it on. The water would be cool enough for formula when she needed it. She picked up a remote and turned off the television.

'Meantime,' she continued, 'why don't I put you in your daddy's van?'

Morven lifted the baby seat and carried Cherub out the front door, singing *hush little baby, don't say a word…*

They moved past the man's muddy Vauxhall Astra towards a late-model Mercedes panel van. The baby seemed contented as she strapped him in, but as she closed the passenger door he began to wail. Morven knew he didn't like confined spaces, and wouldn't abide a whole lot more of these shenanigans. She would have to get a move on.

Then, straight to her brain and soft as a whisper, the angel Kushiel made a clever suggestion. The young woman listened and smiled. 'Good thought,' she told him.

She hustled back to the shed. 'I've changed my mind about your car,' Morven told the man. 'Where are your keys?'

'Trouser pockets,' he said weakly.

She moved to the corner where she'd tossed his clothing.

'If you're taking my car,' he rasped, 'are you going to…?'

'Hold your horses,' she told him. Pocketing the car

keys, she spotted a pair of pliers dangling on the wooden wall. ‘Your nail gun did a bang-up job,’ she warned him. ‘This is probably going to hurt.’

He snorted weakly at the irony. Tears ran from his eyes.

The young woman had to dig into the man’s torn flesh to get a grip on the nail’s head. He shrieked as she gave a series of muscular tugs, jerking the three-and-a-half-inch spike back and forth until she could yank it out of his wrist. The result was bloody. By the time Morven started on the other one, the man had quieted. His eyelids fluttered.

‘Hey, you still in there?’ she called. ‘I want you to be awake for this.’

Morven tossed away the second blood-slicked nail and stood. Fortunately, the man’s feet were pointed at the shed’s door. It was simple to grasp his ankles and slide him outside onto the grass. From there, ground frost made it easy enough to pull his bulk to the gravel driveway. The man hadn’t made a sound since his series of shrieks in the shed, but he wasn't quite dead either. She hoped he was still listening.

‘The day of calamity is at hand,’ Morven told him, ‘and doom will come swiftly.’

She slid into the driver’s seat of the man’s Astra. She

didn't often quote the Bible – it wasn't necessary when angels sent her frequent revelations – but just then it had seemed apt. She put the car in gear and lurched forward over the man's prone figure. The chassis bounced like it was hitting a speed bump at full throttle.

For some reason the second impact, driving over him backwards, proved easier.

By then his body wasn't moving at all. Morven wondered whether to do it again – a belt-and-braces, better-safe-than-sorry kind of thing – but Kushiel told her it wasn't necessary. The young woman got out of the car and stood over the man's corpse. A recent death was always a solemn occasion, no matter how it had happened. She withdrew the card that featured Kushiel, the Rigid One of God, and wiped it carefully before laying it on her victim's chest. Then she waited for some fitting final thought to drop, but none did.

Only the words *serves you right*.

The same thing Morven had thought when she killed Cherub's daddy.

The reminder of Cherub snapped her back into the present. He was still squalling in the van. It was difficult to do all the angels commanded and look after a baby as well.

Still, she thought, *we all have our crosses to bear*. By now, the water in the kettle would have cooled enough to make the formula.

Morven pulled into the car park of a roadside hotel just within the orbit of the M25 motorway. It wasn't fancy – facing an allotment and next to a petrol station – but it was inconspicuous. In fact, it was one of two inconspicuous hotels Morven currently kept rooms in. Both times she had paid cash for the week ahead. She'd fancied booking herself into swankier hideaways, but any nicer places might have balked at her appearance. Especially right now. Morven had washed as best she could in Jeff's sink, but still… she wasn't fresh as a daisy. She urgently required a shower and some sleep. Killing people was harder work than her angels had let on.

'You stay put, my little Cherub,' Morven told the baby. 'Mummy's not going anywhere without you. Just need to make a trip to the cash machine.'

She got out of the van and slid open its side door. She squinted at the supermarket bags that lined the opposite side. Crouching and kneeling, she tugged one towards her. The bag toppled and spilled thick bundles of banknotes across the floor. She re-stuffed it, keeping back a small brick of twenties. She planned to get a sausage roll at the petrol station. And a bag of crisps and a Dr Pepper, too. Morven hoped Cherub would be a good baby and let her rest. That's something else the angels hadn't warned her about – what busy work it would be to kill people while caring for a baby.

The young woman carried out her short-term plan – petrol station, room, shower – in a daze. Her mind thundered and crashed with loud thoughts:

I've been reckless, and if
I was doing this alone they might
Have killed me, and then
What would my little Cherub have done?
But they didn't, because I'm not alone, and that's
Because the angels are with me.

The angels could always be trusted. Maybe they hadn't warned her of everything, but they'd certainly guided her through some complex whoops-a-daisy whenever she needed them. Like when she had killed Cherub's daddy, Greg. Had that only been a couple days ago? Morven had been at the farm in Dorset when they'd told her now was the time. Greg's newest van was missing, and she knew –

she just knew, even without asking anybody – that he'd gone to the pied-a-terre in London. She hadn't even needed to think before grabbing the keys to the old Transit van from the hook in the kitchen. She took Cherub, too – she knew she wouldn't be coming back. It was true that that horrible woman Lorna had caught her fitting the baby seat into the Transit's passenger side, but Archangel Af had been right there on hand, whispering a few convincing lies to tell. Soon she and Cherub were driving through the New Forest. Morven kept the baby from crying by singing songs about blind mice and little donkeys. Af was there in the van, too, telling her what to say to Greg when she got to West Kensington.

Thinking of Archangel Af reminded Morven that she'd used the last of his cards in Kensington. As she'd told Jeff not long before she'd run him over, she needed to get more. That would be her next step – but not now. Not until she'd slept. Tomorrow morning, she and Cherub would drive down to Surrey to visit Mother Edwina.

It had been so long since she'd been in Mother's presence. Mother Edwina would give her more cards. And maybe she would have some advice on how to approach that one final name on Morven's to-do list.

FOUR

The headquarters of The Supplicants of Dusk was also its founder's home. Mother Edwina Koch lived in a large redbrick house in a cul-de-sac on the northern edge of Weybridge. The place was still known as The Retreat, though it had been a long time since Mother Edwina had allowed her Supplicants to stay there overnight, or even on Dark Holy Days. Mother also discouraged the faithful from showing up uninvited. Despite this, Morven had failed to announce her arrival. She knew Mother Edwina well enough to understand something. The more time you gave Mother to think about something, the more extreme her response might be. All Morven wanted was to admit… well, at least some of what she'd done, and then get some advice. She did not plan to tell Mother she'd killed Jeff Sawyer only days ago, because Jeff wasn't all that important. But by sending Greg to the underworld, she'd really thrown a spanner in the works. Greg had been a big donor to the Supplicants. He'd also looked after a number of them – if you could call it that – on his farm. Morven hoped that Mother Edwina would understand that Morven's mission came directly from the Heavenly Kingdom. Mother had always said, you can't contradict the angels.

Mother answered the door herself, on Morven's second knock. Mother stared for several seconds, lips thin and eyes wary. She broke her gaze only when she realized they were in public. Peering over Morven's shoulders, she scanned the street for neighbours. Then she hustled Morven and Cherub inside.

She glanced briefly down at the baby in his pram. Save for this, there were no formalities. 'Did you drive?' Mother asked tightly.

'Yes, and don't worry,' Morven told her. 'No one will see. I parked in the lay-by on the main road.'

Mother's lips grew thinner. 'I presume you've taken his new Mercedes van?'

Mother knows about Greg, Morven thought. Mother always knew. The angels told her everything, always.

Two other people appeared in the foyer. One was a

well-muscled Supplicant, whom Morven had never seen before. Behind him was a young woman Morven already knew. The two women made meaningful eye contact.

The well-muscled young man said, 'Mother? Is everything okay?'

'Yes, Raymond – everything is fine,' Mother Edwina told him. 'I won't need either of you for the time being. Morven and I will be in the conservatory.'

Mother Edwina's tone made it clear – Raymond and the girl with him should stay out. 'In fact,' she went on, 'both of you should go upstairs. I'll call when you can come down.'

Raymond bowed. Morven widened her eyes at the girl and angled her head towards the downstairs loo. 'I need to use the bathroom,' Morven told Mother. 'I think Cherub's nappy weighs more than he does.'

Cherub did need a new nappy. His old one was so soggy it felt like a bag of warm suet. Morven lay her baby on the toilet seat, his arms and legs dangling from its edges, and slipped a fresh nappy under his used one. It was a trick taught to her by necessity. She had learned to have the new nappy in place before uncovering the baby. Then Morven would remove the tape securing the old one, whisk that nappy away, and cover the baby with the fresh one as quickly as possible. It was the only way to prevent Cherub weeing straight up into the air. He'd hit her in the eye once.

Behind Morven, the loo door opened. The young woman pressed herself into the cramped space. 'Morven!' she said.

'Hey, Cara,' Morven said, 'I'd hug you if I could, but Cherub here would fall down and go boom. Don't want him cracking his little skull on the floor tiles.'

Cara hugged Morven's back awkwardly. 'I've thought about you,' she began. 'Wondered how you are.' She straightened up. 'There've been so many rumours. Raymond hasn't said much one way or the other, but when someone from the farm rings Mother, I hear things.'

'And I wish I could tell you everything,' Morven said. 'But if I start repeating the whole story now, we'll be here till tomorrow.' Morven secured Cherub's new nappy and yanked up his trousers. 'Now, you be a good baby,' she told him, 'and give Aunt Cara a sloppy baby kiss.'

She handed Cherub to Cara, who didn't wait for him to show affection. She covered his face with kisses of her own.

‘We weren’t sure you were really here,’ Morven told Cara. ‘Back at the farm, I mean. When you disappeared. They said Mother had chosen you specially to serve her, but for all we knew someone might have…’

Morven let the thought hang in the air.

‘I’ve been here the whole time,’ Cara confirmed.

‘Bet you were relieved to get away from the farm.’

Cara sighed. ‘This is no picnic, either,’ she said. ‘Mother’s hard work to keep happy.’

Even such a vague complaint made Morven squirm uncomfortably. Negativity against Mother sounded a lot like criticism of the Celestial Kingdom itself. ‘Well, I was jealous,’ Morven told Cara.

‘You were pregnant,’ Cara said. ‘She couldn’t have chosen you, even if she’d wanted to.’

‘She wouldn’t have, anyway,’ Morven said, and then grinned. ‘I’m a troublemaker.’

Cara glanced behind her at the closed toilet door. ‘I know we don’t have a lot of time, but could you at least tell me–’

‘Whatever you’ve heard,’ Morven interrupted, ‘it’s all probably true. That’s all I can say for now, Lovely. But I’ll come back if I can. We’ll talk.’

Abruptly, the door jerked open. The muscled bulk called Raymond stood before them. He looked at Cara, Cherub in her arms, with disdain. 'Give the baby back,' he ordered her.

Swiftly and without protest, Cara handed Cherub to Morven. As soon as she had, Raymond's hand shot out and pinched her ear. She drew in a breath. Raymond twisted, and she released a sharp cry.

'Mother,' Raymond said, 'has told us to go upstairs.'

'Then we should go,' Cara said.

With that, Raymond let go of Cara's ear and stepped back into the hallway. Cara gave Morven a sad goodbye smile and squeezed past her minder.

Raymond surveyed Morven will dull eyes. 'Mother is waiting in the conservatory,' he said.

Mother sat in front of a pot of tea and a plate of biscuits. A bag of yarn rested at her feet, and a half-finished crochet blanket was draped across a side table nearby. Here was a private side to Mother so few got to see. Morven parked Cherub's pram next to an upholstered chair and sat him up inside of it.

'That child needs a pushchair,' Mother said. 'He's

getting too big for the pram.'

'I'll buy him one,' Morven said.

Mother looked at her with concern. 'Do you have money?' she asked.

'Scads of it,' Morven replied.

She sat down, checked out the biscuits and smiled. Mother's taste in food had always lacked pretension. She may have been intimate with every angel in the Celestial Kingdom, but Mother still knew chocolate-covered Hob Nobs tasted good.

'Speaking of money,' Morven said. 'I brought you a gift.'

She leaned back so she could reach Cherub's changing bag, which was wedged on the plastic shelf under his pram. She rooted to its bottom. 'Donations,' she said.

One-by-one, Morven withdrew five thick bundles of banknotes, and set each side-by-side on the table. She counted them out as she did so: 'Donation Number One… Donation Number Two…'

Mother stared implacably as each bundle appeared before her. 'Oh, look – stolen money,' she said. 'Do you expect me to thank you?'

Morven shook her head innocently. She hadn't told

Mother the money was stolen.

Mother remained frozen for several seconds more. Then, in a single effortless movement she half-rose from her chair, swept up the cash and dropped it in her bag of yarn. 'How much did you keep for yourself?' she asked.

Morven shrugged benignly. When it came to Mother Edwina, there was no point in denying things. But, anyway, the money wasn't really stolen. Greg had no use for it now. Morven bent towards the tea pot. Once she had poured for herself and Mother, she slid half a biscuit into Cherub's chubby little fist. At first the baby gummed its edge into soggy chunks, but soon discovered licking the chocolate was more satisfying. Morven slurped and munched as she gazed across The Retreat's garden. The grass had turned olive with frost, as though Archangel Uriel had graced it with his coldest breath. Beyond the towpath, a lone canal boat was moored on a narrow bend in the Thames.

'What made you kill Greg?' Mother asked tightly.

Morven smirked. She'd been right. *Everything – that's what Mother knows*. She listened to a floorboard creak above the kitchen; the few staff were staying upstairs as ordered. Morven spread her palms as if caught bang-to-rights. 'Which naughty angel grassed me up, then?' she

asked.

Mother snorted. ‘Lorna told me,’ she said. ‘And that girl’s no angel, believe me.’ She stirred her tea but did not drink.

Lorna! Morven thought. *Maybe I should have killed her, too.* But Morven was new to heavenly executions and hadn’t seen widely enough, not even with what Mother called her ‘angel glasses’ on.

‘She saw you leave the farm in Greg’s old Transit van. The police found that vehicle in his parking spot in Kensington. That means you swapped it for the Mercedes. And now that Mercedes is a hundred yards from this house.’ Mother stirred her tea again. ‘And I’ll bet it’s simply stuffed with Greg’s cash.’

Uncharacteristically, Mother threw down the spoon in disgust. It clattered on the table and fell to the floor. ‘You tell me not to worry when you’ve put our entire order in danger.’

A trill of surprise rippled through Morven. It felt like harp music wafting through her body. Could it be that Morven understood something Mother didn’t? The thought was akin to blasphemy – and yet…

‘There’s not a single smidgeon of danger,’ she

explained. 'It's what needed to happen.'

Mother stared at her with sharp little eyes. 'Why?'

'The angels told me.'

Mother Edwina blew a raspberry. 'That's what you'll say to the police, is it?'

Morven snorted softly. 'This is so far beyond the police – they can't even see it,' she said. 'To them, it's like shadows. I mean, if a shadow killed another shadow, how would you know?'

Mother's jaw flexed. 'They're already investigating,' she said. 'I've told Lorna to keep her mouth shut and instruct the farm staff not to cooperate, but you've almost certainly left evidence.'

'Evidence?'

'DNA.'

Morven looked uncomprehending.

'Forensics?' Mother said. She flicked her fingers helplessly and raised her voice. 'You're driving his car! They'll catch you soon.'

Morven smiled at her from her heart, the way Mother and all the angels had taught her. Beatific – that was the word Mother used for that smile. Morven knew they wouldn't catch her... she just didn't know why. Maybe she'd die. Maybe Archangel Raphael would help her escape, as once he had shepherded Tobit to the city of Rages. Whatever way things played out, everything would turn out right as rain. 'I'll be just fine,' she said.

'It's not you I'm worried about, you stupid girl,' Mother snapped, even louder than before. At this, heavy footsteps began to descend the staircase. 'Everyone in Greg's organization is a member of the order. And you've left one of my bloody cards on his fucking body. How long before they're banging on my door?'

'Mother?' a deep voice called uncertainly. 'Is everything all right?'

'Go upstairs,' Mother said.

The footsteps clumped back up the steps. Morven pursed her lips sadly. Mother was confused – she wouldn't throw spoons and swear like that if she weren't. 'I had to leave the card,' Morven told her, 'because I put Greg into the care of Archangel Af. He needed to know who to follow during his descent into the underworld.'

Mother was so upset about Greg that Morven decided it was best not to tell her about Jeff. She had assumed Mother would know about him already, but in this case the angels had kept that information from her. This strange truth seemed almost impossible. Why would any heavenly being hide something from Mother, of all people? Mother, who usually knew – and *needed* to know – everything? Then again, who was Morven to challenge the judgement of the Celestial Kingdom?

'Speaking of the cards,' she ventured, 'I'm running a bit low. I'm completely out of Af, and I only have two Makatiels left. Could you give me some more, please?'

Mother's jaw ground like she was chewing bones. 'You want more cards,' she said flatly.

'Yes, please.'

'Those cards,' she told Morven, 'are not yours to have.'

Morven felt her head twitch backwards. 'You've always given them to me before,' she said.

Mother's voice turned sarcastic-sweet. 'You've never left them on a fucking body before. In fact…' She held out her hand. 'Hand over the ones you have left.'

Morven experienced something she had never before felt in Mother Edwina's presence – a swell of defiance. How this small rebellion had risen in her ever-faithful soul, Morven did not know. It was a first. But then, so was the fact that the angels were hiding things from Mother. 'They're not mine to have?' she asked. 'Well, they're not yours to deny, either. They belong to the Kingdom.'

'I represent the Kingdom on Earth,' Mother hissed.

Morven pondered this. It was still true. She stood and walked calmly to the foyer, where her parka hung on a hook. She rifled through one of the deep pockets and pulled out her diminished deck. Swiftly, she flicked through it, and flicked through her remaining angels: Lahatiel, Hutriel, Rogziel. Finally, she came upon Shoftiel – a beautiful young woman with black wings, and a deadly angel of punishment. She was perfect. Morven felt a pang of guilt as she slid the card into the coat's inner breast pocket. Ordinarily, she was not a deceiver. She returned to the conservatory and handed the rest of the cards to Mother Edwina.

'That's all of them?'

Morven nodded, pleading with the angels not to grass on her.

Fortunately, they didn't.

'OK,' Mother said. 'This is for you.' She handed Morven a cheap-looking mobile phone. 'It's pay-as-you-go and untraceable. I've programmed the number of another pay-as-you-go phone into it. If you need to get through to me, use it. If I want to speak to you, I'll ring this phone.

And you'd better answer.'

Morven dropped the phone into Cherub's nappy bag.

'I should make you leave the van,' Mother added. 'I own it now – the order is Greg's sole beneficiary. But you'll need it to flee, and you need to go fast.' She stared out to the boat moored in the Thames. 'I don't care where you go,' she went on quietly, 'but make sure it's far away. And if you're caught, I had nothing to do with this and you were not here today, do you understand?'

'Yes, Mother,' Morven said contritely, grasping the handle of Cherub's pram and angling him towards the hallway.

Mother led them to the door. As Morven shrugged on her parka, she felt for the card nestled in its breast pocket. As her fingers pressed against its edges, she breathed the last name on her list.

A standard bank bundle of fifty-pound notes contains £2,500. The ones Morven had given to Mother Edwina were not standard. As far as Edwina could guess, there was close to double that in each bundle. Around £25,000 in total. Under normal circumstances, Edwina would have put it in one of the order's bank accounts. Sometimes Greg had made similar cash offerings, and she'd deposited them openly. There was no reason not to. The Supplicants of Dusk was a religious order, and as tax-free as the Anglican Church.

But these were not normal circumstances.

'Put all this in the safe,' she told Raymond. He scooped up the bundles in his large hands. As he was leaving the room, she asked, 'Is Cara still upstairs?'

'Yes, Mother.'

'Keep her there. You stay put, as well.'

When Raymond was out of earshot, Edwina retrieved another mobile from the assortment of phones stashed in her roll-top writing desk. She had a man in London who kept a similar mobile. Whatever unknown number rang that phone, this man knew it would be either Edwina, Greg, or one of very few other Supplicants. Edwina did not have his number stored, but dialled from memory.

When he answered, she said, 'I'm presuming by now, you'll know who killed Greg.'

'Not yet,' he said, 'but trust me – my people are working on it.'

'You don't know?' she asked sceptically. 'Really?'

'Should I?'

'I'll give you a clue,' she told him. 'Our faithful Supplicant Greg was murdered by a chicken coming home to roost.'

When she heard nothing but the hiss of white noise on the phone, Edwina shouted, 'The little girl, for Christ's sake! That bonkers one from Greg's farm.'

Edwina thought she could hear a catch in her man's voice as he said, 'Morven?'

'Yes, Morven,' she snapped.

'You're sure?'

'She was just here. An unannounced Saturday morning visitor.'

'And you let her get away?'

'What was I supposed to do, kill her?' Edwina caught a glimpse of herself in the mirror above the sofa. She wore the expression – indeed, the entire face – of a bitter old woman. When she pictured herself in her mind's eye, she always saw someone carrying a heavy burden with fortitude and dignity. Of course, in that mental mugshot, she also looked about twenty years younger.

'OK, OK,' the man said. 'We both need to calm down.'

With effort, Edwina softened the muscles around her jaw. 'You have to handle this,' she said. 'It's your responsibility.'

'I know,' he assured her. 'And I can. I'll give everyone Morven's name and description. Trust me,' he concluded, 'we'll find her.'

'You'll *find* her?' Mother spat. 'That's your plan?'

Again, she heard nothing but silence. Edwina sighed deeply – she was surrounded by high-placed idiots. Some people didn't rise to the level of their incompetence, they shot well past it, incinerating everything in their trail. 'Tell me this,' she went on. 'When you describe the girl to the authorities, how will you explain knowing that she killed Greg?'

There was another long pause. 'You're right. I wasn't thinking,' he admitted. Then his tone grew more decisive. '*You* need to do it. After all, she came to you. You could ring Surrey police and report the visit.'

'What?'

'She victimised you, too,' he said insistently. 'Invaded your home. She's just a girl you barely know – a girl with mental health issues, at that – who's become obsessed with your teachings. You're lucky to be alive.'

Edwina could feel the dull throb of a headache forming behind her forehead. She hoped that wherever he was speaking from was private. 'And they'll ask me questions about her,' she reminded him. 'About her life on the farm.'

'Those are things you simply don't know,' he said in a breezy tone. 'Why would you? She was a member of your congregation, nothing more.'

'That'll work until they catch her,' Edwina said. She had told Morven to keep her mouth shut, but Edwina knew the girl was one of life's deadly innocents. She only knew what she thought the angels were telling her. 'She'll talk,' Edwina concluded, 'and once the authorities sort out the sense from the nonsense, we're all fucked.'

She could hear her man's heavy breathing, distorted by the mouthpiece of his cheap phone.

'I've told her to disappear,' Edwina went on. 'She's got a van stuffed full of Greg's cash, so she won't be destitute. If she listens to me, we might all have a chance.'

The girl would have to stay in Britain, of course. Morven did not have a passport. Then again, she did not have an official identity, either. Wherever she went, she wouldn't be missed.

'Of course,' Edwina went on, 'that baby is going to limit her options.'

'Shit!' the man cried. 'She has the *baby* with her?'

'She'd hardly have left it at the farm. Lorna would have tossed it into the ganja fields.'

'Oh, shit,' the man repeated. 'Shit.'

'What's important from your end,' Edwina told him, 'is that the girl is not caught. Is that clear?'

He made an inarticulate sound.

'Not caught,' she repeated. 'And to be clear, I mean allowed to escape.'

'How can I guarantee that?' the man almost cried. 'The Met have an active homicide investigation underway.'

'That's not my area of specialty,' Edwina said. 'Fortunately, it is yours.'

She noticed her head was still aching, and her jaw was tight again. 'Treat this as though your life depended on it,' she told the man. 'Because it really, really does.'

Before he could respond, she pressed the phone's red button and rang off.

All our lives depend on it, Mother Edwina thought.

FIVE

Sara bent over a display case in the hush of a New Bond Street jewellers. The place was decorated in a theme of understated cream-and-beige; even its marble walls and fluted columns looked light and tasteful. This mild backdrop offset the dark line of mahogany cases. Strategic lighting made each piece of jewellery sparkle. A rich Indian carpet, the same size as the floor, drew everything together. The proprietor had arrayed a number of items atop a glass case for Sara's perusal.

It was a few days before Valentine's Day, and Sara had decided to make this year's gift to Jamie special. The two of them had been through so much in the last several months and, throughout, Jamie had kept his good nature. A year ago, that might have bothered Sara. She'd been frustrated by that very light-heartedness in the face of problems she could never share with him. Although Sara would never have wished the misfortunes that befell Jamie in his tenure at Thorndike Aerospace, they had reframed her entire relationship with him. Jamie's cheerful fortitude reminded Sara what a wonderful partner she had.

'I think this one,' Sara said.

The proprietor complimented Sara on her excellent choice. As he began clearing the other items from the glass cabinet top, he acknowledged someone on the other side of the door. He buzzed her in and promised he'd only be a minute more. Sara looked behind her, where there stood a striking woman in her early twenties. She must have been at least six feet tall, and wore her hair in a broad afro dyed blue at the tips. The woman's wardrobe caused Sara a moment of puzzlement. It seemed at odds with her surroundings: she was dressed in tracksuit bottoms and a hoodie branded with the logo of a chain of gyms. Immediately, Sara felt a small stab of shame for judging the woman on the clothing she wore – obviously, the proprietor had a more nuanced understanding of who belonged in his shop of pricey treasures.

'That is lovely,' the woman marvelled. 'Valentine's Day?'

Sara smiled in acknowledgement.

She whistled softly. 'You must love your partner a lot.'

‘I do,’ Sara said, handing the proprietor her AmEx card.

The woman laughed merrily. ‘Or else you feel guilty about something.’

When Sara didn’t return the laugh, the woman held out her hand. ‘I’m Daniela,’ she said.

Sara shook, and told her how lovely it was to meet her.

The woman grinned and replied, ‘Obviously, it was destiny.’

A slightly odd reply, Sara thought as she keyed in her PIN. In fact, it bordered on creepy. She accepted her parcel, thanked the proprietor and left the shop. Outside, Sara paused in a recessed doorway to fit the small bag inside her handbag. When she looked up again, the striking woman named Daniela was passing by her at a meandering pace. She smiled at Sara.

‘Didn’t find what you were looking for?’ Sara asked her.

‘Whatever makes you think that?’ the woman replied. ‘As it happens, I found exactly what I needed to find.’

A few nights later, Sara and Jamie sat on a blanket on the floor of their living room. Dinner had been Sara’s idea: a picnic in February. She had picked it up earlier that day from Harrods' Food Hall. The high-end indoor picnic consisted of wagyu sirloin, potato salad, truffles, caviar, and a variety of breads. Sara had served it with a pinot noir. As they ate, Jamie said, 'This is incredible. All of it.' He wagged his head. 'Though I wish you'd let me choose the wine.'

Sara started. 'You don't like this?' she asked.

'The pinot? It's great. Goes so well with the beef. It's just that…' He grinned. 'I know you like Chardonnay.'

Sara wrinkled her nose. 'I wouldn't have chosen it for today's picnic.'

'Maybe not, but usually, right? I mean, if you were to buy one really expensive bottle of wine, it would be a Chardonnay.' He paused dramatically. 'That's why I got you this.' From the side of his chair, Jamie produced another bottle. 'Happy Valentine's Day,' he said.

Sara laughed. 'I didn't think we were doing presents yet,' she said.

'I couldn't wait,' he said.

Sara squinted at the label. '2009,' she read. 'A good year for American Chardonnay… and, yes, it does look expensive.' She leaned over and kissed him. 'Thank you. It's the second best gift you could have given me.'

‘Second best?’ Jamie asked. As it dawned on him, he drew in a breath and threw his head back. ‘Of course. A kitten.’

Sara smiled. ‘Just saying.’

Jamie shrugged. ‘Well, know knows?’ he said. Glancing at the bottle, he continued, ‘Ask me how much it cost.’

Sara gave him a look of exaggerated reproof. ‘No!’ she said. ‘That would be vulgar.’

‘Over two hundred pounds,’ Jamie told her with glee.

Sara shook her head in exasperation. ‘We’ll enjoy it together,’ Sara said. ‘One day soon, we’ll spend a day playing hooky – and we’ll drink this.’

She returned to eating the beef.

Jamie smiled in anticipation.

Sara stopped mid-chew. ‘What?’ she asked around her food. ‘You want your gift now, too?’

Jamie feigned indifference, albeit quite badly. ‘Not necessarily,’ he said unconvincingly. ‘Later will be fine.’ Suddenly, he smiled with comic-book-villain cruelty. ‘We’ll just talk about the investigation instead. I notice they haven’t asked you to do anything for a while, and I’m wondering whether that’s because you haven’t come up with an answer about that card…’

'OK, stop! You win,' Sara cried. She huffed comically and tossed a fist-sized package his way. 'Here – take it.'

Laughing, Jamie caught the gift and tore off the wrapping paper. When he saw the green box with its Rolex insignia, he stopped. 'My God,' he whispered. 'You didn't.'

'Open it,' Sara said.

Jamie snapped open the box and gazed down at the steel watch with its elegant royal blue face. 'A Perpetual,' he said. 'This is… it's… it's about thirty times more expensive than the wine I gave you.'

Sara grinned and shook her head. 'Not at all.' She made a dumb show of calculating. 'More like twenty-three times.'

'Why?' he asked in all innocence.

'Because I've never given you anything this nice before,' she said, 'and that was an oversight.'

Jamie had been right, though – little had happened on the investigation, and Sara had begun to feel like a consultant in name only. The weekend came and went. Sara and Ceri spent Saturday shopping in the West End, had dinner at an Indian restaurant and a nightcap at a folk club's Country and Western night. On Sunday, they went their separate ways, Ceri doing what she called *bimbling about* – whatever that meant – and Sara spending time with Jamie in Brixton. Now it was Monday morning, and Sara was still in her dressing gown, a cup of coffee before her. Jamie sat across the table, pecking away at an essay on his laptop.

Sara's mobile sounded its saxophone.

'Dr Jones,' a voice said. 'It's Joe Bennett calling. We met at West End Central.'

'I remember, Minister,' Sara said.

Jamie raised his eyebrows. *Minister?* he mouthed.

'I'm sorry to call you first thing on a Monday morning, but I was wondering if you'd be available to meet?'

'Err – of course,' Sara said. She pointed to her chest, indicating to Jamie that the minister was asking for her. He offered an exaggerated frown to show he was impressed. 'When would be convenient for you?'

'I was thinking of this afternoon,' the Minister for Policing said. 'Are you available?'

'If you need me,' Sara confirmed. 'I assume you're in Westminster?'

'I won't be this afternoon,' Bennett said. 'Would you be willing to meet me up in Hampstead?'

'I can go anywhere,' Sara said. 'Just give me the address.'

'I thought we'd stroll on the Heath,' the minister said. 'It's like my second home. I'm something of a keen ornithologist, if that's not too grand a title.' He chuckled modestly. 'Really, I'm just a bird watcher.'

'And is the watching good now?' Sara asked.

Jamie made a puzzled face. 'What is he watching?' he whispered.

'It's been fine for months,' Bennett replied. 'Last September I was on Parliament Hill and saw osprey migrating. But, really, I prefer the bushier areas of the Heath.'

'That's lovely,' Sara said, hoping she had sounded like she meant it. 'Where will I find you?'

'Meet me at four o'clock outside the Hampstead Heath Rail Station,' Bennett said. 'We'll stroll around the ponds.'

'I'm looking forward to it,' Sara said, and rang off.

'You're meeting a minister?' Jamie said.

Sara nodded. 'All in a day's work for a crime fighter like me,' she said. She considered for a moment and added, 'Did I sound insincere?'

'A few months ago,' Bennett told Sara, 'I spotted a lesser kestrel just over there. See?' He pointed to the branch of a barren tree. 'That's rare.'

Sara followed the minister's finger and tried to look impressed. Bennett waved to a dense patch of shrubbery. 'This time of year is good for woodcocks, but you have to come in the evening. Right now, they'll still be asleep in the bushes.' Next, he gestured with his chin towards the treetops. 'If you're here at dusk, you might also see a tawny owl.'

The Minister for Policing was dressed like a model from an RSPB brochure. He wore an olive waxed jacket and a camouflage-patterned boonie hat. In his right hand, he carried a pair of pocket binoculars. 'Have you ever been bird-watching?' he asked.

'I don't make a habit of it,' Sara said. 'But as a child, I lived near a place in the Cambrian Mountains where they feed red kites. Sometimes the family would go and watch them.'

'What a splendid childhood you must have had,' Bennett said. Sara faked agreement with a smile. Bennett was the first person connected to policing who didn't seem to know her history. 'You know,' he went on, 'for a long time, Wales was the only place in the country you could see red kites. Now they've been reintroduced to England, and they're doing very well indeed. Sometimes, you can even see them here, over the Heath. Magnificent bird.'

Sara nodded. Just as she had almost decided the minister was simply looking for a bird-watching companion, he changed the subject. 'These cards,' he said. 'What a mystery, eh?'

'Somebody will know where they come from,' Sara said.

'You think?'

'It's a certainty. The only question is, will we find out before someone else is killed?'

'Another victim?' Bennett asked. 'Do you think that's likely?'

'Hard to say,' Sara said. She considered. 'Possibly not.'

The minister looked relieved. 'Why do you say that?'

'You've seen the evidence. Mr Blackadar and his killer were having sex. She stabbed him during the act. That sounds to me like there was a personal motive. The card she left may have had some significance between the two of them.'

Joseph Bennett stared into a thicket of trees, following

his own pathways of thought. He nodded absently.

'Minister,' Sara ventured, 'why have you asked me here? I mean, alone. It seems unorthodox.'

'How so?' he said.

'I'd think the Senior Investigating Officer should be present at a meeting like this.'

Bennett smiled coyly. 'He doesn't like bird-watching. As for your handler – Detective Sergeant Mir – I don't know what she likes.' Bennett folded his binoculars and slipped them into his pocket. 'You're here because I want to ask you a favour,' he said. 'I'm always kept up-to-date on the facts of a homicide investigation. What I seldom hear is the speculation.'

'Speculation,' Sara repeated.

'It's the things people suspect but can't prove that are often meaningful,' he explained. 'You must have found that in your own career.'

More than you know, Sara thought.

'The press has asked for comments from me. So far, I've avoided saying anything. However, my silence can't carry on indefinitely. If I understood what the thinking is on the ground, I could avoid jamming my foot in my mouth,' Bennett concluded.

Surely, Sara thought, *you'll say the same bland things all politicians say*.

'So, you want me to spy for you?'

'You are not a police officer,' Bennett pointed out. 'That means you're free to tell me things the constabulary is not.' He removed his hat and ran his fingers through his richly-dyed hair. 'I'd like to hear whatever you're thinking, that's all.'

SIX

A couple of days later, Sara and Jamie were watching the seven o'clock news when Sara saw Joseph Bennett again – this time on their television screen. He stood in the central lobby of the House of Commons. Bennett was answering a reporter's questions about matters unrelated to policing. He spoke in a tone of amused high-handedness that irked Sara for reasons that had nothing to do with politics. She'd been thinking a lot about the minister ever since their meeting in the woods. Sara didn't like being used as a pawn, and suspected that was the role Bennett had assigned her. She muted the television's sound.

'What do you think, though?' she asked him. 'About Bennett. Is what he's doing normal?'

'Taking you bird-watching? Not many politicians would do that.'

'I mean trying to use me as his…' She groped for the word. 'As his *snitch*.'

‘That’s more like a politician,’ Jamie said. He gestured towards the silent screen. The television lights washed out the wrinkles in Bennett’s face, and made his dyed hair shine like the surface of a chestnut. ‘Just look at him – they’re a sneaky lot by nature.’ He angled his head thoughtfully. ‘What was Adeela’s reaction?’ he asked.

Sara released a breath slowly and heavily. ‘I haven’t told her.’

‘Why not?’

‘She’d see it as interference.’

‘Well, it is.’

‘But then she’d inform her superintendent,’ Sara went on, ‘and that would create rather a lot of tension.’

Jamie chuckled sardonically. ‘If Bennett is meddling, he deserves the tension.’

‘Maybe – but he wouldn’t suffer at all. The investigation would.’

Jamie nodded. ‘You’re probably right. Maybe it’s best to wait and see. But if he puts any more pressure on you, you’re going to have to spill the beans. Anything else and you’d make yourself complicit.’

Sara shook her head slightly. She was complicit in enough things already. ‘Well one thing’s for sure,’ she said.

‘I won’t become his informant.’

She noticed that Bennett had disappeared form the screen, and turned the volume back up.

An hour later, Sara was going over paperwork related to the new practice when she was interrupted by the music of her mobile.

‘Can you make it up to Hertfordshire?’ Adeela Mir asked. ‘Police up here have found another body.’

‘Oh, good heavens,’ Sara exclaimed.

Jamie looked up from his phone with eyebrows raised. *What is it?* he asked without words.

Mir, Sara mouthed.

A new victim? he replied silently.

Sara nodded gravely, and he shook his head with equal solemnity. In truth, she did not feel grave; she was surprised by the tingle of excitement that ran up her spine. ‘Same M.O.?’ she asked Mir.

‘I wouldn’t have said so,’ Mir told her, ‘except that–’

‘There’s another card,’ Sara guessed.

Mir grunted in acknowledgement. ‘That’s why they alerted the Met. At least the picture’s prettier this time,’ she said.

Sara told Mir she should be able to get there within the hour. Then she realized how hurt Ceri would be if she weren't invited along. Sara knew that bringing her friend would border on the unprofessional. Still, the long-term consequences of ignoring her would be more tiresome than giving her what she'd want.

'Detective Sergeant Mir?' Sara said. 'Would it be OK if I brought Ceri along?'

Jamie made an exaggerated gesture of surprise. Sara mimed a sigh and he grinned. They were both used to appeasing Ceri Lloyd. Mir did not answer; there was nothing but a hiss on the line. Sara added, 'She might have something to contribute.'

Jamie raised his eyebrows. *She might.*

Sara imagined Mir closing her eyes as she recalled the inappropriate comments Ceri had made previously. She wondered if she were putting her credibility on the line by championing her old friend. 'That won't be necessary,' Mir said finally. 'Inspector Lloyd is already here.'

'What?' Sara blurted.

'What'd she say?' Jamie whispered.

Questions flooded Sara's mind. Why was Ceri there? Had Mir called her first? And why? How had Ceri got to the scene? Why hadn't anyone picked up Sara at the same time?

Jamie still stared. Sara smiled at him grimly and shook her head. *It's nothing.* She found she didn't want to ask questions in front of her partner. She wasn't entirely sure why. Maybe it was just embarrassment that Ceri had been asked to the scene before she had.

Instead, all Sara said was, 'Never mind. Just give me the address.'

Sara used a navigation app to guide her to the site in Hertfordshire. By the time she was on the right lane, she no longer needed it; Hertfordshire Scene of Crime officers had floodlit the area. The glow served as Sara's own personal homing beacon. Hertfordshire Police had taped off the property's perimeter, and Sara had to join a short parade of cars parked on the lane's edge. It seemed the vehicles belonged mostly to journalists, who now elbowed each other along the barrier. Two television reporters stood at a distance, each blinking at the ground as their camera operators fiddled with lights. Sara approached the constable who guarded a break in the tape. Flashes strobed, and she heard an old hand bark out her first name. She didn't bother listening to his question.

'Sara Jones,' she told the constable. 'I'm a consultant with the Met.' He nodded her through.

The house itself was relatively modern – 1970s, she guessed – with a sprawling front garden bracketed by fields. At the far end of a gravel drive were two cars. A Ford Focus sat nearest the lane, and behind it, an older Vauxhall Astra had been isolated by tape. Immediately behind the Astra stood a white popup gazebo, erected to hide the body from the gawping journos in the distance. Ceri had spotted Sara and was trudging down the drive to meet her.

'We've got our connection,' she called, her breath shooting steam through Scenes of Crime's light. Reaching Sara, she angled her head towards the gazebo. 'Jeffrey Sawyer. He was 44 years old and – listen to this – he used to live in Poole.' She raised her eyebrows meaningfully. 'And Poole is in Dorset.'

'So, Dorset's the connection?' Sara asked.

'If it's not, it's a hell of a coincidence,' Ceri replied. 'A second victim with another freakish card, and both bodies hailing from Dorset.'

Ceri swivelled on her heel and led Sara up the drive.

Their feet crunched softly on the gravel.

'Where's DS Mir?' Sara asked.

'Adeela's in the house. Hertfordshire has jurisdiction, so she really can't do much. She's observing as a sergeant talks to the victim's wife.'

'The wife found him?'

'Apparently she'd spent a fortnight caring for her mother in Southampton. She got back to find Mr Sawyer on his driveway. Hell of a time to find him. There's bloating, decomposition, and *plenty* of aroma.'

'Eugh,' Sara said.

'I haven't got to the worst of it,' Ceri said. 'He'd been tortured. He's got a man-cave out in back, and he was held there for a while. It's chock-full of power tools, which the offender put to some creative uses.'

Sara winced. The bile in her stomach rose again.

'That's not all. Then he was squashed by his own car.' Ceri pointed. 'That Astra over there. The offender drove over him.'

'Improvised murder weapons,' Sara observed. 'Same as in Kensington.'

'Seems like it. Busked it with whatever was available,' Ceri agreed.

'And messily, too. Violent, bloody. That suggests it could be personal,' Sara said.

'Could well be,' Ceri agreed. 'A great-big goddamned grudge.' She angled her head towards the white gazebo. 'I'm sure Adeela can get you in to examine the body.'

'I don't need to,' Sara said, too quickly.

'Suit yourself,' Ceri said.

'What are you doing here, anyway?' Sara asked. She sounded more irritable than intended.

Ceri stared across the driveway. 'Helping.'

'You know what I mean.'

She waved her hand, as though the explanation were simple. 'When the Met got the call from Hertfordshire Police, Adeela stopped by your new home. You weren't there, but I was. She asked me along.' Ceri scanned the floodlit site. 'We had to get up here quickly, so we couldn't wait for you.'

'I see,' Sara said.

At that moment, Adeela Mir emerged from the house. She clocked Sara and Ceri and headed over.

'How's Mrs Sawyer?' Ceri asked.

'Distraught, naturally,' Mir told them. She looked to Sara and said, 'Thanks for coming.' Sara nodded.

'Mrs Sawyer has confirmed a connection to the other victim,' Mir went on. 'She thinks Greg Blackadar might have ordered a hit on her husband.'

'What?' Sara said.

'Of course, that's impossible, based on what we know.'

'Hang on a second,' Ceri said. 'Why does she think that? What's the connection between the two men?'

'Cannabis,' Mir replied. 'Apparently, Sawyer served time for supplying. When he lived in Poole, he was a mid-level dealer.'

'And Blackadar…?'

'Grew the stuff on his chicken farm. Sawyer brokered it to street dealers. It was a small-time operation. When Sawyer was arrested, he never gave Blackadar's name – according to the wife, he thought Blackadar owed him for that. He was put out that his old business partner didn't seem grateful enough. They fell out over it.'

Sara buttoned the top collar of her coat; as the night wore on, it was getting colder. It would make sense that Sawyer's wife would jump to conclusions. She didn't know that Blackadar was also dead. Or that Sawyer, and very likely her husband, were murdered by a woman.

'Can I see the card?' Sara asked.

‘I’ll see what they say.’ Mir gestured for Sara to wait. She trudged towards some Hertfordshire officers standing near the gazebo.

‘Once I’ve photographed it,’ Sara told Ceri, ‘I’m going home. If you want a ride, get your things.’

Ceri grimaced. ‘I’ll stay,’ she said. ‘They may need me,’

‘For what?’

Ceri hardened her jaw. ‘I can be quite useful, you know. Adeela will take me back.’

Not long afterwards, Sara trudged down the drive towards the police tape. Her eyes were on her phone. This image featured the same border as the previous one, and had been painted in similar garish hues. Its subject was a handsome young man with flowing hair and robes. He brandished a streak of fire in his right hand. Unlike the rather generic demon on the previous card, this one was clearly an angel image. Then again, what she’d been thinking of as a demon might well be an angel too. It all depended on the tradition the image came from; there was no consensus when it came to angels. This particular character’s shaft of flame suggested he might be the Archangel Michael… but maybe not. Several angels were depicted brandishing fire in one tradition or another.

Sara stopped near the constable guarding the perimeter exit. She opened her emails. Immediately, one of the television journalists called out her name. News of who she was had spread among the reporters. A light swung in her direction and threw purple spots into her vision. Sara ignored the woman and closed and opened her eyes, trying to focus on her phone's screen. She called up the mailing list she had made recently. It was of contacts who were experts in the same arcane waters Sara occasionally swam in. None had got back to her yet about the first image, but she attached the clearest photo of the new card and asked for speculations.

'Dr Jones?' the television journalist said. The young constable at the tape looked at Sara questioningly. He could deal with the intrusion if she'd like. Sara shook her head softly.

'Yes,' she replied neutrally.

The journalist introduced herself as a news reporter for the regional BBC outlet and asked if Sara would be willing to appear on camera. A camera was already pointed in her direction.

'I can't,' Sara said.

‘Dr Jones, what’s your role here?’ another reporter barked. ‘Has the Hertfordshire constabulary called you in?’ Sara pretended not to hear.

‘Would you be willing to be interviewed later?’ the television journalist said.

‘You might as well tell us,’ the reporter said loudly over the TV journalist. ‘We know why you’re called into these things. Are there occult trappings?’

The constable pointed his finger at the man and shouted, ‘You pipe down.’

Sara concentrated on the woman from the BBC. ‘I couldn’t give an interview unless the police agreed,’ she said. ‘And that’s unlikely. Now, please excuse me.’

The constable ordered the reporters to clear a space for Sara. Before she walked the gauntlet of press towards her car, Sara glanced back up the drive. Ceri and Mir still stood where she had left them. Sara narrowed her eyes - it looked for all the world as though Ceri was accepting a cigarette from Mir.

It must be gum, she thought. Ceri wouldn’t smoke so soon after a heart attack.

Then Mir popped a lighter and Ceri leaned into the flame. A cloud of smoke billowed into the floodlights.

SEVEN

That Thursday morning, Morven lazed in her hotel room bed with Cherub at her side. She'd bought breakfast already from the restaurant downstairs. The toast had been cold and the eggs reconstituted, but the coffee had been good. And Morven always felt irrationally pleased by those little plastic pots of jam. She never used them, she just fiddled with them as she ate. Now Morven felt pleasantly full of fat, sugar, and caffeine. Cherub was sucking contentedly on a bottle of Follow-On Formula. *Organic!* the tin said. *Full Cream!* There was also a little printed lecture about how breastfeeding was better than using the product you'd just paid for, but Morven couldn't imagine putting up with all that kerfuffle. Gummed nipples were something she did not need.

Morven had morning television playing at a low volume. She found it awfully boring. She had been watching way too much of this kind of rubbish ever since she and Cherub had fled the farm and started their angelic mission. She wondered whether she shouldn't buy a book to read. Up until recently, Morven had read quite a lot. That was thanks to her papa. Morven knew Papa had been used by Greg like another piece of farm machinery… but that hadn't meant he was stupid. He'd just been unlucky. Papa and Mummy – the mummy Morven never really knew – had fled Glasgow maybe twenty years ago for a better life. Instead, they found nothing but low-paid servitude, from the top of England all the way down to the bottom. With each menial job it had become harder to feed and shelter themselves. They'd been kids themselves then, and when Mummy got pregnant, they'd found their way to Greg. Greg would've been in his early thirties at the time, and he already owned the farm – an inheritance – and had bought his first rental property in Bournemouth. He was a Supplicant by then, too; Andreas and Mother Edwina had found Gregory Blackadar when he was young. Greg offered Morven's parents a place to stay in trade for food and board. To a young couple about to have a child, it seemed a good deal. Trouble was, they never left and Greg never paid them.

Morven grew up on the farm. Her birth had not been

registered, and she'd never been to school. But she'd heard an awful lot about the Celestial Kingdom. And in a way she'd been home-schooled by her papa – probably earlier than a lot of kids start. She couldn't recall Mummy dying, but she remembered all the hours Papa had stolen for her after that. Those were good times, when they would sneak off beyond the chickens, out to the weed fields or greenhouses. They'd smuggle books like contraband, giggling about the illicit reading they were going to do. The sense that they were getting away with something made Morven want to do it all the more. In the really early days, Papa had just read to her. Morven remembered a blocky cardboard book about cars, and a whole series about a family of teddies who did wonderful things together. One read: *We've all gone on holiday. The sand on the beach is hot. Look! The palm trees are very tall.* Later the books got more complicated, but by then Morven was reading them to Papa. By the time he died a few years back, Morven was borrowing books from Greg or anyone else who had them. She never asked, but always replaced them. She could read quickly. A year or so ago, Lorna had given her a beating for taking a book without permission. Morven hadn't felt guilty – Lorna had been 'reading' it for months and the bookmark still protruded from an early chapter.

I really should have killed that girl, Morven thought.

Since she had seen Mother on Saturday, Morven had devoted herself exclusively to mummy and baby time. She no longer had those early books her papa had read to her, but she had them memorised, and had repeated them to the baby like favourite family stories. Morven and Cherub had also visited the zoo in Regent's Park and the Museum of London at the Barbican. There, Morven had hoped to see the massive chunk of fatberg that had been pulled straight from the sewers of Whitechapel. She was disappointed to hear that it had been taken off display. Until it returned, a cheerful museum employee told her, she could watch a live stream of the attraction online. No she couldn't, Morven thought. She didn't have a smartphone, and there was no way she was going to visit the library just to watch a chunk of congealed fat, wet wipes and nappies hatch flies in a glass case. Nonetheless, these excursions had helped to blot out Morven's uneasiness about the way she had been received at The Retreat. She had expected Mother Edwina's empathy – indeed, her help. But Mother had not seemed pleased to see her. She had not been happy that Greg had died, either – even though it was what the angels had decided. It had been clear the angels had kept things from Mother. This fact had unsettling implications that troubled Morven.

She pulled the bottle from Cherub's mouth. It made a popping sound and immediately he protested. 'You can have it back in second,' Morven told him. 'But first you need to burp.'

She laid him heavily over one shoulder, his forehead pressed against the padded headboard affixed to the wall. She patted Cherub's back. When he was once again pressed next to her side and sucking greedily, Morven picked up the remote and found the news channel. Suddenly, her heart raced. There – right there on television – was a picture of Jeff's house in the dark, flooded by bright lights. Police were swarming all over the gravel driveway. Morven released a moan of wonder. *This new report was all about her!* One of the coloured information bars at the bottom of the screen said the images had been taken last night. She slid up the headboard and leaned forward in rapt attention. Concentrated. The voiceover was saying a lot of words, but none of them amounted to much. These reporters didn't know anything. In a way, she guessed that was good – safer, anyhow – but in another way, it made the report less interesting.

The report cut to an on-the-street interview, grabbed that very morning with Minister for Policing Joseph Bennett. The minister wore a casual jacket and jumper and stood in front of a row of posh white houses. His hair looked freshly dyed. Morven edged away from Cherub and sat further up on the bed. 'The Bedfordshire, Cambridgeshire, and Hertfordshire Major Crimes Unit is investigating this awful event,' the Minister was saying.

An off-screen reporter reminded Bennett that Jeffrey Sawyer's murder came not long after the grisly murder of Gregory Blackadar in London.

Morven gave a small cheer. *Both* her killings had been mentioned!

Bennett chose to take this fact as a veiled query as to whether the killings might be connected. He moved to deflect such speculation. 'Last year, there were one hundred and thirty-five murders in London,' Bennett said. 'Mr Blackadar's death was the ninth this January. Every single death is a tragedy. I'm concerned about all murders.'

'That isn't all you're concerned about, arsehole,' Morven jeered at the TV.

The news report switched back to images of last night's

murder scene. There was a shot of a woman trudging down the driveway towards the camera. She appeared to be in her late thirties. The woman had spiky auburn hair, an expensive-looking coat, and one of those beige Burberry-check scarves around her neck.

'Dr Jones,' an off-screen reporter called, 'what's your role here?'

The woman did not answer. Another unseen reporter asked her if there were 'any occult trappings' to the murder. It seemed like a stupid question until the report said *occult trappings* were exactly what this woman was into. Her name was Sara Jones, and she was a psychiatrist who helped the police. Some old footage showed her at an investigation in Wales, ducking under police tape at the bottom of a hill. Morven had never been to Wales.

The footage returned to last night, and showed Dr Sara Jones walking away from reporters and moving towards a blue Mini. Morven slid off the bed, careful not to disturb Cherub, and found a pen. On the back of her hand she wrote, *sara jones/blue mini*.

There was something about this psychiatrist that intrigued Morven. Maybe the angels were sending Morven a message. Maybe this woman would somehow become important to her. Morven decided she needed to find out more about Dr Sara Jones.

The only question was, should she do it before or after she killed TV star Stewart Delaney?

Between the times she'd killed Greg and when she'd killed Jeff, Morven had checked into two different hotels. They were only separated by a few miles, but it had seemed smart to have a backup. Morven hadn't known whether she'd need to dash from one of them in a hurry. Running for an almost-identical hotel nearby would never have been a long-term solution, but it would buy her time to hide and pull her thoughts together.

Morven decided to find out more about Sara Jones first. There was no rush with Stewie – she knew where he lived. Since they'd killed off his character in that soap opera, he had been staying home a lot. Sometimes when Morven was at the farm, someone would mention how Stewart was up for a big part in so-and-so's movie, or that he was being considered for such-and-such a TV show. In the end, though, he was never in any of them. Stewart would almost certainly be home whenever Morven needed him to be.

Also, killing people took its toll. Morven got tired even

thinking about having to do it again. She'd really need to gee herself up to carry on with the Kingdom's plan.

Morven loaded their toiletries and some clothing into the van, and strapped Cherub into his car seat. She figured if she had to drive into town, she might as well show her face at the other hotel. It wasn't far from the High Street, and she could walk to the library from there. Besides, she'd had to pay extra for parking at that one. She might as well use it. Once they had arrived at Hotel Number Two, Morven left the pram inside the van – she could pick it up again on the way to the library. She carried Cherub and their belongings into the lobby.

Their room was on the third floor. As they waited for the lift, Morven heard a voice sounding from the reception desk. 'I think you're in the wrong hotel,' the voice said.

Morven froze. She fixed her gaze above the lift's doors and watched the numbers counting down. She cringed as she heard the receptionist rise and emerged from the recessed office. 'Seriously,' he asked, 'are you visiting someone?'

'We have a room here,' Morven replied without looking at him.

'Did you move?'

Slowly, she spun around. She looked at the receptionist – a chubby man with dark, curly hair. Morven had seen him before. 'You're the guy from the other hotel,' she said. It rang out like an accusation.

'I'm the manager there,' he confirmed.

'What are you doing here?' she asked.

'It's the same chain,' he told her. 'I'm filling in.'

'Ah,' Morven said. She'd known her hotel rooms were similar, but hadn't realised she'd booked into two identical hotels. 'I reserved a room here for my mother, actually,' Morven said. 'She's a classical musician, though, and she's been delayed in Vienna.'

'Why didn't you book her into the one you're staying in?' he asked.

The lift dinged and its doors slid open. 'That dump?' Morven said, and stepped in quickly. 'Not nearly close enough to town for Mumsy.' As the doors shut, she added, 'She's very cosmopolitan.'

Even on a Thursday, the High Street pavements were crowded with shoppers. Morven nipped into the Co-Op for a package of chocolate Hob Nobs. Cherub would be a good baby if he could lick and gum his way through the afternoon. In the library, Morven paid for an hour's worth of internet time. There were three computers side-by-side. Two were taken, but the one on the right side was free. Morven parked Cherub just behind her and logged on. She found that Sara Jones was surprisingly easy to research. It didn't take long for Morven to learn what Sara had been up to in Wales. The investigation she'd been part of was awful, and it led, in a roundabout way, to the death of Sara Jones's brother. He had been a bigwig at some weapons company, and it sounded like he was pretty unpleasant, too. The papers speculated that Rhodri Jones became unhinged when he was attacked by the crazy psychic guy Sara was trying to catch. Whatever the truth, that brother had gone on to kill a young woman, and then himself. Well, good riddance to him, Morven thought. Hurt a young woman and you deserve to die.

'Have you got a biscuit?' Behind her, someone was speaking in a syrupy voice. 'Is it nice? You like biscuits, don't you? Yes, you do.'

It sounded like someone talking to a dog. Morven half-turned to find a man in late middle-age kneeling in front of Cherub. Her first reaction was shock. She'd had no idea that strangers approached each other in libraries. This intruder-of-her-personal-space had a receding hairline and a large mole on the left side of his chin. He might have been almost-handsome in an old man sort of way, except for his silly pug nose. Cherub stared at Mr Pug Nose dispassionately, as though he were a dull cartoon. Mr Pug Nose looked up to Morven and smiled. 'What his name?'

Morven tensed and dropped her gaze. She glowered at the right back wheel of Cherub's pushchair. It was white, but its middle had been stained the colour of street dirt. 'He doesn't like strangers,' she muttered.

'Ah,' Pug Nose said. 'Well, he's a lovely boy.'

Morven did not reply, or even look at him. She remained frozen in her half-turn until he scooched sideways and faded from her peripheral vision. Then she cleaned Cherub's mouth with a baby wipe and replaced his tacky Hob Nob with a new one.

Turning back to her research, Morven soon discovered that Sara Jones's parents had been murdered by a local drifter when she was only a teen. That touched her heart. It touched her so much that the last of her jangling nerves about Mr Pug Nose dissolved into a feeling of warm pity. Morven could relate. She had never known her mummy – she'd died when Morven was a wee baby – but her dad had passed on only a couple years ago. It wasn't easy, losing a parent in your teens. She and Dr Jones shared something in common. Morven decided she wanted to see this Sara Jones woman up close. Maybe not talk to her, but at least have a look. Morven was pretty good at finding people online. Sometimes, Greg had let her use his computer, and she'd researched plenty of things. She knew there were sites she could use that drew from the electoral roll. That was how she'd found both Jeff's and Stewart's addresses. Those sites didn't tell her everything, of course – not unless she was willing to pay. Like, they'd say what street someone lived on, but not the house number. And they'd give an age range – say, forty-to-forty-five – but not the person's exact age. Morven would gladly have paid for that extra information, but she didn't have a bank account. She had a bunch of money stuffed in a van, but there was no way to push that into the internet. In the end it didn't matter. Morven knew she could learn enough to find anyone, with a bit of time and legwork.

At some point, the woman who'd been using the computer next to Morven's had left. Morven only realised this when the seat was taken by Mr Pug Nose. He was holding a library copy of *The Sun*, which he laid on the keyboard. 'I wanted to apologise,' he whispered. 'I should have asked your permission before speaking to your child.' Mr Pug Nose tried to smile, but it came out more of a simper. 'I live alone,' he explained. 'Sometimes I forget what's proper etiquette.'

Proper etiquette? This guy used creepy words. Morven stared fiercely at her screen.

'What are you looking up?' he asked.

Morven could feel her breathing grow more laboured. Pug leaned in closer. Much too close. He smelled like chemist-shop aftershave. 'Are you searching for someone?'

Morven's teeth clenched so tightly her jaw hurt. She relaxed just enough to talk quietly. 'There was a guy before,' she said, eyes still on the screen. 'He used to bother me now and again. I didn't know him too well, but in the end, I ran over him with his car.'

That hadn't been all she'd done, of course, but Morven didn't feel like getting descriptive. There was no point in over-egging the pudding. 'Another guy used to bother me all the time. I knew him better. Really well, in fact.' She forced herself to turn her head and look straight at Mr Pug Nose. 'Know what I did to him?'

He twitched his lips. A kind of shrug.

'I stabbed him in the eye.'

Mr Pug Nose's expression flitted in a second from shock to irritation to concern. Then it settled into something like disbelief.

'With scissors,' Morven added slowly.

Now Pug was the one to look away. He cleared his throat uncomfortably. 'People shouldn't bother you,' he said softly, staring at the table.

'True,' Morven agreed. She swivelled back to her screen. The man tugged his paper from the keyboard and retreated. With his departure, Morven could feel her muscles slackening. Her judgement softening. She guessed Mr Pug Nose wasn't a bad sort, really. Lonely, probably. He'd said he lived alone. Maybe his wife died a long time ago. Maybe he had no kids to visit. No friends, even. Maybe they'd all died or moved somewhere. But, really! What kind of dimwit talked to a young girl in a library? A young girl with a *baby* at that. Playing with fire, that's what that was. Morven wondered if the man had a personal Guardian Angel. Mother Edwina said some people did, but not everyone. According to Mother, people were assigned a Guardian Angel if they had specific need for one. Otherwise, they could just access any angel in the Celestial

Kingdom. That's what the Supplicants of Dusk did. They had no need for a personal one, because they were on good terms with all of them. Morven decided that Mr Pug Nose, being lonely and not a Supplicant, probably had a low-ranking angel of his own. She said a quick prayer to that particular being, to abide with Mr Pug Nose in his time of loneliness and bothering people in libraries. She suggested to the angel that Mr Pug Nose should at least be taught some manners. Having put the problem under the aegis of the Kingdom, she could focus once again on the work before her.

The records showed there were dozens of people in London named S. Jones. But – better – there were only six named *Sara* Jones. The age ranges given for four of those six Saras were either too young or too old to be Morven's Sara. The other two were both in their thirties, which seemed about right. One lived in a nasty part of north-east London, which wasn't promising. The other lived in Brixton, which might be. Morven made note of the street, and looked it up on Google Maps. Street View showed that one end of the road housed a council block, and the other had a Roman Catholic school. Between the two were gentrified houses of a kind Morven could picture Dr Jones living in. And better than that, the photo showed a blue Mini Countryman parked outside. Morven checked the fading ink on the back of her hand, just to be certain. Sure enough, it read, *sarajones/bluemini.* The car on Street View was just like the one Sara Jones had got into in the news footage.

Morven noted the approximate location of the car on the street, and stood. She fussed with Cherub, cleaning his face and hands and making sure he was strapped into his chair. As she pushed him past one of the reading tables, Mr Pug Nose stared intently at the library's copy of *The Sun*.

EIGHT

Back in late November, Sara, Jamie, and Ceri had holidayed in a resort in the south-western corner of Mallorca. Although not far from the pile-'em-high fleshpots of Magaluf, the complex they'd stayed in catered to an older clientele. Here, Sara and Jamie – neither of them too far shy of forty – were considered youngsters. Selecting the locale had been Ceri's job, and there had been some advantages to her choice. Save for the occasional infestation of lounge cabaret acts, the evenings were quiet. During the day, they found the pools nearly empty. That is, once they'd learned to avoid the clockwork appearance of elderly lap swimmers who refused to get their hair wet. Sara tried not to swim at the same time as them. Otherwise, she'd be burned by a death-stare fired by decades of pettiness. The resort was especially quiet on the days management had laid on coach tours to Valldemossa or Palma.

On the afternoon it had happened – three days into their stay – they'd been in the indoor pool. The sky was sunny, but November is still late autumn, and the temperature hadn't climbed past 17 degrees Celsius. Indoors or out, Ceri had proved herself to be an impressive swimmer. She attributed her talent to those early-morning practices she'd suffered as a youth on the Aberystwyth swim team. Ceri and Jamie had grown quite competitive. They did not race together, since Sara refused to referee. Instead, they set stopwatches on their phones and tried to beat each other's times.

Ceri had just climbed from the water after an impressive effort. She dripped her way to a deck chair and rooted through her swim bag. She found and lit a cigarette.

'I don't think you can smoke in here,' Sara called. Her words echoed between the tiled walls until they were reverberating noise. Ceri stood at the side of the pool and took a celebratory drag. She blew the smoke high above the water and focused on Jamie, who was standing in the shallow end.

'Beat that,' she bellowed. Then she stiffened and crumpled to one side; her cigarette dropped into the water. A second later, Ceri had joined it with an ungainly splash.

It was just before four thirty on Saturday afternoon. Sara and Ceri sat side by side on the battered sofa in the Brixton flat, as Jamie leaned forward in his matching leather chair. In the Six Nations rugby, Wales would soon take on Italy. Jamie had the television turned on with the sound muted. Ceri followed the Six Nations passionately, and Jamie liked rugby well enough, despite the fact that it wasn't cricket.

Sara and Jamie had seen a lot of Ceri since the three of them had taken that ill-fated trip to Mallorca. There, they had enjoyed exactly three days of fun-in-the-sun before Ceri had plunged into the pool with her myocardial infarction. She'd spent the rest of the holiday in a hospital ward in Palma. Over Christmas, Jamie and Sara cared for her in Penweddig, and now Ceri had joined them in London for who-knew-how-long.

'So, the vehicle,' Jamie said to Ceri. 'How many times did she drive over him?'

'Once more than she needed to,' Ceri replied with a chortle.

Jamie nodded seriously. 'And before that?'

'She'd dragged him from the shed. Tortured him with his own nail gun.'

Jamie gave his professional grimace – the kind he may have offered around a table at Scotland Yard during an especially gruesome briefing. It was something Sara had not seen in a while.

He's enjoying playing copper so much, she thought.

In all their recent time together, Ceri had never once brought up the events of last spring, when Sara was driven off a road in the Brecon Beacons by the partner of Jamie's erstwhile boss Gerrit Vos. Officially, police had not connected that road accident with Vos's murder in London; forces did not routinely compare notes, except in unusual circumstances. Those two events had not been unusual enough to make it on to the forces-wide HOLMES system. Sara's accident was put down to narrow Welsh roads, excessive speed, and misjudged overtaking. As for Vos's murder… it too had seemed cut-and-dried. Dozens of people had witnessed Vos's associate, Levi Rootenberg, commit the crime.

Still, Ceri was both observant and nosy. Sara was sure she'd spotted the glaring connections between the two events and had asked around. What conclusions Sara's friend had drawn, she did not know. And, unusually, Ceri had been circumspect enough not to let her know. Today,

Ceri and Jamie were bonding over safer police topics – like the murder investigation Sara was currently involved in.

'And who found out about the victim's drug connection?' Jamie asked.

'The wife told us,' Ceri said. 'By the time Adeela and I got to the scene…'

Next to Sara, Ceri gave Jamie a blow-by-blow of the evening's events, from the time she climbed into Adeela Mir's CID car in Marylebone. The mention of DS Mir caught Sara's ear. She felt an unexpected prickle of irritation. Sara was flummoxed by the comradeship Ceri seemed to share so suddenly with Mir. She was also annoyed by the way they were using her to enable their budding friendship. Ceri had no status on the investigation, so officially she was simply present as Sara's assistant – a supportive presence, as requested by the consultant.

Immediately after thinking this, Sara felt ashamed. A third party, watching her thoughts, would suspect jealousy. Would they be right? Sara was uncertain. It wasn't as though Ceri didn't have other friends and pastimes that had nothing to do with Sara Jones. She always had, from the time Sara had first met her. In Wales, that seemed natural – and Ceri had hobbies that Sara would never choose to take up. Country music she could just about tolerate. And while she wasn't put off by Welsh nationalist politics, she would never want to spend hours in a community hall plotting Plaid Cymru campaigns. What was different was that this new friendship was budding here, in London, and on the job.

Still, Sara thought, *I'm probably just jealous*.

The match was about to start. Jamie had just turned up the volume when Sara was jolted by Take That telling her she had a phone call.

'Hello?' she said.

A man with a pleasant Irish lilt replied. 'Dr Jones, I'm sorry to ring you on the weekend, but I thought you'd want me to.'

'Who is this?'

'It's Monroe Collins at Trinity.'

'Ah,' Sara said, 'Professor Collins.'

Jamie and Ceri looked at Sara with their full attention. 'Who?' Jamie mouthed.

'One moment, please,' she said into her phone, then told Jamie and Ceri, 'I've asked some old contacts for advice about the cards,' she said. 'This one's from Dublin.'

She waved her hand in the way that meant *I'm just*

going to take this somewhere you're not. Sara wasn't certain why she didn't want Jamie and Ceri listening to her conversation. Whatever the reason was might be similar to why she felt jealousy over Ceri's friendship with Mir. Regardless, she slipped into the bedroom. 'Professor Collins, thank you for ringing,' she said. 'I assume that you didn't send an email because–'

'Because I have answers you'll want immediately,' Collins said.

'I appreciate that,' Sara told him. 'What do you know?'

'Have you ever,' Collins said, 'heard of a little cult called The Supplicants of Dusk?'

The Supplicants of Dusk was an esoteric group founded in the early 1980s by a civil engineer named Andreas Koch. In both his native Germany and in England, Koch had combined his background in conservative Christianity with an interest in secret societies. According to the order's official history, Koch's fascination with the esoteric came from a revelation he'd had on a walking tour of Bavaria. The Celestial Kingdom was real, he'd discovered, and more unified than anyone had ever realised. Angels were real, too, and all of them worked for the Kingdom. There were no fallen angels, as some religions believed – simply heavenly servants whose responsibilities were not always pleasant. 'It all comes from the same place,' he had said. 'Light and darkness, peace and evil. All angels work to one divine end.' It was one of his most-quoted aphorisms, and appeared in the order's scriptures, *Sermons of Dusk*.

The implication was that the so-called fallen angels were as holy as any, and more powerful than most when it came to darker tasks. It would be foolish not to invoke them.

Andreas Koch might have been a visionary, but he was a terrible cult leader. He had no head for organisation, and didn't really want acolytes fawning over him. He preferred engineering and hiking. He thought that now he'd shown everyone the truth, they could simply read his book – which he'd written with his wife Edwina – and pray to whatever angels they wanted. Edwina Koch had other ideas, though. Between them. they agreed that while Andreas was the true prophet, Edwina was the celestially-chosen Head of the order, with a heavenly mandate to organise the Supplicants and grow the faith. This she did with gusto, introducing the angel cards early on, and creating rituals and holy days. Edwina exploited Andreas's contacts list of like-minded occultists, and soon had a tight band of followers who would converge on their retreat in Surrey for spiritual growth. They would also give large offerings of cash – something Edwina was always insistent about – as regularly as they could.

It wasn't until Andreas died of colorectal cancer in 2006 that Edwina took the spiritual title *Mother*. Unlike many leaders of cults large and small, Andreas was not glorified in death. Edwina seemed content that her followers focus on the angels rather than her late husband, who now resided with the archangels in the underworld.

Professor Collins explained all this to Sara in a long, eloquent monologue. Sara had listened raptly, only becoming distracted when, about half-an-hour into their call, she'd heard groans from the living room as Italy scored the first try. Sara found herself wishing she could audit Monroe Collins's courses. His students were lucky. Sara herself had taught at a university, and knew how difficult it could be to keep listeners engaged during a lecture – which was more-or-less what Collins had just delivered. By the time he'd finished talking, Sara had covered pages of her Moleskine with tiny handwriting, saying very little in case she missed something important.

She thanked the professor, said she would follow up on his input, and promised to keep him updated

When she returned to the living room, the first half had just ended. Jamie killed the volume, looked over and raised his eyebrows. 'Anything?'

'Maybe,' Sara said noncommittally. She feigned interest in the muted half-time analysis. 'How's the match?'

'12-7 to us,' Ceri told her. 'We should be doing better.' She waved her hand at the screen. 'We're playing *Italy*, for heaven's sake.'

Sara realised that, just as she had not wanted them listening to her call, she also did not want to explain about Mother Edwina Koch and her Supplicants. It seemed a good guess that the killer was affiliated with the order, and very possibly a True Believer. It would be hard to explain the fetishistic behaviour displayed by those cards in any other way.

'We had a good start,' Ceri was saying. 'Dan Biggar took a penalty kick. I rate Biggar. Watched him play for Ospreys once.'

If what Sara suspected were true, she was going to have to share her news about the Supplicants with DS Mir. But not yet.

Ceri patted the sofa. 'You going join us for the second half, *fach*?'

'Err, yeah,' Sara replied. 'I'll make coffee first.'

Sara moved into the galley kitchen and filled the kettle. She poured beans into the grinder. Maybe, she thought, she didn't want Ceri to know because she didn't want Mir to know. Not yet, anyway. Sara finally knew where the cards had come from, but nothing else. All she could report at the moment was a bit of odd history from an Irish Sociology professor. She worried about how thorough the Met would be in their investigation without more knowledge. They might simply ask the Surrey police to have an informal chat with Edwina Koch. Without any understanding of the fringes of belief that groups like this one inhabited, any police officer would be bound to miss things.

Sara would explain everything to Mir very soon. But not until she had travelled to Weybridge and had a conversation with Mother Edwina.

NINE

The Supplicants of Dusk did not advertise the location of The Retreat. The order did not even have a web page, and the scant references online offered a post office box in Weybridge as a contact address. However, The Retreat was also Edwina Koch's home, and personal addresses were fairly simple to find. Sara had found that so-called 'Mother' lived in a prosperous neighbourhood on the northern edge of Weybridge. She had decided not to call first. The element of surprise was worth the gamble that she may have taken an hour's drive for nothing.

As she drove along the A3, Sara found herself thinking not of Edwina Koch, but of Jamie. He had been keen to have Ceri around yesterday afternoon, and Sara suspected it had little to do with the rugby. Rather, it was the police talk he'd been attracted to. Jamie hadn't said a single negative thing about his law degree… but he'd never seemed excited by it, either. Each day he went to classes, or the library, or stayed at home to write a paper, and he did it all with his usual dedication to duty. But talking to Ceri, enjoying police work vicariously through her, seemed to bring him alive in a way his studies didn't. He missed police work. Sara had to accept that he might even feel jealous of her for still being involved in it, without him.

Maybe Ceri was the wrong choice, she thought with a chuckle. *I should take Jamie along on investigations as my emotional support friend.*

It turned out that The Retreat – Mother Edwina's place of religion and tax-exempt home – was a large, redbrick mansion that backed onto the Thames towpath. Sara drove around the sweeping cul-de-sac and parked outside the house. It occurred to Sara that today was Sunday – even if Mother Edwina were home, there was also a chance she might be leading a Sunday service among her supplicants. Sara had no idea if that was something these people even did. Indeed, she had no idea what she would find or the reception she would receive. Maybe she'd find herself running away from a snarling dog.

Sara walked up the path and rang the bell next to the double doors. A well-muscled young man in a black button-down shirt and pressed black trousers answered.

'I'm looking for Mother Edwina.'

The man's expression was slack, eyes unfocused. Slowly, his gaze lowered to Sara's hands. 'You're a doctor?' he asked.

Sara followed his line of sight. She felt almost surprised to see her leather medical bag gripped in both fists so tightly her knuckles had whitened. 'In fact, I am,' she said.

'Mother called you?'

For a moment, she considered saying yes. It was an untruth guaranteed to get her inside the house. However, that lie would also be revealed as soon as this doorman fetched his mistress. 'Not exactly,' Sara confessed. 'I mean, it's not why I'm here.'

'Then why are you here?' the man asked.

Their circular conversation lasted a further two minutes. Sara discovered that one-hundred-and-twenty seconds was a long time to try to bluff her way past a wary subordinate. In the end, she managed to convince him it would be prudent to let Mother Edwina decide whether to see her or not. Safer than risking Mother's wrath by taking the decision himself. Even with this stark choice, the man considered this proposition for several seconds before telling Sara to wait. After he'd closed the door, Sara stood in the milky winter sunlight, smiling to herself. No true flunky wanted the burden of decision-making – or to face the consequences of having guessed wrongly.

The door was opened again by a woman who looked to be in her late sixties. Edwina Koch had a narrow face, thin lips, and soft grey hair. Today it was a little unkempt; she had not been expecting company. Mother Edwina's pale blue eyes were large and expressive. Sara had expected to see wariness or dull hostility there, but those eyes showed nothing but warm interest. 'My, my – you've confused Raymond,' she said. Her tone was gently teasing. 'He wondered why I'm receiving a house call.'

Sara chuckled, trying to match the woman's pleasant tone. 'Sometimes I forget I'm carrying my medical bag.'

'He was surprised, that's all,' Mother Edwina said. She patted down her hair. 'But I wasn't,' she went on. 'I knew you were going to visit.'

Sara kept her voice light. 'You did?'

'I didn't know it was going to be you specifically, you understand… but I knew a stranger would come to my door today.' Mother Edwina's hands now smoothed wrinkles in her simple cotton blouse. 'Sometimes I sense these things.'

Before she could stop herself, Sara brushed up against Mother Edwina's mind. She found it as tightly self-contained as a walled city. Almost certainly, Mother Edwina was not psychic.

'Do you know why I'm here?' Sara asked.

'Of course,' the woman replied. 'But it may not be for the reason you think you're here.' She pulled the open door wider and took Sara gently by the elbow. 'You're here because an angel told you to come to me.'

With the slightest pressure from her fingertips, Mother guided Sara inside. The foyer's walls were clad with large ceramic tiles – shiny white with light-grey marbling. The floor was tiled in darker grey. The effect was clean and modern, totally out of keeping with the redbrick façade of the Victorian mansion. 'And if an angel brought you here,' Edwina continued, 'then it's where you belong.'

'Well… thank you, Mrs Koch,' Sara said politely.

'Call me Mother,' Edwina replied. She waved an arm slowly in the air. 'This is The Retreat.'

'You have a beautiful home,' Sara went on. 'And, in a way, I think I *was* guided here by angels.'

Mother Edwina's narrow eyebrows raised. Sara withdrew her phone. 'Two of them, in fact,' she said, 'though I don't know their names.'

She held up her screen; the image was of the blood-spitting demon. Mother clocked it, and for a moment her large eyes flashed. Sara could not tell whether that indicated surprise, irritation, or even fear. She swiped to the photo of the prettier angel. That was the picture Sara had taken at the murder scene. Mother Edwina had composed her expression, and stared at the photo dispassionately.

'These cards are yours?' Sara asked.

'They belong to all Supplicants,' Edwina said. 'Those are religious artefacts. Devotional tools. They're very important to my order.'

'These particular cards,' Sara went on, 'were found on the bodies of two murder victims.'

Edwina hesitated, then her head twitched towards the stairs. 'Raymond!' she called.

From above: 'Mother?'

'Keep Cara upstairs and away from the windows. I'll be strolling in the garden.'

'Why did you tell Raymond to keep Cara away from the windows?' Sara asked.

They walked slowly down the long stretch of lawn,

towards the Thames towpath. Mother Edwina had not given Sara the choice to stay inside. 'Those two are nosy,' Edwina replied. 'They'd stare at me all day if I let them.'

'That's not nosiness,' Sara replied. 'They're protective of you.'

Edwina snorted softly. 'They're hoping to see me talk to angels.'

Sara turned around to look at the house in the near-distance. The haziness of the sun had made all its colours soften; The Retreat looked more like a pastel drawing than bricks and mortar. She and Edwina had left two dark trails of footprints in the wet grass. Sara drew in a deep breath of crisp air. This woman certainly led a pleasant life out here among the angels. Although Sara had broached the topic of murder back in the foyer, neither woman mentioned it now. The subject hung in the air like a front of low pressure as they talked instead about Mother's life, here on the outskirts of Weybridge. Sara discovered that, besides Raymond, one young female Supplicant lived in The Retreat. Cara was maid, cook, and anything else Mother wanted her to be. Raymond seemed to be a combination social organiser, doorman, and security guard. As for Mother herself, she hinted vaguely at all the deep cosmic responsibilities laid at the feet of one who knew the workings of the Celestial Kingdom.

When they reached the towpath, Edwina thrust her hands into the pockets of her waxed jacket. 'Shall we stroll or sit?' she asked.

Sara gazed along the path that followed a bend in the river. *Sit where?* 'I'm up for a walk,' she said.

Edwina pulled a dubious face. 'Not sure I am,' she said. 'I didn't realise how cold it would be.'

Mother Edwina led Sara a few metres along the path to the place where a well-kept canal boat was tethered. 'This is my private meditation room,' she said. 'Climb aboard.'

Inside the boat, they sat on an L-shaped sofa angled around a tiny dining table. Edwina now seemed ready to discuss business. She asked to see Sara's photos again. Swiping between them, she said, 'You told me these were found on murder victims?'

Sara nodded. 'If you read the news,' she said, 'you've heard of them.'

'I have little interest in the world's decay,' Edwina told her. 'Things tend to crumble whether I witness them or not.' She smiled beatifically. 'The angels tell me all I need to know.'

'The victims' names,' Sara persisted, 'were Gregory Blackadar and Jeffrey Sawyer.'

Sara watched Mother Edwina's face. Her neutral expression did not change, but Sara noticed tears begin to well at the bottoms of her eyes. Smoothly, Edwina pulled a cotton handkerchief from the sleeve of her jacket and dabbed.

'Af and Kushiel,' she said quietly. 'Those are the angels on the cards.'

'Were Mr Blackadar and Mr Sawyer members of your faith?' As Sara asked this, she withdrew her notebook and scribbled the names *Af* and *Kushiel*.

Edwina watched her write. 'Those are very powerful angels indeed,' she noted. 'Af means anger.' She indicated Sara's notebook. 'You should write this down. God created him at the beginning of the world. He is an angel of destruction, forged from black and red chains. Once, he swallowed up Moses himself. Temporarily, as it happens…'

Pointedly, Sara put down her pen. 'At the moment,' she said, 'I'm more interested in the victims than in Moses or angels.'

'Please – write,' Mother commanded. 'If you want to

understand the cards, this is important. Kushiel is known as the rigid one, because his role is to punish. He is one of the rulers of the underworld.'

To appease her host, Sara picked up her fountain pen and made a quick note about each angel. Edwina's tightly-neutral expression softened into something close to contentment. 'It's a long process,' Edwina said understandingly. 'I mean, the journey to the truth. You're making a fine start.'

Sara wondered whether this tactic of attempted conversion was something Mother Edwina used as a distraction technique, or whether she simply tried it on all her visitors. 'You may not want to tell me about your relationship to the victims,' she said softly, 'but I guarantee, the police will find out. If either of those men ever donated to your order, you'll have detectives knocking on your door in just the same way I did.'

Edwina's pale eyes stared levelly at Sara. 'I thought you were the police,' she said.

'I work with them,' Sara replied. 'I'm a consultant psychiatrist. I specialise in crimes that centre around religion or fringe beliefs.'

'Aha!' Edwina said, raising her eyebrows. 'So you

encourage people to think you're an expert.' Her thin lips twisted into a smile. 'Yet, here you are asking about angels, just like any seeker. You should be telling me a thing or two.'

Sara grinned without mirth. 'OK… I know both angels depicted on your cards are fallen.'

Mother Edwina mimicked a yawn. 'That's so trite,' she said. 'What does *fallen* mean? It's not a description you'll find in the Bible, you know.'

'No,' Sara agreed, 'the concept of fallen angels comes mainly from some pseudepigrapha attributed to the prophet Enoch.'

'My, my,' Edwina said, 'you might just be an expert after all.' Subtly, she leaned forward. 'Tell Mother Edwina what drew you to such a lurid profession.'

The last thing Sara wanted was to open up to a religious charlatan. But at least she had piqued Edwina's interest, and such attention could be used. 'If I tell you, will you let me know whether Mr Blackadar and Mr Sawyer were members of your faith?'

Mother's smile grew less mocking. 'It's a deal,' she said soberly.

For a moment, Sara considered inventing a facile lie.

She rejected the thought almost immediately, suspecting this canny old lady would see right through it. Instead, she braced herself to tell a small fraction of the truth. 'My parents were murdered when I was young,' she said. 'There was a teenage boy. He was a member of a local group of oddballs. The police told us he'd done it.' She forced a smile. 'From there, I guess I became interested in oddballs.'

Mother Edwina stared at Sara so intently, it was as though she were trying to memorise her features. 'But that oddball,' she said finally, 'was not the one who killed your parents… was he?'

An uncanny sensation tingled down Sara's spine. This woman may not be psychic, but she was eerily perceptive. Sara knew all about Cold Reading – the ability to make accurate guesses based on body language and intonation. But even knowing this, there was something about Mother Edwina that compelled her to make confessions. Her gaze dropped to the table's wood-grain laminate. 'No, he didn't do it,' she admitted softly. 'My older brother did.'

When Sara looked up again, Sara saw genuine compassion in Mother's eyes. Still, instead of offering words of comfort, the woman simply fulfilled her side of the bargain. 'Both Greg and Jeff were Supplicants,' she informed Sara. 'Greg was one of the first to join the order. My late husband recruited him, and he was always faithful. Jeff came later, because of Greg – they had some sort of business relationship.' She cocked her head in thought. 'I always suspected Jeff of insincerity. He never participated and I don't think he really believed. Jeff joined the order the way some men join the Freemasons. It was good for business.'

'And who killed them?' Sara asked, making notes.

'I don't know.'

Sara stopped writing and ran her fingers along the platinum coating of her pen. 'I'd say the cards indicate it was another member of your order.'

Mother smiled almost tenderly. 'I'm sure you would say that,' she agreed. 'In exactly the same way you thought a teenage oddball killed your parents. Sometimes we're very quick to jump to conclusions… don't you think?'

Sara dropped her gaze again. They sat together in that silent tableau for seconds that felt like for ever. Finally, in her peripheral vision, Sara saw Mother slide from behind the table and stand. Mother was short enough not to hunch, despite the boat's low ceiling. Sara understood that their meeting was over. She looked up and nodded. 'Thank you for seeing me,' she said.

'It's not goodbye,' Mother Edwina said. 'The angels have assured me of this. We will talk again.'

Carefully, she moved along the boat's narrow length. 'We need to,' Mother added. 'Expert or not, you still have a lot to learn.'

TEN

The Sunday afternoon traffic had been light, and Sara was back in London within an hour of leaving Mother Edwina's cul-de-sac. As she drove along the south side of Clapham Common, Sara gazed over the acres of dull winter grass and thought of Edwina, at the end of her garden, sitting quietly alone in her canal boat. Sara still did not know if this religious figurehead ever held services on Sunday. Or any other day of the week, for that matter. However, Sara's attitude towards Edwina Koch was not nearly as harsh as she had expected it to be. The woman had probably been lying to her – the trouble was, Sara was unsure about what. Mother Edwina had admitted ownership of the angelic cards without hesitation. Maybe she'd been telling the truth when she claimed not to know who had killed her followers. Maybe she was right to point out that it hadn't necessarily been a member of her order.

Then again, Sara thought, *maybe I've been lulled by the*

ceramic tiles and the waxed jacket and the canal boat – by the sheer normality of it all.

If so, it was a rookie mistake unworthy of her experience. Despite having repeatedly encountered the banality of evil, Sara still subconsciously expected every occult figure she met to be some sort of bizarre nutter. She was predisposed to liking Mother Edwina Koch simply because the woman did not wear spangled robes, adopt a highfaluting spiritual demeanour or sacrifice animals in her presence. Sara could only think about Edwina's compassionate gaze and the no-nonsense way she had answered Sara's questions about… well, about spiritual nonsense. It was easy to understand what Mother Edwina's followers saw in her.

Sara decided she would ring DS Mir today and give her the broad strokes of the story: both victims, and the cards found on their bodies, came from the Supplicants of Dusk. Their leader claims not to know who within her order would have killed the men. Sara was sure that Mir would want police to interview Edwina Koch. She would arrange a fuller debrief for tomorrow morning.

When Sara reached her street, she noticed that Jamie's Range Rover was still parked by the school, exactly where it had been when she'd left. She hoped the parking space they both favoured, right in front of their house, would still be free. Sara regretted that there was no parking allowed on the cobbled Marylebone mews outside their new home. She had already arranged long-term spaces for herself and Jamie at a 24-hour indoor car park nearby. But it would be expensive, as well as less convenient. When Sara pulled up in front of the house, she saw a bedraggled young woman standing on the pavement a few doors down. Sara may not have noticed her at all, but this woman – a girl, really – was standing next to a baby's pram. Sara wasn't certain whether it was the girl's age or something more, but the mother-and-child dynamic felt very wrong.

From her safe distance, the young woman watched Sara unblinkingly.

Sara grasped her bag from the passenger's seat and got out of the car. She returned the young woman's gaze. 'Hello,' she called. In Sara's old job at the London Fields Support Service, she had treated many homeless patients, and they had all shared the same wary, haunted look that this girl wore as though born to it. 'Are you OK?'

The young woman nodded solemnly and backed up a few feet, pulling the pram along with her.

‘It’s a chilly day,’ Sara told her. ‘Would you like a cup of tea? Maybe a sandwich?’

Her only reply was a shake of the head.

‘Look,’ Sara said. ‘I’m a doctor.’ She held up her bag. ‘At least let me look at your baby. I can make sure she’s all right.’

‘He,’ the girl said.

‘I beg your pardon?’

‘You said *she*. He's a boy.’

‘I apologise,’ Sara replied. ‘Well, this is my house.’ She pointed with her bag. ‘That’s my flat right there, through the big window. If you’d like to come in…’

The girl began to shake her head fiercely. Sara suspected she was overwhelmed by such an unfamiliar offer. She tried to find other words of comfort, but before she could the girl muttered something that might have been *no thank you,* and spun the pram around. She pushed it at speed down the pavement, towards the council flats at the bottom of the road and well away from whatever danger she felt Sara might represent.

When Sara entered their flat, she found Jamie watching more of the Six Nations, a glass of beer in hand. The match pitted Scotland against France. Although Jamie was an England supporter, Sara knew today he would become an honorary Scot, just as he had been an honorary Welshman yesterday. Sara had watched France play once already this season, when Wales had come from a zero score at halftime to defeat the French 24-19. Even she had to admit, that had been an exciting second half. Sara only watched rugby when Wales was playing.

'Where were you?' Jamie asked, eyes still on the screen.

She tugged back the net curtains and peered onto the street. 'I just met somebody outside,' she said. 'A girl – late teens, I'd say. She looked homeless.'

Jamie shook his head. 'That's always sad to see.'

Sara let go of the curtains and turned. 'This was worse. She had a baby.'

He looked up. 'Did you ask her in?'

'She ran away.'

Jamie shifted forward in his seat. 'Why don't we get in the car?' he suggested. 'We could drive around – have a look for her.'

Sara unwrapped her scarf and began to unbutton her coat. 'We wouldn't find her,' she said. 'And even if we did, we couldn't force her to accept help. This girl didn't want to talk to me.'

Jamie sat back in his chair. He looked to the television once more.

Sara hung up her coat and wandered into the bedroom. She closed the door against the sound of rugby commentary. Sitting on the bed, she slid off her boots and thought about the baby. What if he were ill? She should have rushed over and looked in that crib. She'd been far too polite to that silly girl. Sara sat back on the mattress, a pillow wedged against the small of her back. Her fingers brushed against her neck and pulled out the silver Eye-in-the-Pyramid pendant she wore there. She gripped the warm metal tightly between her fingers, fighting a strong urge to lie down, go into a trance and try to explore this young woman's life.

That's not how you're doing things anymore, Sara.

She had made new rules for a reason. Sara had agreed with herself that, if she were ever hit by a psychic impression so strong she could not ignore it, she'd pay attention. Otherwise, she would not go looking for trouble. Sara sensed that meddling with this young woman would bring her nothing but grief. What would she do if she went searching psychically through this woman's life and saw something she should act on? Would she trust the vision?

Last time this happened, Sara had put her life in danger, and then killed a man.

Which is why there are new rules.

With a swivel, she kicked her legs off the bed and stood. She would force herself to forget about this young woman and her baby. Sara picked up her phone and dialled Adeela Mir's mobile. After she had made her report about Mother Edwina Koch, she would join Jamie in the living room, even though she didn't care about the prospects of either Scotland or France.

Morven had made it back to her room at the hotel. She'd switched on the TV, boiled the kettle, mixed formula, and changed Cherub. Now she lay on her side next to him. She'd wedged a pillow under his upper back so he could easily drink his bottle. In an East London petrol station, Morven had bought a big bag of Walkers – smoky bacon flavour – and a Dr Pepper. Now, she worked her way methodically through the crisps, reaching over Cherub to pinion a few of them at a time. Her heart was pounding. It had been doing that for the entire hour-long drive back to the hotel. It was no surprise that Morven had caught sight of Sara Jones, but she hadn't expected the woman to *speak* to her. Or, even better, to show concern for Cherub! That had been amazing.

Morven hadn't said much back. What could she have said to Sara Jones? Even informing her Cherub was a boy had seemed like confiding too much. But Morven hadn't needed to speak. Sara Jones spoke, and that was what had mattered. It told Morven something really important. It had sent her a message.

Mother Edwina had once said that angels communicated in many ways. The most reliable was direct communication: an inner voice with clear instructions. But the Celestial Kingdom offered messages in other ways, too – and one of those was how people treated us. If a Supplicant had a bad day, it may be the angels' way of telling her she was off course. By the same token, if someone were kind to a Supplicant, this might be the angels' way of telling her she was on the right track. Then events would transpire in her favour. Morven was certain this had happened in Brixton. Here was a doctor, a *psychiatrist* no less, trusted by police with their most puzzling cases. And there were Morven and Cherub, just blending into the pavement, and Sara Jones noticed them and said kind things. What else could that have been but an angelic message?

The message said, *all is well.*

It said, *You're on the right track.*

It said, *the time is right.*

And, finally, it was. Through Sara Jones, the angels had told Morven to act. They had let her know that her days of zoos and fatberg museums were over. The angels had instructed Morven to complete her task.

It was time to kill the actor.

Late on Sunday evening, Sara packed a small overnight bag. She had arranged to meet DS Mir the next morning at nine o'clock, and also wanted to swing by her new home before heading over to West End Central. She didn't need anything at the Marylebone house, but thought she should touch base with the builders. Sara realised she would have had to rise early to do both, and decided to head into Central London that evening. She hoped Ceri wouldn't mind sharing the bed.

She said goodnight to Jamie and locked the front door, thinking vaguely about when to put the flat on the market. It all depended on when she and Jamie could move. The contractors had told her the date they planned to be finished, but she didn't quite believe they would. Because of this, Sara had not yet scheduled any patients for her new practice – even though her oldest client, Andy Turner, would have booked twice-weekly sessions for the rest of the year. Similarly, Sara wasn't willing to risk temporary homelessness by selling the Brixton flat too soon. She would rather carry both mortgages for a while.

Walking to the streetlamp-orange pavement, Sara stifled a yawn. As she thumbed the key to her car, she glanced at the spot where she had seen the teenage mother hours before – and, without warning, her senses began to tingle. Maybe it was no more than the memory of that girl and her baby, but Sara felt as though she were being watched. That was not a sensation she wanted to have late at night in a Brixton street. Sara looked up and down her street, but saw no one. Still, the eerie feeling persisted. *It could be misplaced guilt*, she thought. She was still haunted by this afternoon's encounter.

There was nothing you could have done for that girl, Sara reassured herself. *She didn't want you meddling.*

She forced herself to get into the car, pull on to Brixton Hill and join the late-night traffic into Central London. She imagined her unexpected visit would wake up Ceri. Her friend needed a good night's sleep so she could spend her morning inspecting freshly-poured cement, or saying things like, 'Have you checked this with a spirit level?' That was Ceri's idea of a good day. Sara supposed it was good therapy for a certain personality type after a heart attack.

Sara left her car at her new, twenty-four-hour garage at Portman Square and walked to the mews. When she entered, the smell of concrete, plaster, and timber was mingling with the aroma of cigarettes. She started. *Cigarettes?* At the crime scene, she had definitely seen Ceri – a recent non-smoker – accept one from Mir. Sara hadn't mentioned witnessing that lapse to Ceri, but she'd hoped it would be a one-off. It was disappointing to think it wasn't.

'Hello?' she called.

The house's kitchen was on the ground floor, tucked behind the room Sara would use as her practice. As she approached it, Ceri emerged. She wore her oversized man's shirt and pyjama bottoms. She carried a glass of wine in each hand. 'What in hell are you doing here?' Ceri demanded, surprised to find Sara in her own home.

As Sara explained, she noticed her friend carried two

glasses of red wine. 'Is the other one for me?' she asked.

If it is, she thought, *then Ceri is as good a psychic as I am*. Sara had not told her friend she was coming.

Before Ceri could respond, Sara heard footsteps descending the stairs behind her. Ceri looked up – Sara saw her eyes widen. She turned to find Adeela Mir at the bottom of the steps, robed in Ceri's dressing gown.

Mir smiled shyly. 'Good evening,' she said.

Too quickly, Sara grinned and made an odd noise. She'd meant it as a greeting. Instead, she sounded like someone trying to recall a foreign word. Ceri frowned at her accusingly. 'We went to dinner,' Ceri said defensively. 'Just a couple streets over that way.' She pointed vaguely. 'Then Adeela was tired.'

'And a bit drunk,' Mir added.

'She didn't want to drive home.'

'Honestly, I couldn't have.'

'So, I told her she could stay here.'

Ceri stared at Sara levelly, as though daring her to contradict the story. With her back to Mir, Sara offered Ceri an expression of wide-eyed innocence: *I didn't suggest anything otherwise*. 'Of course,' Sara said. 'Sergeant Mir can stay here anytime.'

Ceri held Sara's gaze longer than was comfortable, then handed her one of the wine glasses. 'You can have this,' she said flatly. She passed the other glass to Mir. 'I'll get myself another.'

'Are you staying?' Mir asked.

'I was planning to,' Sara said.

'That's no problem,' Mir said hastily. 'I was about to go home.'

'You said you were planning to stay.'

Mir set down the glass. 'I've sobered up,' she said. 'And I can take a cab.' She waved her hand towards the stairs. 'Just let me get my things together and I'll be out of your hair. But I'll see you at West End Central in the morning, yes?'

'Nine o'clock,' Sara confirmed.

'Well, let me warn you,' Mir said. 'My SIO's going to give you a proper bollocking for not telling us about this cult woman before you went there.'

'There was nothing to tell.' Sara angled her head. 'Now there is.'

From the kitchen, Ceri hollered, 'That was the last of the wine. I'm making coffee. It'll take a moment. Sara – you wait there. Adeela, you go upstairs and get dressed.'

Mir gave an exaggerated shrug that meant, *who am I to argue?* With a grin, she said, 'Bossy, isn't she?'

To Sara's relief, Ceri had not joined her at the West End Central police station the next morning. Maybe she'd just heard all she needed to hear about Mother Edwina. Or maybe she'd had her fill of DS Mir for the morning. Once Mir had changed into her uniform, the three women had shared a quick cup of coffee on Sara's bed. For Sara and Ceri, the encounter had been strained. They had both tried to act normal – and Ceri was always at her strangest when trying to act normal. As for Mir, she had not seemed awkward at all. Once in uniform, she'd acted as though her presence in Sara's home were just another routine visit from the Met.

All through their hasty coffee party, Sara's eyes had kept drifting to the shard of ceramic tile that sat next to her bed. Six crushed cigarette butts nested in its ashy centre. Sara had fought the urge to ask Ceri why she was risking her health. She also wanted to know why Mir had a uniform in Ceri's bedroom. It was unlikely she'd worn it to dinner last night.

The meeting at the station was not nearly as formal as

Sara had expected it to be. Sara provided all the information she could and Mir entered it into the HOLMES system.

'It's a useful link,' Mir said of the Supplicants. 'The Superintendent will certainly want her interviewed, because of those cards.'

'Will you do it?' Sara asked.

'He'll probably send a request to Dorset,' Mir said. 'A detective constable there can handle it.'

'I don't know how much Edwina Koch knows,' Sara said, 'but I suspect it's more than she's saying.'

'At the moment, that's only speculation,' Mir said. 'We don't have evidence to act immediately.' She gestured to her laptop, even though it was closed. 'Over the weekend, I'd half-decided we should release those images to the press.'

Sara nodded. It would have been the right move.

'I was planning to consult the Superintendent about it today.' Mir pursed her lips. 'And if we *had* revealed the cards,' she said. 'I was planning to ask you a favour.'

'Oh?'

'I was hoping you might start giving media interviews.'

Sara shuddered. 'Why?'

‘Because of your reputation. If we’d needed to publicise the cards, you would have attracted more press than I could. You could explain them.’

Sara smiled. ‘You mean, in that lurid way the media likes. They could ask about devil-worship, occult rituals, blood sacrifices…’

Mir smiled. ‘Exactly.’

They were silent for a moment. ‘I’m glad you didn’t need to ask me,’ Sara said finally.

That wasn't a surprise to Mir. ‘Ceri warned me you might say no.’

And she would have. Sara had never been comfortable in the spotlight. She was not one to keep a scrapbook of press cuttings. She chose not to recall the times *The Daily Mail* had used her name in the same headline as Satan’s. When Rhodri died immediately after the Aberystwyth investigation, Sara was besieged by calls from the press. She’d known they wanted more than comments about the serial killer Eldon Carson. They wanted all the old dirt on her dysfunctional family. They wanted tragedy and tears. And her brave story of recovery and moving on.

Sod that, she had thought.

‘I’m not sure if there’s much left for you to do on the

case at the moment,' Mir said. 'That is, until something else happens that we can't explain. The lead you've given us is good. For the moment, we can take it from here.'

'Believe me, that's a relief,' Sara said. 'I was happy to help, but there are other things I could get on with.'

'Great,' Mir said, and then hesitated. 'Officially, I'd like you to be ready to jump back in, though.'

'Of course.'

'So, if anyone asks,' Mir confirmed, 'you'll tell them Ceri is still assisting you on the investigation, OK?'

'Ceri?' Sara repeated.

Mir nodded. 'Since she'll be in London a while longer, I thought she could continue to help me.'

Sara could think of nothing to say. She felt herself blink.

'But the only way that can happen is if we keep explaining her presence through you. You don't mind, do you?'

'Err – no.'

Mir grinned and shrugged in a *what-can-I-say* manner. 'I just like having her around,' she explained.

ELEVEN

A few days later, Morven sat on a black sofa in the living room of Stewart Delaney's house in Chiswick. She'd wanted to arrive early in the morning, so she'd catch Stewart in. Of course, he didn't have an acting role at the moment, so he might have been home at any time of day. Morven had plunked Cherub on the carpet; now he toyed moodily with a television remote. He was being a fussy baby today – maybe the room's lingering odour of incense was too much for his little lungs. Morven recognised that smell: storax resin. It was one of Mother's favourites. Or maybe Cherub's grumpiness was because he hated small spaces. This living room was tiny.

Stewart's place was made even more oppressive by its dark grey walls and black furniture. Morven and Cherub both preferred bright colours. She supposed Stewart thought all this darkness was sophisticated, or maybe actors were just inspired by gloomy palettes. One thing Morven did like was a big oil painting that hung atop Stewart's mantle, illuminated by its own dedicated wall light. It was of a fierce angelic figure with massive black wings, surrounded by insects. Morven didn't know specifically what angel he was supposed to represent, but the painting was pretty cool. Under it, on the mantle itself, was the room's one oasis of brightness. Reflecting the painting's wall light were two metal statuettes. Stewart had won them by playing a nasty character on that soap opera.

Currently, Stewart was in the kitchen making hot chocolate. He knew Morven liked that. Whenever he'd come to the farm, Stewart would bring Morven a tub of fancy cocoa powder. Sometimes, there would be ginger in it and sometimes coconut. Once, the cocoa was peanut butter flavoured! That memory almost made Morven feel bad about killing him.

Still, she *was* going to kill Stewart. Really, she should have done it last week, before she'd driven over Jeff. Jeff had been a nobody, really, and hadn't deserved to die second after Greg. Although Jeff had visited the farm regularly, Greg had only given Morven to him twice. Both times, Jeff had been pretty brutal in what he'd done to her. That was why, when she'd gone to his house last week,

Morven had been rather brutal back to him. Not that the dolt had understood why any of it was happening. He hadn't even recognised her! Greg always claimed Jeff was a Supplicant like the rest of them, but there had not been a single flicker of familiarity in his eyes when she'd shown him the angel cards. That Jeffrey Sawyer had been a great big poser and Morven was glad he was dead.

'Morven, love,' Stewart called from the kitchen, 'do you want anything to eat?'

'No thanks, Stewie,' she called back.

Stewart was no fake. Once there was a time when Mother had come down to the farm. It had been like a Royal visit – they'd cleaned for days beforehand. Stewart had driven all the way from London just to be in Mother's presence. It had been Easter then, and Stewart brought Morven a big chocolate egg. That weekend was another of her treasured memories. *If only the angels were willing to spare Stewie*, Morven thought. *I could drink my cocoa, let him do whatever he wanted to me, and then leave*. But the angels had been firm in their instructions. And they were probably right… technically, Stewart was way guiltier than Jeff.

The Celestial Kingdom didn't tell Morven in advance

how to kill people, but she trusted the angels to send last-minute inspiration. With Greg, it had been those scissors. With Jeff, a lingering session of nails and tyres. Now, Morven's eyes drifted to the awards on the mantle, and she thought maybe one of them would do for Stewart. They looked heavy. His death would come quickly. Stewart deserved that at least.

Morven would need to make sure Cherub was out of the way, though. When she hit Stewart with that heavy thing, his blood would spatter like a tree branch in a wood chipper.

Stewart came in with two mugs of cocoa and placed one on a low black table next to her. 'Sorry there's no whipped cream,' he said.

Morven noticed Stewart's hair was growing back in. She'd never seen him with hair; he'd had to keep his head shaved for the soap opera. He had recently lost that job when his character was flung from a bridge by some big-time gangster he'd been cuckolding.

'Have you seen Mother recently?' Stewart asked.

'No,' Morven lied.

'Well, how's Greg?'

'Good,' she said.

That answered one question, anyway. Morven had wondered whether Stewart knew Greg was dead. Nobody had told him, which might also be why he'd seemed pleased to see her.

'Is he at the flat in Kensington?' Stewart asked.

'Not right now, no,' Morven replied.

At least, she didn't think he was. They must have removed his body by now.

Stewart dropped down next to her on the sofa. They sat perpendicular to the mantle, which meant they could both see the trophies. Morven wondered how she was going to reach one without arousing suspicion. Stewart took a sip of his chocolate and placed the mug on the carpet. He bent back up and eased an arm around Morven. 'Then why are you here?' he asked.

'In London?' She looked away, and felt the weight of his forearm on her shoulders. 'Errands,' she said.

He grunted acknowledgement. With his free hand, he stroked her tummy. 'Thank the angels for errands,' he said.

Stewart hooked her sweatshirt's elasticated hem with his thumb. He hoisted the fabric enough to slip his hand underneath. Morven felt the cool of his palm slide up her skin. She never wore a bra – she didn't really need to – and soon Stewart's index finger was circling her right nipple. 'How about that?' he breathed. 'It's like I'm reading Braille.'

'You say the most romantic things,' she told him.

Stewart pulled away his hand and untangled his arm from her shoulder. He clasped Morven's hem with both hands and tried to tug her shirt over her head.

'No, wait,' she said. 'Cherub's here.'

'So?'

'I don't want him watching us.'

Stewart snorted. 'He won't know the difference.'

'Can I put him on your bed?'

He pulled away with a good-natured sigh and said, 'Sure. Upstairs – first on the left.'

In Stewart's bedroom, Morven lay Cherub in the centre of the king-size bed. Cherub squirmed and started to fuss again. The baby could sit up, and was pretty good at dragging himself by the arms. Morven wished she could find something to entertain him, so he wouldn't crawl to the edge of the mattress. She looked around the room. There were bottles of cologne on the dresser… but Cherub would only squirt them in his eyes. There were some plants, a few framed photos, a couple of paperbacks... Morven crouched down and looked under the bed. There she saw a stack of magazines, a heating pad, a cricket bat, and a suitcase with a red pom-pom tied to the handle. That was it! Babies loved pom-poms. Deftly, she untied the puffball and tossed it to Cherub. He took it happily and began to gum the wool.

'Now, you stay there,' she told him. 'Things are going to get hectic for a while, and I'll have enough on my hands without you thumping to the floor.'

Morven paused, then looked back under the bed. She'd only half-noticed the cricket bat the first time. As far as she knew, Stewie didn't play. Maybe he kept it under there for protection. Which was ironic, Morven thought, as she grasped its handle and headed towards the stairs.

In the hallway downstairs, she rested the bat against the wall and moved into the living room. Stewart now lay on the sofa stark naked. He'd left his bits of clothing on the carpet where they'd landed. Stewart looked at Morven and grinned. 'You're overdressed,' he said.

'I guess I am,' she replied.

And it was true – it would be best to be naked. Once she'd hit Stewart in the head, his blood would spray like mist in an atrium. Skin was so much easier to wash than fabric. 'Stay right there,' she told him.

In the hallway, Morven shucked off her sweatshirt and trousers. She folded them carefully and lay them on the stairs. Her pop socks and pants went on top. Then she picked up the bat. Morven braced herself and found the centre of her being. She was ready.

From the living room, she heard Stewart's voice. 'I'm really glad you came, sweetheart,' he was saying. 'I've missed you.'

Without warning, a wave of anguish overwhelmed her. Morven could feel the warm wash of misery soaking through her muscles. It weighed them down and made the bat too heavy to hold. She let it wilt in her hands, until its toe pressed against the floor. It appeared Morven wasn't ready after all. *Stewie has been so nice to me*, she thought. *He was always kind in a way that others weren't.*

Kind or not, the angel Lahatiel whispered to her, *what he did to you was wrong.*

What he did to you was rape, agreed the angel Pusiel.

But she couldn't kill Stewart, Morven protested. Why had she ever thought that was possible?

If Greg and Jeff had to die, said the angel Hutriel, *this one has to die, too. Same crime, same punishment.*

'Morven?' Stewart called. 'What's taking so long?' His voice grew gooey-playful: 'Do you need help undressing?'

Please, Morven begged the angels.

She could feel their rigid insistence. The Kingdom was firm on this.

Morven closed her eyes. She breathed deeply. Blotted doubt from her mind. The Celestial Kingdom was inerrant, she reminded herself. The angels always knew what was what. Compared to them, she was just a babbling ninny whose thoughts would lead her astray.

She gripped the bat tightly. Opened her eyes.

Then she leapt. Morven sprang into the tiny living room, brandishing the bat. She swung it hard; its edge impacted against Stewart's shoulder. She imagined she could hear bones cracking under his bellowing scream. Morven hoisted the bat again – but Stewart managed to jerk his foot upwards and shove forcefully against her hip. Morven spun. The bat swivelled wildly. Stewart rolled off the sofa and, with his undamaged side, tackled her to the floor. Morven's breath whooshed out of her lungs. She thumped onto the carpet as Stewart grappled for the bat. Morven may have been stronger than she looked, but she was no match for Stewart. Even when he was wounded and barking in pain. He slammed the bat with his forearm; Morven's hand cramped as the heavy chunk of willow flipped from her grasp.

Upstairs, Cherub started to cry.

Morven could feel Stewart's sweat as he slid up her body one thrust at a time. With each jolt, the roughness of the carpet burned her back. Soon they were face-to-face. Stewart's weight pressed down on her. His breath huffed wetly against her cheeks. He grasped her wrists and forced them above her head. Within seconds, Morven was trapped.

'Are you fucking crazy?' Stewart spat.

Eddies of contradictory sensations battered Morven. There was a swell of elation at not having killed Stewie, but also a backwash of fear for what he might do now. Her mind churned with confusion – why had the angels allowed this fiasco? Morven's breath caught on the phlegm damming her throat. In rapid, staccato puffs, she sucked air. Hyperventilation swelled into sobs.

With his knee, Stewart nudged apart Morven's legs. Spitting into his good hand, he reached between them. He made her slick with saliva. Fumbling, he adjusted himself.

Pushed into her. Stewart's thrusts were lopsided. Despite his pain, he didn't take long to finish.

He lay on top of her, inside but motionless. His head dropped, face pressed to the nape of her neck, forehead on the floor. They both breathed heavily. Morven's eyes were inches away from his damaged shoulder. It looked awfully wonky.

'Were you trying to kill me?' he asked, voice muffled.

Morven sniffed. Swallowed. Nodded.

He raised his head. 'Why?'

'Get off me,' she said.

Stewart rolled onto his back and huffed in pain. Now Morven stared at the ceiling. It was the only thing painted white in the entire room. A brown water stain had marred one corner. The stain had seeped right under the coving.

'Is Mother cross at me?' he asked.

'I wasn't doing it for Mother,' she said sullenly. 'She loves you. Loves that you're on TV.' She sniffed again. 'That you *were* on TV.'

'Then why?'

Morven struggled upwards. She glanced around the room for paper handkerchiefs. There weren't any. She chose one of Stewart's socks and squatted. He watched dispassionately. Stewart did not react when she tossed the soiled sock into the hallway like litter. Stiffly, Morven kneeled and knee-shuffled to the sofa.

Then why?

It was a fair question. Since she'd failed to kill Stewart – and wouldn't try again, no matter what the angels said – at least she could explain why she'd tried.

Morven settled on the sofa, brought her knees up and hugged a pillow to her tummy. 'Greg's dead,' she said.

'What?'

'Jeff, too. Did you know Jeff?'

Stewart's mouth opened a couple of times before the word *how?* formed.

'I killed them,' she told him simply, and stared up at the water stain as though it contained all her memories.

Stewart Delaney had eased himself off the floor. Now he sat in a chair, a cushion supporting his damaged shoulder. Morven had told him how, after her papa died, Greg started taking a personal interest in her. How he'd said she could retire from tending to the weed, and help around the house instead. She described how, from then on, Greg would come to see her when she was alone. Sometimes it was in her room at night, but not always. If the house were empty, it could be almost anywhere, at any time. Greg would always ask if she were OK. He'd put his arm around her. Comfort her. Sometimes, Greg's comfort could take an awfully long time.

Later, he started giving her to selected friends. That lasted until Greg had shot Cherub into her tummy. After that, Morven was off limits to anyone but him. Of course, Stewart already knew that part. In fact, when Morven started describing it, he interrupted. Cherub was crying upstairs.

Morven fetched the baby and prepared a bottle, and now sat back on the sofa with Cherub in her arms. Stewart had pulled on his trousers and now was holding a pack of frozen cod against his damaged shoulder. Morven told him about the well of mixed feelings she'd experienced when Cherub was born, from elation when she'd look at his chubby new-born face to the constant sense that none of it should have happened.

And especially about how the angels had started speaking to her directly, telling her what she needed to do.

'The angels thought I should die?' Stewart asked incredulously.

'I thought they did,' she replied.

'Are you sure you heard them?' he asked. 'I mean, are you certain it was them and not your own thoughts?'

Morven understood, but asked what he meant anyway.

'Maybe you only think you heard angels,' he suggested.

'Maybe I'm crazy – is that it?'

'No,' Stewart insisted. 'It's just that… what we had was different.' His good hand groped the air in front of him, as if trying to grasp the words. 'It wasn't like I was…' His voice trailed away.

'The angels said you were,' Morven told him. 'They said you were just another rapist.'

Stewart dropped his hand and adjusted his package of cod. He stayed silent for a long time. Finally, he asked, 'What about Cherub? Did you take him along, the way you've done today?'

'When I killed those people?' she said. She looked down at the baby tenderly. He sucked greedily on his bottle. 'Of course I did.'

Stewart frowned at her uncomprehendingly.

'Well, where else would he have been?' she said defensively. 'He belongs with his mummy.'

'Morven,' Stewart said, 'it's not right. You can't

endanger a baby like that. This new life you've chosen, all this crazy business–'

'The angels chose it!' she insisted.

'Whatever's caused it,' he continued earnestly, 'it's dangerous, and it's no place for a baby. I'm on your side, really I am. But you've got to give Cherub to someone who can take care of him.'

'Who?'

'Social Services,' Stewart said.

'They'd arrest me!'

'Then leave him anonymously. Call and tell them where to find him. Drop him off at a hospital.' When Morven yelped, Stewart pressed on urgently: 'I know it sounds cruel, but it's just the opposite. It's the only way to keep him safe.' Morven started shaking her head violently. Stewart slid back to the floor, wincing, and took her hand. 'Ask the angels,' he urged her. 'Look into your heart and ask them what to do.'

Morven squeezed her eyes tightly. She snapped, 'Stop talking now.' She pouted, eyes down, expression sullen, and finally muttered, 'I'll think about it.'

'Good,' Stewart said. He stroked one of her eyelids with his thumb and Morven reopened her eyes. 'There's one more thing I need to tell you,' he said. 'And it's something I thought you knew already.'

She looked at Stewart expectantly.

'Greg wasn't Cherub's father,' he said, and Morven shot him a wide-eyed look of puzzlement.

Stewart cleared his throat, and told her all of the facts she hadn't known. As he did, the mushy-sad sludge clogging Morven's mind drained away. Rapidly, everything became sparkling-clear, and she knew she would need to form a new plan. Morven licked her lips. Considered her options.

'I'm going to want to keep your cricket bat,' she told Stewart.

TWELVE

Edwina Koch was in a Marks & Spencer's café. The anonymity of malls always gave her a contented glow. Edwina especially liked sitting at their food courts and in-store restaurants – places of solitude, where she didn't have to worry about being *Mother*. This particular mall was so close to Heathrow, customers could hear the airplanes taking off and landing. However, like most of those habituated to the soundscapes of London, Edwina was not disturbed by the shrill whine of the aircraft engines. She was drinking a cup of coffee when her mobile rang. The caller ID told it was Stewart – the soap actor. Edwina frowned. She'd trusted few Supplicants with her personal details. Those she had were expected to call one of the unregistered pay-as-you-go phones.

'Why are you ringing me on this number?' she demanded. 'Don't you have the right ones?'

'I tried them,' Stewart said. 'You didn't answer.'

'That's because I'm out,' Edwina snapped. 'I don't carry them all with me, do I?'

'This couldn't wait,' Stewart told her. 'Do you know where I am? The Charing Cross Hospital. That little bitch just tried to kill me!'

'What?' Edwina said. 'Who?'

'Greg's little girl. Morven! Did you know he's dead?'

'Greg? Of course.'

When Edwina did not elaborate, Stewart pressed on. 'She's going around killing other Supplicants,' he said. 'And she's got her kid with her – the baby! You knew about all that, too, didn't you?'

Edwina lowered her voice. 'Shush,' she commanded.

'She hit my shoulder,' Stewart complained. 'With my own cricket bat. I think it's broken.'

Edwina set down her coffee and rubbed her forehead. The girl had been ordered to disappear. Then, it seemed, she went straight to this fucking actor with murder on her mind. Morven had an agenda – and Edwina was pretty sure which individuals she was targeting.

'This needs to stop,' Stewart continued. 'That Frankenstein's Monster you've created is still on the loose.'

'I didn't create her,' Edwina hissed quietly. 'She's a legacy from those Scottish pikeys Greg enslaved.'

'She has her *baby* with her,' Stewart repeated. 'My shoulder's broken.'

'I told you,' she said, 'I'll deal with it.'

'You'd better,' Stewart said. 'Because I'm willing to stop this if you can't.'

Edwina tensed. 'Meaning?'

Stewart cleared his throat. 'I'm telling you now – I am prepared to go to the police.'

Edwina trembled with sudden rage. Who was this soap opera prick, telling her what she had to do? It was true that Stewart Delaney's support had been good for the Supplicants of Dusk. He may not have been an A-list actor, but he was willing to go on the record. As soon as *The Sun* got wind of Stewart's involvement in the order, interest had risen a hundred-fold. At the time, that had meant a lot. But an actor's fame was ephemeral, and Stewart wasn't on television anymore.

'Stewart?' she asked. 'I'm curious. When you go to the police, what exactly will you tell them?'

She heard Stewart exhale. 'What do you mean?'

Edwina smirked. 'I'm just wondering how you'll

explain that the child you've been raping has suddenly grown angry with you.'

Edwina Koch dropped her midday purchases inside the house and ordered Raymond to take them upstairs. She picked up her half-finished blanket and bag of wool and made her way down the garden. Now she sat alone in her boat, producing an intricate chain of puff stitches. An iPad streamed late Sixties folk-rock at a low volume. Although Edwina called her house The Retreat, her true retreat was here, bobbing on the banks of the Thames. This canal boat was the one place that was Edwina's alone, a refuge even more liberating than a mall cafe. Not even Raymond and Cara were allowed down here.

Edwina had surprised herself by bringing that psychiatrist aboard on the weekend. She'd wanted the woman out of the house, and out of earshot of the staff. Edwina had intended to walk with her along the towpath, but the day had turned cold. That had been enough for Edwina to violate her own sacred space. *I must be slipping*, she thought. Had Sara Jones been a Supplicant, she would have considered such an invitation the highest possible honour.

Then again, had Sara Jones been a Supplicant, Edwina would have never asked her onto the boat.

One of the things Edwina liked to do down here was speak to her long-dead husband. That was something she couldn't do in a public food court. Andreas had never seen this boat – she'd bought it several years after his death – but Edwina always felt his presence here. And, as she had done so many times before, today she felt the need to apologise to her husband's spirit for all her shortcomings.

'We're in a bit of a mess, Dre,' she said to him. 'Your old friend Greg's last hurrah may have sunk me. He never could resist putting his paws all over that girl of his, and I was too greedy to put him in his place. He just kept donating, and I kept quiet. I'm sorry for that. I don't want it to wreck what we created.'

Had he been alive, Andreas wouldn't have managed to control his friend either, Edwina thought. Her husband had been a real visionary, but a terrible leader. That's why she'd assumed control of the order in the first place.

'And lately,' Edwina admitted, 'I have taken my eye off the ball. I should have seen trouble brewing on that farm. That blabbermouth Lorna used to call me, bitching about all the problems Greg allowed to fester in his businesses. I took her calls because sometimes I learned something everyone else was afraid to tell me.' Edwina laughed. 'More than once, one of them would ask how I knew something. I'd always say it was the angels.'

And who's to say it wasn't? Edwina asked herself. For all she knew, that was how angels communicated.

'But I ignored Lorna's warnings. I'm sure she even mentioned the girl – Morven – by name. Lorna told me she was going mad. I said to her, childbirth can do that.'

This weekend's visits from Morven and the psychiatrist had been wake-up calls. Edwina had slipped up recently, but the run of misjudgement was over now. The order was at stake, and she was the only person who could clean up the mess.

'Anyway, darling Dre,' she concluded, 'you don't need to worry. I'll think of something.'

Edwina set the blanket, wool and hook on the small table and slid from her chair. Carefully, she eased her way along the narrow aisle.

'And Dre?' she said in parting. 'If you see your friend Greg in the underworld, tell him not to worry, either.'

Stepping off the boat, she added, 'Somehow, I'll find a way to avenge him.'

Throughout the 1960s, Edwina Fisher's family had been active members of the Evangelical Group within the Church of England. Even at primary school, Edwina would devote several hours a week to visiting the local university campus, working with older colleagues to recruit for the Student Christian Movement. Despite her tender years, Edwina proved herself to be the best recruiter and shrewdest organiser on campus. In the early 1970s, she began university. By that time, Edwina's wing of the Evangelical movement was being threatened by harder-line Charismatics who bore little fealty to the Church of England. One of the rising stars in that fundamentalist movement was an intense German engineering student with a studied frown. His name was Andreas Koch.

The relationship between Edwina Fisher and Dre Koch started as an evangelical Romeo and Juliet story. Soon Edwina realised Dre's personal ideology had drifted in significant ways from the Christianity either of them espoused. When not poring over his engineering texts, Dre had made a study of so-called fallen angels within apocryphal literature. When they were alone, he would spin elaborate theories for Edwina – stories that would have shocked his conservative brethren. His were tales in which demons worked for the Almighty, and traditional morality was a scriptural misinterpretation followed by fools. Dre would back up his notions with befuddling proofs. His philosophy combined history, scripture, folk tales, and perhaps a touch of imagination. Dark angels could do dark deeds, Dre had said, but sometimes those deeds brought light to the dim majesty of the Celestial Kingdom.

Often, love can act as the soil in which new beliefs grow. As Edwina fell more deeply in love with Dre, his words appeared to make more and more sense. And the thing about Edwina Fisher was, once she'd accepted an idea, her mind would burn with ways to promote it. It was Edwina who had encouraged Andreas to write down his thoughts in a special journal. After that, she had engineered his break with the Charismatics, and those notes led him to formalise his own theology. Soon, Edwina was helping him to write the book that would become the cornerstone of the Supplicant movement, *Sermons of Dusk*. From their marriage in 1980 and through the subsequent founding of their order, Edwina had acted as cheerleader for, and enforcer of, Andreas Koch's dark exegesis. Dre had a mystical mind, but Edwina showed aptitude for leadership.

Those skills served her well after her husband's premature passing from cancer in his early fifties. After a suitable period of mourning, Edwina Koch became Mother Edwina, shepherdess to the chasms of the underworld.

Had Edwina ever believed the theology she shared with her flock? The answer was complicated. Raised an evangelical Christian, Edwina Koch had always been capable of accepting claims that required faith in the absence of proof. And so, even as she drifted between waves of belief and doubt, Mother Edwina had spoken with confidence of fallen angels doing evil for the sake of good.

Edwina had always been secure in the knowledge that her stories would not be contradicted – at least within her order. But there was another type of challenge, not so readily overcome by ferocity of will. That was the challenge of circumstance, of how far she might put the darker tenets of her faith into practice. Edwina's morally-flexible theology had made accepting donations from questionable sources – including the drug-dealing slaver from Dorset, Greg Blackadar – much easier. But what did those morals say about even darker behaviour? Edwina knew that, within Dre's philosophy, it was possible to justify almost any act. But she had never been tested to any worrying extreme.

Not until Morven, the murderer, started creating havoc among the Supplicants of Dusk.

Edwina knew she would be expected to tame her order's out-of-control psychotic. If she didn't, the whole structure of her order might tumble down. For days she had struggled with the options. Leaving Morven to her own devices was not one of them. Edwina knew Raymond would do anything for her… but could she really ask him to take on the burden of stopping the girl?

Was there any other way?

It wasn't until the wee hours of Monday morning that Edwina Koch finally committed to a course of action. Before she could even countenance silencing Morven directly, there was one more thing she could try.

She would see if Morven could be convinced to silence herself.

It was just after dawn on that same day in early March. Morven was awakened by a sound emitting from the shelf beneath Cherub's cot. It took her a moment to realise it was the phone Mother Edwina had given her. Swiftly, Morven snapped to her senses, rolled off the bed and rooted through the nappy bag. She pressed the phone's button.

'Morven, it's Mother,' the voice on the other end said. 'I'm sorry to be calling so early. Can you talk?'

'Always, Mother,' Morven replied. She glanced over at Cherub, who twitched on the bed in a colourful baby dream. Morven had never received a call from Mother Edwina before. This was a special moment in her life. 'What service may I do for you?' she asked in the order's formal greeting.

'Relax, darling,' Mother said. Her voice sounded awfully sweet - almost contrite. 'I have to start by apologising,' she went on. 'Back when you came to visit, I was terribly unpleasant to you. I didn't mean to be. I was so shaken by your tragic circumstances that I forgot my manners.'

Morven started. Intense love gushed through her heart for Mother Edwina. Morven felt ashamed at how she had occasionally doubted her since the trip to Weybridge. 'Mother, you weren't mean to me,' she said. 'I should have called you before I came to The Retreat. And I shouldn't have presumed you'd give me more cards just because I wanted them.'

'No, dear, that's all unimportant,' Mother said. 'I am

pleased you've apologised – and I'm sorry, as well. But that isn't why I've rung you.'

Morven listened to the traffic pass on the road below. Even at this early hour, the area was busy. 'Then why, Mother?' she asked.

'Something very important has happened,' Mother told her. 'Something with deep implications for you.'

Morven stilled, so not even the faintest rustle of fabric would obscure Mother's words. She grimaced towards the traffic outside. 'I'm all ears,' she said.

'Last night,' Mother began, 'I felt unaccountably restless. It was as though some heavenly purpose was eluding my grasp.'

Morven tingled at the idea of being disturbed by a heavenly purpose. Mother was so lucky.

'Finally, I went upstairs to bed,' Mother went on. 'I don't know how long I slept before a dim grey light filled my room. It was the light of the underworld.'

'*Home of those dark angels we revere with trembling and awe*,' Morven quoted from memory. She glanced out the window. The sun was rising, and Morven could imagine that the light in the Celestial Kingdom being the same shade of dusky blue.

‘Without warning, the angel Shoftiel herself appeared before me,’ Mother told her, ‘and her black wings embraced me.’

Immediately, Morven forgot about the light and gasped. *Shoftiel!* That was the angel whose card she had kept back from Mother. The card still in the pocket of her parka.

‘I felt nothing but profound calm,’ Mother continued, ‘and the understanding that what was about to be said could not be questioned.’

Morven’s muscles twitched. She wondered if she’d got it wrong. Was the Kingdom displeased with her? Had they chosen Shoftiel as secret proof of their displeasure?

‘Shoftiel,’ Mother went on, ‘told me you visited Stewart Delaney.’

Morven felt as though she’d been punched. ‘I didn’t kill him,’ she blurted.

‘But you intended to,’ Mother said confidently.

And it was true. *Mother knows everything,* Morven reminded herself. *Angels tell her stuff like this. I was wrong to doubt her.*

‘It was Shoftiel herself who prevented you from carrying out that abominable act of disobedience.’

Morven’s chest rose and fell in tiny gasps. She thought

about how heavy the cricket bat had been this morning. How it had dropped to the floor, almost of its own accord.

'Mother, I –'

'Quiet!' Mother ordered. 'The dark angels need no apologies from you. In her role as Judge of God, Shoftiel has ordered me to pass along two commands. She says you must carry out these instructions to the letter.'

'Anything,' Morven agreed. 'Tell me what I have to do.'

'First,' Mother said, 'you must surrender Cherub.'

Suddenly, Morven's hyperventilation ceased. Breath eased out from between her lips. Her muscles sagged. 'What do you mean?'

'I mean, the angels watched as you attacked Stewart with your baby present.'

'Cherub was upstairs!'

'He was also there when you killed Greg and Jeff.'

Morven's mouth half-opened, then closed. When had the angels told Mother about Jeff?

'You are to give up Cherub for adoption,' Mother ordered.

Stewart had said much the same thing, Morven thought. But if the angels had been watching them, maybe he'd said it because they'd made him. And perhaps now they'd spoken to Mother because Morven hadn't listened.

'Mother, I'm sorry,' Morven said. She looked at Cherub and felt ill. The last thing she wanted was to give up the love of her life. Cherub was her only companion. But Morven also knew defying the Kingdom always led to harsh punishment. The angels they followed were pretty hardcore about transgression. 'Did the Kingdom tell you how I should do this?'

'The angels,' Mother told her, 'said you must do it without being seen.'

Morven heard herself snort. Of *course* she had to do it without being seen! That's not what she'd meant. But she did not want to make Mother angry by pointing out how obvious that was. 'But how, Mother?' she asked. 'Where did they say I should take Cherub?'

Mother paused. 'They say you are to find a branch of Social Services,' she said, 'and leave Cherub there. Our dark angel has assured me he will be adopted by a wealthy family and prosper in life.'

Morven bit her lip. That was precisely the kind of banal reassurance you got when someone was trying to influence you. She wondered whether angels were capable of humouring people. Then she shuddered and dismissed the terrible thought. 'It will be an awful thing to have to do, Mother,' she said.

'I know, child.'

'But once I've done it,' Morven went on, 'what do the angels say I should do then?'

'Oh, Morven, this is so difficult for me,' Mother whispered with a catch in her voice. 'I want you to know how much I love you.'

'I love you, too, Mother.'

'You must also understand that sometimes we need to trust the Celestial Kingdom, even when its guidance is hard.'

'I do, Mother,' Morven assured her. 'I have always trusted the Kingdom.'

'I know you have.'

Morven heard Mother take a long breath. Finally, Mother Edwina said, 'The angels have informed me that your mission on earth is over.'

Morven opened her mouth to speak, but couldn't think of any words to put there.

'They tell me the Kingdom is very proud of you, and that plans are underway to receive you into the underworld with great celebration.' Morven could hear Mother take another breath before she concluded, 'Once you're sure Cherub is safe, you are commanded to end your life.'

THIRTEEN

Morven and Cherub sat in a patch of green next to the Thames. The old *London A-Z* Morven had found in Greg's glove compartment said the place was called Victoria Tower Gardens. She and Cherub played on the grass with some shiny plastic cubes as Morven thought about suicide.

Morven had never considered killing herself. She'd thought about murdering other people, of course – otherwise she wouldn't be in this pickle. She had also pondered dying, at least in the abstract. Morven had always known the path she was on could result in her own demise. But there was a calm conviction that came when you hobnobbed with celestial beings. On the occasions Morven had killed, she'd understood it was with the direct guidance of a host of fallen angels. And if her mission caused her to die, that would be with the angels' OK as well. It was true the act of actually ending her own life – of hanging, or jumping, or cutting – was a new idea. But Morven had to assume her death had the blessing of the Celestial Kingdom, because Mother had ordered it. That had been only a couple days ago, but already, Morven had come up with a plan.

The first thing she needed to decide was how to kill herself. A number of the methods she'd thought of seemed awfully complicated. Some seemed painful, too… or really risky. The thought of *failing* to die, of ending up some sort of drooling object, wasn't pleasant at all. After plenty of consideration, Morven had decided the best way to go would be from gunshot wounds. They seemed the quickest way to make yourself dead, if you held your nerve. The problem was, Morven was in England, where it wasn't easy to find a gun in a hurry. Farmers had shotguns, she knew, but that general understanding didn't help a lot in the here-and-now. That was what had led her to her plan, and brought her here, to check out these gardens.

Morven cleaned away the plastic cubes and put the baby into his pram. She moved to a bench next to the Thames, pushing Cherub back and forth slowly as he sat upright in the too-small buggy. The biggest wrench over the next week would be leaving this wonderful child. Giving up Cherub would be as hard as surrendering her own heart.

Still, looking back, Mother's demand hadn't been much of a surprise. Really, Morven had known in her heart of hearts it would have to happen. Cherub deserved the most attentive mummy he could have, and she wasn't it.

Morven's plan fell into three parts. First, she would savour one last week of mummy-and-baby time. They had already been to the zoo and a museum. Over the next several days, they'd have even more adventures. Maybe a trip on the London Eye. Or a boat along the river. Morven knew Cherub wouldn't remember any of it – or her – as he grew up, but she wasn't doing it for memories. This was a way to say goodbye. Second, during that time, Morven would also return to the library, where she would learn all about the adoption process and how best to give up Cherub. Once Cherub was safely on his way to a new and better family, Morven would be free to return here to the gardens. That was where the third part of her plan would come into play. She would kill old Joe Bennett as he munched his lunchtime sandwiches… and do it slowly enough for the police to shoot her dead immediately afterwards.

The rest would be in the hands of the angels.

Sara and Jamie had decided to play hooky. It was nearly a

month since Valentine's Day, and they'd promised each other a time all to themselves, without interference from universities, builders, or murder investigations. Jamie was expected to attend a seminar that day, but had emailed his sincerest apologies. Sara decided the contractors would get on just fine without her. As for Ceri… no doubt she'd spend the day fighting crime with her new best friend.

Sara and Jamie had allowed themselves to spend the morning in bed. The pricey Chardonnay had been in the fridge ever since Jamie gave it to Sara; they'd started drinking it at 11 a.m. It wasn't long afterwards that Sara received a call on her mobile.

'Sara? It's Joe Bennett.'

Sara set down her wine, wrestled the sheets off her legs, and sat up. 'Good morning, Minister,' she said.

'I'm sorry I haven't rung you since our last meeting,' the Minister for Policing said.

'Sir?'

'It's a busy life in politics these days.'

Silently, Jamie motioned to Sara. She raised her eyes to the heavens and shook her head dramatically. 'No worries, Minister,' she said. 'I understand completely.'

'I'm surprised you haven't rung me,' Bennett said

pointedly.

'Minister?' Jamie whispered. 'Don't let him spoil our day.'

'I hear you had some drama with a young woman outside your house,' Bennett went on.

'A homeless mother, sir,' Sara said.

'Well, you see,' he replied, 'that is precisely the kind of thing I'd have hoped you'd alert me to. I did ask.'

'Did you?'

'When we met on the Heath.'

'Of course,' Sara stammered. 'Honestly, it didn't occur to me. I had no idea you'd be interested.'

'Well… mental note for next time, eh?' Bennett said.

As briefly as she could, Sara relayed the story of meeting the young woman outside her house. It was a less-detailed version of the tale she'd told Mir. 'Do you think she's connected to the case?' Sara asked in conclusion.

'No, no,' Bennett said. 'Not necessarily. But at the moment, any unusual occurrence is worth reporting.'

Sara *had* reported it, and felt a flush of anger at the minister's high-handed presumption. Jamie must have sensed her irritation; he offered her a look of puzzled compassion.

'If anything else out of the ordinary happens,' Bennett said, 'just let me know.'

Sara looked at Jamie and bugged out her eyes. He chuckled. 'Of course, sir,' Sara said pleasantly.

'And we'll get together for another chat quite soon, okay?'

After a late lunch, Sara and Jamie ventured out. The weather was mild for late February; Sara unearthed a Burberry trench coat that usually didn't appear until late March. Jamie wore a sports jacket. Walking towards Brixton Hill, Sara found herself venting about the strange time she'd been having with Ceri. 'I'm supposed to keep saying Ceri's hanging around the investigation because *I* want her,' she told Jamie. 'The truth is, Ceri and Mir are collaborators. They're using me to keep her on the case when she has no official role.'

'I'm sure Ceri can help in many ways,' Jamie said. 'She has the experience.'

'She's told all this, too,' Sara replied. She checked her watch. They were on their way to the local cinema. Sara and Jamie had agreed to catch all the films they'd been too busy to see prior to the awards season. This afternoon's movie was a period comedy that had done well internationally.

'But honestly,' Sara said, 'she's still here because she and Mir have become…'

'Friends?' Jamie interrupted. 'What's wrong with that?'

'I'm not jealous,' Sara replied.

'I didn't say you were,' Jamie noted. He hesitated before adding, 'You know they're… well, *more* than just friends, right?'

Sara barely heard her partner's words. As they passed the redbrick-and-glass expanse of the Lambeth Civic Centre, the prickle of angst she had felt about Ceri shifted suddenly into a different sensation. Sara was overcome by an intense feeling of being watched. It was like being picked out by a spotlight.

Jamie studied Sara's silence and took it as discomfort. 'I know how unsettling such a dynamic must be,' he said soothingly. 'Not just personally, but professionally, too. You were asked to join the investigation, not Ceri.'

Sara nodded vaguely.

Jamie sighed. 'But it's none of our business,' he concluded, and switched to nattering about banal logistics. He mused aloud about the best time to put the flat on the market and which estate agents they should speak to. Sara tried to listen, but was more concerned about her lingering feeling of being on display. She scanned the area, half-expecting to see the young mother and her baby. Since their encounter on Saturday, the girl had become a presence in Sara's mind, a shadow cast over all other events. She was nowhere to be seen… however, Sara had been right. She *was* being observed. Leaning on the metal railing at the Lambeth Customer Centre was a tall woman. Sara did a double-take at her track bottoms and hoodie, which bore the logo of a chain of gyms. However, it was the blue-frosted afro that jogged Sara's memory. This was the same person who'd spoken to her when she'd bought Jamie his Rolex – the one who had introduced herself as Daniela. Now the woman stared, direct and unflinching, as Sara and Jamie walked towards her. When Sara stared back, they locked eyes. The woman nodded solemnly.

'Sara?' Jamie said.

She swivelled her head. 'Sorry. What?'

'I was talking about timings,' Jamie said. 'Putting the flat on the market, moving to Marylebone, kicking Ceri out of our bed…'

'Oh, right,' Sara said, walking past the woman.

'Timings.'

The woman who called herself Daniela was in the cinema, too. Sara felt her presence a few rows behind herself and Jamie. When Sara had got up to visit the loo, the woman watched her with undisguised interest. On her way back, Sara was tempted to lean in close and ask exactly what she wanted. Instead she just breezed past, eyes fixed ahead. Sara did not want a messy confrontation in Jamie's presence.

Once the credits were rolling and they'd left the cinema, Sara told Jamie she would meet him at home – she wanted to pick up a few things at the chemists. Walking down Brixton Road, Sara looked for signs of her human shadow; the woman was nowhere to be seen. Sara finally spied her in the Superdrug near the station, glancing absently at makeup. This time, they did not make eye contact. The woman was biding her time. Sara paid for her goods and left the shop, then bought coffee at the Pret A Manger across the road. She chose a table and waited. It wasn't long before Sara noticed the woman crossing the street, the blue tips of her hair gleaming in the sun. She entered and slid into the chair opposite Sara. Sara had braced herself for an edge of antagonism in their meeting, but, immediately, a flush of warmth seeped through her.

'I don't know if you remember,' the woman said calmly. 'But we've met before. My name is Daniela. Daniela Atta.'

'Sara Jones,' Sara replied automatically.

'I know,' said Daniela with a kind smile. 'I've been watching you.'

'You seem to have been stalking me, too,' Sara replied. 'How long for?'

Daniela shrugged. 'A while.'

Sara took a slow sip of her coffee. 'Then you have far too much time on your hands,' she said.

Daniela wrinkled her nose. 'I didn't say I'd been *following* you the whole time,' she said. 'I have a job to go to, just like anyone else. But there are lots of ways to watch someone. You of all people should know that.'

Daniela's guileless stare burrowed into Sara's head. Sara forced herself to blink and let her gaze drift away. She realised what she was feeling was fear. If this woman were saying what Sara thought she was, then Daniela Atta was the last person she wanted to meet right now. Given the events of the last several months, knowing another psychic would not be the wisest lifestyle choice.

'What do you do for a living?' Sara asked.

Daniela plucked at the logo on her hoodie. 'I work at a gym,' she said. 'Personal trainer.'

'Ah.'

'How are the anti-depressants working?' Daniela asked.

Sara looked up sharply. Daniela did not wait for an answer. 'They seem to be doing some good,' she continued. 'Dr Shapiro would be pleased. But still, you've been so worried about that girl with the baby. And yet, you've never even considered looking for her with your mind.'

Sara's face tightened.

'You know,' Daniela concluded, 'the way Eldon Carson taught you to.'

Sara pursed her lips. Her thoughts rode swirls of emotion. Half-formed questions surfaced in their eddies and broke apart, leaving only one: if this woman knew about Eldon, did it also mean she knew about last summer? About Tim Wilson?

'I know a lot about you,' Daniela responded. 'And I could find out more. But the point is, *you* can discover things, too.' She waved her hand airily. 'For example, you could learn everything you want to know about that girl and her child. You could do it right here, now, in this shop. Just close your eyes and ask the question.'

Sara cast her gaze over the café, with its tables of customers devouring avocado wraps and sipping juice.

'Or you could go home and lie down,' Daniela added.

She looked at Sara eagerly, taking her lack of response as acquiescence. 'So, which will it be?' she asked with vigour. 'Do you want your questions about her answered?'

Sara paused until the silence was uncomfortable. Finally, she replied, 'No.'

'No?' Daniela repeated. 'Are you sure?'

Without asking permission, Daniela reached out and touched the chain around Sara's neck. She slid it between her fingers until a silver disk appeared from under Sara's shirt. Engraved on it was Eldon Carson's Eye-in-the-Pyramid symbol. 'The fact that you wear this,' she said, 'suggests otherwise.'

Daniela let the pendant drop against her chest. The muscles in Sara's legs twitched with the urge to jump up and dash from the shop. 'Of course I felt bad for the girl,' Sara snapped. 'She looked too young to have a baby, and I didn't know if they lived on the street. But that's the extent of it.' She tucked the silver disk back under her shirt. 'Why would I want to know more?'

Daniela cocked her head. 'That's the question, isn't it?' she said. Then she shrugged pointedly. 'But maybe you should.'

Sara could feel the tightness of her face, the way her cheeks trembled with strain. 'Who *are* you?' she asked.

'I told you,' the girl said lightly. 'My name's Daniela Atta. And don't worry… I'm not going anywhere.'

Daniela stood and moved towards the door. Over her shoulder, she added, 'We'll have plenty more chances to talk.'

So far that week, Morven and Cherub had visited the Museum of Childhood, the aquarium, and the London Eye. Now they were back at the library. The place was almost empty this afternoon, and Morven did not have to contend with any nosy old men asking rude questions. Cherub had another Hob Nob gripped in his hand and was contented. Morven knew he wouldn't be nearly as happy if he understood what they were doing there.

Morven now sat before a computer, Googling web pages about adoption. She knew giving up a baby could be a long and difficult process – more than Mother had let on. Still, that did not worry her. Morven had no plans to follow the rules to the letter. What she needed to know was where babies were kept before they went to their new homes. That was where she'd take Cherub. She imagined a kindly nurse finding the baby in a government hallway and thinking, *Oh, look – this would be the perfect child for the Johnsons*. Morven had to trust the angels that such a thing could happen. In order to carry out her plan, Morven would have to leave Cherub at the adoption place within the next few days. Certainly before next Wednesday. It would be sad, parting like that so suddenly… but Mother had been right. Murder and babies simply did not mix.

Morven frowned at the search engine. Even the widest parameters led her to sites offering a range of unhelpful advice. At least, it wasn't helpful to Morven. She simply wanted to know where to find the right building and how to leave Cherub there without being questioned. The web pages advised her to go to 'her local authority' and speak to its 'children's services department.' There were vague references to 'the agency arranging the adoption.' Failing all that, Morven learned she could get guidance from a social worker, or even the Citizen's Advice Bureau. She really doubted they'd give her the information she needed. All this faffing about was new to Morven – she'd never had to navigate the labyrinthine procedures of government. Morven found understanding these instructions like trying to interpret smoke signals.

After a few more fruitless searches, Morven turned to Cherub. His face was mucky with chocolate and wet crumbs. She wiped him clean. 'Well, baby boy,' she said, 'this saga is going to take longer than I thought.'

Morven wondered exactly what to do about that. She still had her date with old Joe to worry about. Now that Morven had made up her mind to kill him, she really didn't want to drop that part of the plan. At the same time, Morven knew it would be a step beyond any crime she'd allowed herself to commit before. In the world of the Supplicants, Joe was the one untouchable. He was the person Mother protected with all her might – the guy really was that important. Under any other circumstance Morven would have bowed to Mother's wishes and left him alone. She'd only decided to kill him because it was the best way for her to die as well. Besides, in such an ambiguous situation, Mother would probably forgive her ghost.

Morven tucked away the soiled wet wipes and pushed

Cherub out of the library. Things never changed as fast as you thought they were going to, she reflected.

On the high street, Morven smiled down at her son. 'Looks like you'll need to tag along on one more adventure with Mummy,' she said.

FOURTEEN

Morven had checked out of each of her hotels that morning. After what she planned to do today, the police would put two and two together. Before visiting the library yesterday, Morven had assumed she'd be without Cherub by now. Then, her plan had been to leave the hotel, drive to Central London, torch the van with all Greg's banknotes still inside, kill old Joe, and end her own life. Now she would need the van, as well as the money, for a while longer.

Morven knew Prime Minister's Questions would start at noon. When it was over, old Joe was likely to want his lunch. She imagined other politicians took lunch at their desks, or over meetings. Morven was lucky her enemy was as fond of his me-time as he was about bird-watching. If Joe were true to form, he'd eat in the Victoria Tower Gardens, binoculars aimed at the trees. With that in mind, Morven parked in a car park directly across from where she'd need to be. For a moment, she wondered whether to leave Cherub in the van. Immediately, she rejected the thought. There was no guarantee she'd be able to come back to Greg's van at all, and it would be heart-breaking to have to part with Cherub in that way. She imagined him squalling in his car seat as the underground garage was in lockdown. Who knows how long he would stay there before he was found?

No, until Morven could find him another home, Cherub needed to be with his mummy.

She removed the baby's pram from the back of the van. She had promised Mother she'd buy a proper pushchair, but things had been so busy recently. Morven got the pram ready and set Cherub inside. She leaned into the cab of the van and tugged out Stewart Delaney's cricket bat. Balancing the heavy chunk of wood on the pram's plastic shelf, she wedged the bat's shoulder behind the handle.

'There we go, my little Cherub,' she said. 'Now everyone will think we're going to play mummy-and-baby cricket!'

Morven imagined herself standing, bat at the ready, as Cherub bowled her a slider. She chuckled at her little joke. As an afterthought, she reached into the van and removed several bundles of cash, placing them in the pram's bottom tray, just in case.

Morven passed a statue of a woman she'd never heard of. The woman's stone likeness stood on a tall plinth, looking down benignly on the pigeons that pecked the pavement beneath her. Diagonally ahead, stone benches lined the pathway close to the Palace of Westminster. Morven thought it likeliest old Joe would perch there. Morven chose the bench farthest from the street. The sun was shining, and she found it quite pleasant to rest on the bench, just waiting.

Her thoughts turned to Stewart. That lad was a real conundrum. Morven had been so sure the angels had told her to end his life. He was just another rapist, they'd said. And yet when it came right down to it, Stewart had fought her off. Morven wondered whether she'd allowed that to happen. After all, she hadn't wanted Stewie to die. Or maybe the angels had kept him alive so he could tell her the truth about old Joe Bennett. Had that been the plan all along – to send her to Stewart's house with one intention, then twist it all around when she discovered the truth? Morven wasn't sure, but she was glad she hadn't killed

Stewie.

Joe Bennett was a very different kettle of fish. Before Stewart spilled the beans, Morven hadn't even considered harming the man. He was too much of a bigwig, she'd thought. Too important to Mother and the order. Everyone said how useful he was to the Supplicants of Dusk. That was why Greg had allowed him to… well, to do whatever he wanted. But Stewart's words had changed everything.

And maybe the angels directed Greg's words, she thought. *And maybe they want me to be here now, too.* Even if Morven weren't able to fulfil Mother's request and die just at that moment, killing Joe was a holy thing to do.

Morven looked away from the river to the line of benches spread out to her right. Suddenly, a jolt of adrenaline shot through her. There, on the bench closest to the road, sat a man, angled three-quarters away from her. He had binoculars pressed to his eyes. They were aimed at a leafless tree on Milbank. It looked like the man was goggling at some kind of finch. Morven rose and stroked Cherub's forehead. She whispered that he should be a good baby, and slid the cricket bat from the pram.

It would have been best to sneak up behind old Joe, but the benches were backed by a low stone wall and a mound of grasses and plants. Morven would have to trust the minister to keep concentrating on finches instead of her. It would be a long few seconds to walk from her side of the benches to his. She decided to take Cherub part of the way. A woman with a baby and a cricket bat was less threatening than a woman with a cricket bat alone. She tucked the heavy willow under her arm. It was hard to hold there, but she found some equilibrium by resting its handle on the pram.

Morven parked Cherub two benches down from old Joe. Joe's eyes were still covered by lenses aimed at the barren tree. She gripped the bat tightly in both hands and made a beeline towards him. When Morven thought she was close enough, she swung full-force. A foot closer and she might have taken Joe's head off. As it was, the toe of the bat caught him just above the left ear. The bat's splintered edge tore his flesh and made blood spatter and spill down his neck. Old Joe let go of the binoculars. Both he and they dropped to the ground. Nearby, a woman screamed. Morven realised she would have to finish Joe off fast. As it was, she and Cherub would have to run for it – too much longer and armed police would dash here from Parliament. And, despite her previous plans, Morven couldn't die today. She stepped forwards and raised the bat once more, like a truncheon this time, bringing it down heavily. It missed Joe's head by an inch and clunked against the pavement. The vibration hurt Morven's hands. Joe shuffled to his right, kicking out at Morven's leg. Morven lost balance, dropping the bat and wobbling unsteadily. With blood drenching the shoulder of his suit jacket, old Joe Bennett rolled onto his stomach, grabbed Morven's foot and yanked. She toppled over his back and he rolled onto her, trapping her against the tarmac, bleeding onto her parka.

'Get the police!' Joe cried to everyone. Then he looked down at Morven's face through his barely-focused eyes and said, '*You.*'

People were watching. Morven whispered, 'Me,' then echoed Joe's cry. 'Get the police!' she screamed. 'I'm being attacked. Help me!'

She could hear the shouts of people in the park: *that man there – a woman with a baby – bat – blood.* To the side, a TV cameraman who had been recording on College Green dashed into the park, his gait clumsy as he tried to steady his camera. A brawny young man charged towards Joe and wrenched him off Morven.

‘Her, you idiot,’ Joe cried, ‘not me.’

‘Shut up,’ Morven’s vigilante said, and kicked Joe in the ribs with steel-toe boots. Bennett yelped. The TV cameraman was advancing, doing his best to frame the action. The vigilante lent Morven his arm for support and she stood, swaying like a new-born foal. ‘Police,’ the vigilante cried.

‘My baby,’ Morven gasped, and staggered towards Cherub.

‘Are you OK, madam?’ someone else asked.

‘It was her,’ the original screaming woman cried. ‘I saw her.’

‘You shut up, too,’ the vigilante said. ‘You don’t know shit.’

Unsteadily, Morven grasped the pram’s handle. Cherub squawked for Mummy’s attention. Morven tucked her chin to her chest and pushed him straight past her vigilante, past the cameraman, through the onlookers, and away down the path.

She pushed Cherub down backstreets through Westminster until she came to Victoria Street. *I failed to kill Joe*, Morven told herself. She repeated it over, in time with her steps: *I failed to kill him. I failed to kill him.*

I failed.

She could hear police sirens in the distance, panda cars speeding towards Victoria Tower Gardens. There was no way Morven could go back to the car park now. She could kiss Greg's Mercedes goodbye for sure. Not to mention all her clothes, and most of Cherub's. And, of course, the stacks of banknotes the van contained. At least Morven had been wise enough to take some of that money with her. She still had a few hefty bundles, and they should tide her over until… well, until she did whatever she'd need to do.

Morven crossed Victoria and made it to St James Park tube station. She bought a Travelcard, then she and Cherub boarded the first train to arrive. It was heading for Wimbledon.

It was that cricket bat, Morven told herself. *It didn't work on Stewart and it didn't work on Joe*. That bat had been a bad choice. She should have bought a knife. *Why didn't I do that?* she wondered. Morven could picture herself walking calmly up to Joe and sticking the flesh under his left ear. Then he'd have been dead for sure, before he even dropped to the ground.

As the tube train juddered to Wimbledon, Morven stood

near its doors. She realised she must look an odd sight – hair all matted, with a baby who'd outgrown his pram. Added to that, she wore a parka stained with fresh blood. Nothing screamed *arrest me* like wearing human blood. As soon as she got to the station, Morven knew, she'd need to take quick remedial action.

Why didn't the angels warn me? Morven chewed at that question like torn flesh on her lip. It was strange – she'd received no angelic feedback at all. No feelings, no voices in her head. Was the Celestial Kingdom cross at her for disobeying Mother?

Have the angels abandoned me?

Leaving Wimbledon station, Morven reached into the breast pocket of her parka and retrieved her one remaining angel card. It was of Shoftiel, the judge. She tucked it into Cherub's bag.

The doubt and self-recrimination pressed on.

They must have abandoned me.

Morven wrestled off the bloody parka and stuffed it into a litter bin. In the ladies' room of a nearby mall, she rubbed herself with hand foam until she was passably clean. Then she and Cherub went shopping. By the time Morven's spending spree was over, she had purchased a top-of-the-line pushchair and new clothes for the baby, a lightweight leather jacket for herself, and a battery-operated men's hair clipper. As an afterthought, she popped into WH Smith and bought a thick paperback. Morven abandoned Cherub's old pram next to an escalator, making sure to retrieve his things and her remaining money before returning to the loo. There, she shaved off her hair until her scalp was covered in fine stubble. She let her hair drop into the sink, and did her best to scoop it up and flush it down the toilet. Morven put on the jacket and took in the effect in the mirror. The impromptu haircut, the expensive leather, and Cherub's shiny new pushchair made mummy and baby look almost respectable. She'd kept the bags from the shops she'd visited, and hung them off the handle of the pushchair. Just another family from out of town, come to the Big Smoke for some retail therapy.

It wouldn't help long-term, of course. Old Joe was an important man. A lot of people had seen what happened to him in Westminster. There would be countless descriptions of a mother and a baby. They'd find Greg's Mercedes van in the car park, stuffed with his money. Soon everyone would know who to look for. Morven had the luxury of staying in Hertfordshire for days, unbothered. Now, she wondered whether she could be safe in Wimbledon for even a night. But she had little choice – a baby could hardly sleep on the street.

As she pushed Cherub down Worple Road, looking for an inconspicuous bed-and-breakfast, Morven thought of her vigilante savoir in the gardens. She hoped he wouldn't get into too much trouble for helping her attack a government minister.

FIFTEEN

Sara half-watched television – a documentary in which elderly celebrities toured foreign countries for some reason she hadn't picked up. Jamie had spent the day at university, coming back to Brixton mid-evening and retiring with a book. Now, Sara could hear the sporadic rattling of his snores. It was just as well Jamie slept; the one thing Sara really wanted to share with him was off-limits. Last week's encounter with Daniela Atta had become a further unnerving complication in her life. Another secret she could not share with her partner. These lonely times of helplessness were when Sara missed Ego the most. Having a cat stretched across her lap demanding praise was a good way to get out of herself.

Since meeting Daniela, Sara had been trying to act normally. She'd kept a long-arranged lunch date with a clinician at the Maudsley who had helped her when she was last in private practice. She'd dropped by the new house and talked to the builders several times. The days had passed in orchestrated banality – other than the sporadic feeling of being watched. Until last week, Sara had attributed the sensation to that young mother and her baby. Actually, she'd secretly hoped the girl truly was following her. Then she could have met her, and offered her child the care he needed. But that was not what had been happening. Daniela Atta had been watching her. And that had become Sara's biggest mental struggle – admitting she'd met another psychic.

You could know everything about that girl and her baby, Atta had told her. *The way Eldon Carson taught you.*

Once, Sara would have grappled for mundane ways to explain Daniela's uncanny knowledge. Eldon Carson's name had been in the news, after all; Atta could have read it there. *But what about the girl?* she'd asked herself. *How could this woman have known about her?* There was no need to play those games now. Sara knew what it felt like to talk to another psychic, and she had no doubt Daniela Atta was one. Still, what this woman wanted, and what her presence implied, were things Sara couldn't consider rationally. There were too many possibilities numbing her mind.

On television, the celebrities pushed their wheeled suitcases through a park, walking away from the camera. They were leaving whatever country they were in for pastures new. There was a trailer for next week's show, set in a different part of the world. Dispassionately, Sara watched the images pass. The ten o'clock news began. The top story featured an assault on a politician in Westminster. MP Joseph Bennett had been ambushed next to the Houses of Parliament, and his attacker had escaped. Bennett was still in hospital, being treated for minor contusions. Sara forced herself to focus. *Bennett!* The Minister for Policing – the one who wouldn't let her alone.

On screen, people described what they had seen. Apparently, a young woman had hit Bennett with a cricket bat and was observed running away, pushing a baby carriage. Sara snapped to alertness. A news cameraman had been near the scene and managed to record the woman fleeing. A fairly clear still had been grabbed from the footage. It showed a teenage girl with matted red hair grasping the handle of a baby's pram. Sara's throat thickened. She picked up her mobile.

'*Allai'ch helpu chi?*' Ceri's voice said. Then she added, 'Oh – it's you. What's up?'

'Are you home?' Sara asked.

'Err, yeah,' Ceri said. 'Is something wrong?'

'Is Sergeant Mir with you?'

'What?' Ceri's tone grew coy. 'Why ever would you ask such a thing?'

'Ceri, this is important,' Sara snapped. 'Is Adeela there or not?'

'Of course she's here,' Ceri admitted.

'Hand her the phone.'

There was a short rustling before Mir said, 'Sara?'

'Today's assault on the Minister…' Sara said.

'Joseph Bennett,' Mir said. 'Horrible. He's in hospital, but I understand his injuries aren't life-threatening.'

'I know who did it,' Sara said.

'What? Who?'

'I'm on my way,' Sara told her. 'Call your Senior Investigating Officer. I'll ring you from my car.'

Adeela Mir had rung her superintendent as soon as Sara briefed her. Sara had told Mir about her interaction with the young mother in front of her home in Brixton. She did not mention Joseph Bennett's phone call to her yesterday. Sara suspected Mir would not have found it suspicious. She would have pointed out that Bennett was merely following up on a promise to ring again. Naturally, he would have raised the issue of the young mother he had heard about. And it was true… Bennett's having asked about a woman the day before she attacked him could, just maybe, be a coincidence. But Sara planned to keep alert to any other, similar coincidences.

As it transpired, the superintendent did not see fit to haul everyone out for a midnight meeting. Sara did not know the name or address of the offender, he'd explained, so there was no immediate action to be taken. However, he requested Sara's presence at the next morning's briefing. Sara decided it was best to stay at the new house overnight. Adeela had driven home to her flat in Hackney, and Sara had shared the bed with Ceri. Her new room smelled of cigarette smoke.

The morning's briefing was held at West End Central. On the room's projection screen was one of the shots taken from the footage of Victoria Tower Gardens. The Senior Investigating Officer, Mir's superintendent, updated his team on the health of Joseph Bennett. He also said Bennett had been interviewed by police from his hospital bed, and had denied knowing his attacker. The superintendent then introduced Sara, who recounted her meeting with the mysterious young woman and her baby, just outside her house in Brixton.

A young man raised his hand. The superintendent introduced him to the team as one of Bennett's advisors. 'I've spoken to the Minister,' he said. 'We both think it's quite possible – even likely – that the offender acted on the basis of a news report.'

'Which one?' the Superintendent asked.

'The report on the BBC, in the aftermath of Mr Sawyer's death.' The advisor sat back in his chair. 'It featured both the Minister and Dr Jones. It's a fair assumption the offender saw it, then tracked down each of them.'

'Her behaviour was different in each case,' Mir pointed out. 'She assaulted Bennett, but not Sara.'

'Perhaps Dr Jones was lucky,' the advisor suggested.

'It's possible,' Sara agreed. After all, Bennett had shown an interest in the investigation, which the girl may have interpreted as a threat. In a similar vein, Sara's role as an expert may have caused her to fear Sara might uncover her exact connection to the Supplicants of Dusk. Maybe she'd been sizing up Sara on the street, wondering whether she should be attacked.

Still, Sara doubted the girl thought of her in the same way as Bennett. This lack of certainty came from the conversation she'd had with Daniela Atta – something Sara could not reveal in this meeting. Atta seemed to imply, at least cryptically, that the girl had a special reason for seeking out Sara.

Why would I want to know more about her? Sara had asked, and Atta had replied, *Maybe you should.*

'Forensics is examining the weapon,' the Superintendent told the team, 'and we're waiting to see if they can match it to Blackadar's and Sawyer's murders.' He looked to Sara. 'We have no direct evidence, but we suspect this girl might be our offender in those homicides.'

Sara nodded, recalling her first meeting with Mir. Then, she'd felt there had been another person present when Blackadar had been killed. Could it have been a baby? It was obvious Daniela Atta wanted Sara to find out by using her psychic powers… but why?

'This morning, we dispatched house-to-house teams to Brixton,' the Superintendent went on. 'They'll cover the neighbourhood door by door, starting with the place where Dr Jones saw the suspect, and working outwards from there. There's a chance the girl lives locally. We'll also review CCTV footage. In the meantime,' he concluded, 'the screenshot of the girl has been circulated widely. We're hoping she'll be spotted by a member of the public.'

The superintendent called on DS Mir, who stood and addressed the team. 'If this young woman is our killer,' she announced, 'it means she also has links to Edwina Koch and the Supplicants of Dusk. We're sending two of our own detective constables to re-interview Mrs Koch today. We'll also be releasing images of the cards to the press.'

Sara raised her hand. 'Then you're making a direct link between this girl and the homicides?'

'Not directly, no,' the superintendent said. 'We'll treat them as separate-but-concurrent investigations. However,' he added, 'both the mother's photo and information about the cards will be out there. If someone wants to put two and two together for us, we'll thank them.'

Sara saw the Inspector make eye contact with Mir. Mir gave a slight nod and stood. 'We'll need to give interviews to the press about those cards,' she said. 'We've already set up an interview on the BBC's news channel. It's likely to receive wide coverage on all their bulletins. We'll also be ready for this evening's ITV and Channel 4 news. The press office is making further arrangements now.'

Bennett's advisor cleared his throat. 'And who will be conducting these interviews?' he asked.

Mir looked down at Sara. 'We'd like to ask our resident expert, Dr Jones, to do the honours.'

.

The six-foot-four bulk of muscle-and-flesh known as Raymond shifted uncomfortably. He had fitted himself into an overstuffed floral chair in The Retreat's conservatory. Mother Edwina sat opposite, watching him closely. She smiled sweetly at his discomfort; Raymond was used to being told to stay out of this room. Mother's iPad lay on the table, displaying the still image of Morven in Victoria Tower Gardens.

'That girl,' she told Raymond, 'is a loose cannon.'

She studied Raymond's slack expression. Others might have taken it for stupidity, or at least disengagement. Mother knew the look was deliberate and precautionary. It was Raymond's way of keeping his emotions masked. However, in Raymond's past year of close service at The Retreat, Edwina had uncovered many of the lad's tells – those micro-expressions that revealed his true thoughts. With Raymond, it was all in his eyes. Mother Edwina could read them like runes. Right now, she knew Raymond was well ahead of her. He had already steeled himself to commit violence on the Supplicants' behalf. He'd done some unpleasant, necessary things for the order in the past, so Mother Edwina had no worries about his competence or willingness. Still, she had never requested anything like the service she was about to demand of him.

'I have been talking to angels all night,' Mother said.

Raymond nodded once. If anything, his expression grew even slacker. Edwina knew she could skip the preliminaries and still find Raymond willing to obey her. However, she needed him to be in the exact mind-set for what was coming. 'I have received instructions directly from the Celestial Kingdom,' she went on. 'They are for the two of us alone to know. But first, you must understand why this conversation is necessary.'

Mother Edwina was aware of what facts that Raymond knew. He was aware that Greg's farm-slave Morven had begun murdering people who'd had the misfortune of getting close to her. He knew Greg was dead, as was a minor Supplicant named Jeff. He did not know about Stewart Delaney, so Edwina started there. She told Raymond that Stewart and Morven had been intimate at the farm. She described Morven's unsuccessful attempt to take Stewart's life, and how Stewart had threatened to go to the police.

That information made Raymond's eyes spark.

Mother told him about her agreement with Morven – that Morven would give up her baby, then quietly end her own life. Raymond's eyes widened slightly at this news. 'That would be a very hard thing to ask of anyone,' Mother went on softly. 'At least, anyone who did not have faith in the Kingdom. I believed Morven had such faith.'

She touched the iPad's sleeping screen, and the image of Morven reappeared. 'Alas, I seem to have misjudged,' she sighed. 'If Morven would only do what she agreed to do, she would arrive this very day in the underworld – and to an angelic fanfare.'

Raymond's face remained slack, but now his eyes shone as he nodded. Mother smiled slightly. This lad was a believer.

'Sadly, Morven's delicate state of mental health has got the best of her. She has ignored her promise to me, and to the Kingdom. Not only that, but she has just committed the most grievous sin. She has tried to murder a man who had protected this order for years.'

‘I am to kill Morven,’ Raymond said.

Mother pressed out her hands, open-palmed and low, as though she were calming an animal. ‘Don’t jump the gun,’ she said. ‘You’re to leave for London on the weekend,’ she said, ‘I will arrange a meeting with Stewart for this coming Monday. Your first task is to finish what Morven started, and kill him. Don’t be too neat about it. Beat him to death with whatever’s handy.’ Mother smiled thinly. ‘It’s what Morven would do.’

She reached into her bag of yarn and withdrew a stack of angel cards, handing one to Raymond. ‘Leave this on his body,’ she said. ‘The aim is to make it appear as though Morven has completed her task.’

Raymond took the card and tucked it into his breast pocket. ‘He’ll be home when I get there?’ he asked.

‘Don’t worry,’ Mother said, ‘I’ll tell him I’m coming to London to take care of this mess myself. He’ll believe me – he knows I don’t want him to contact the police.’

‘And the girl?’

‘I’ll send her to you, as well. If I tell her I’m going to Stewart’s house, she’ll dash there in minutes. Probably bring me a cake.’ Mother fixed Raymond with a hard stare. ‘Make Morven’s death look like suicide. An understandable fit of remorse after finally murdering Stewart.'

He nodded and hoisted his muscular form out of the upholstery. As he walked towards the conservatory door, Edwina added, 'Oh, and Raymond? If Morven brings her baby along, please don't kill it. I'd rather let the police find it in Stewart's house.'

She sat back and smiled benignly. 'We may worship fallen angels,' she added, 'but we're not demons.'

SIXTEEN

Morven and Cherub were required to leave their Wimbledon Bed and Breakfast room by one in the afternoon. Otherwise, they would have to stay for a second night. Morven would have liked nothing more than to hole up here for a week, but the luxury of lingering in hotel rooms was over for good. Morven's picture was absolutely everywhere. That meant she couldn't afford to become a regular face in any one place, even with her newly-changed appearance. The only thing that might hold her and Cherub in this room was uncertainty about where to go next. Morven no longer had the van, and it wasn't like Cherub could be expected to camp in the woods.

Morven was tired, too. It had been a fitful night. She'd kept waking up from surreal dreams, and when she'd finally drifted off around dawn, Cherub woke her again. Now he slumbered once more, but Morven was wide-awake and punchy, eyes on the TV screen. She had taken to watching the news as much as she could; she never knew when there'd be another item about her. Last night, the newsreader said old Joe was in a stable condition, and would likely be released from hospital within the next couple of days. That was such a shame. In her mind, Morven had replayed the attack on him over and over. She worried away at the memory, examining its most minute details: should she have swung the bat half a second earlier? Could she have summoned more strength? Would it have helped to strike his head an inch higher or lower?

And another question – why had the angels allowed this failure to happen? Why had they led Morven to those gardens in Westminster if they hadn't wanted Joe dead? It seemed a lot of kerfuffle just to injure a bloke.

These thoughts zipped through Morven's mind like headlines crawling along the bottom of the TV screen. The newsreader introduced the next story. Morven looked, then scuttled closer. A photo of one of Mother's cards hovered above the newsreader's right shoulder. It was of Af – the angel Morven had left to guide Greg into the underworld. The programme then cut to an interview. There, onscreen, was Dr Sara Jones! Morven gasped – she looked amazing. Poised, alert, intelligent. Dr Jones's makeup was perfect, her hair shone auburn and her clothes were elegant but understated.

Morven so wished she could be Dr Sara Jones.

The reporter asked her about the cards. Dr Jones explained they were depictions of fallen angels used by a New Religious Movement known as the Supplicants of Dusk. This made Morven's sides tingle with both excitement and fear. She knew they'd drag Mother Edwina into this now, just as Mother had said they would.

The reporter asked Dr Jones about the assault on the Minister for Policing. The photo of Morven in the gardens appeared on the screen behind them. Commentators, the reporter said, had pointed out the improvised nature of the attack showed similarities to the murders of Gregory Blackadar and Jeffrey Sawyer. Could the woman in the photo be responsible for those deaths?

'That's a rather big leap to make,' Dr Jones replied. 'Police aren't ruling out anything, but at the moment there's no direct connection between the murders I've been consulting on, and what happened to Mr Bennett.'

That was something, anyway, Morven thought. They hadn't assumed a link between old Joe and the Supplicants. Still, she felt like using the phone Mother gave her to ring and apologise. But, really, what would she be able to say? Mother would be very cross indeed that Morven had gone after old Joe in the first place. Morven couldn't think of anything to tell her that might tidy that mess.

The interview seemed to be wrapping up when the reporter said, 'Dr Jones, do you feel any special empathy for the young woman who attacked the Minister?'

The tingling in Morven's sides grew more intense. The reporter was asking about empathy – for her!

Dr Jones twitched back her head. 'Why on earth would I?'

The reporter feigned innocence. 'She looks to be in her teens, and obviously, she is troubled. You yourself suffered a great deal of trauma in your own teens, didn't you?'

Dr Jones managed to hold her composure, but Morven thought she looked rather peeved. 'I'm not sure this is relevant,' she said.

'Except that it might provide you with insight into the murders,' the reporter pressed on. 'You were fourteen when your parents were killed. Your older brother attempted suicide shortly afterwards. Then, four years ago, tragedy struck again when you were involved in that ill-fated investigation in Aberystwyth–'

Morven had read about that investigation when she was at the library. At the time, it hadn't occurred to her just how awful Dr Jones's childhood had been. They shared so much in common, she and Dr Jones!

'I haven't come to discuss that investigation,' Dr Jones replied. 'I'm here to draw attention to the cards found on the recent murder victims, and to ask the public for any information they may have. That is all.'

'And if the young woman who attacked the Minister is involved in the murders…?'

'That's speculation,' Dr Jones said.

'But if?'

Dr Jones opened her mouth and shook her head in exasperation. 'Then we'll cross that bridge when we come to it.'

The next several minutes seemed like days to Morven. Doubt swelled like flood water, and any excitement she'd felt to hear Dr Jones discuss her had been submerged. The only emotion left on the surface was fear for Mother's exposure. Morven paced the small room, turning every few steps. Her heart pounded wildly. Thoughts knocked against each other like pebbles churned by a crashing wave.

Mother has been implicated in my crimes, she thought.

And that's because I left those cards and

I've really messed things up this time.

Mother had said as much, Morven thought. Mother knew leaving those cards was a stupid idea. Morven's final mistake had been going after old Joe. That had been a massive step too far.

They've already linked me to those other murders, and

I'm going to be caught, that's pretty much for sure.

Unless I do what Mother asked and kill myself.

But she still had Cherub, she thought.

Until moments ago, each of those thoughts would have come sluggishly to Morven. She'd have gathered them up like a patient shepherd, and herded them into the dim light of the Celestial Kingdom. There, they would have been taken under the dark wings of angels. But now all the thoughts came at once, and Morven could not even entrust them to the angels.

Because the angels let me down when I tried to kill

Old Joe, and

What I did to him was caught on camera, which

Puts everyone in danger, including Mother

And now I

Must get Cherub to a new home before it's too late.

Suddenly, without further thought, Morven had the answer. She took a deep breath and waited for her heart to slow. Maybe some powerful entity was still on her side. Maybe it had stopped her from finding out about adoption back at the library because it knew there would be a better option. Finally, Morven could see what that option was. She had found just the right person – so competent and kind – to take care of her baby.

Morven sat on the bed and stoked Cherub's forehead. He squirmed in his sleep. 'You'll need to wake up in a minute, my little Cherub,' she whispered. 'It's time to take you to your new home, with your new mummy.' She picked up the remote and silenced the television. 'You'll like her,' she told the sleeping child. 'Her name is Sara Jones.'

Sara left the BBC's Portland Place studios after recording a radio interview for a late-afternoon current affairs programme. It had been her fifth media appearance of the day. Mir had accompanied her throughout, along with a Communications Manager from the Met's Directorate of Media – a bright young man named Chris. There hadn't been a single interview in which Sara had not been asked for details about her tragic childhood, the events in Aberystwyth, and the murder-suicide perpetrated by her brother. In each case, she'd managed to sidestep the question. *I'm focused on this current investigation, and nothing else,* she'd learned to say. And yet, each refusal sapped a little more of her self-control.

Skirting All Souls' church, Sara said to the Met's Communications Manager, 'So, Chris – that's it then, yes? I'm done now?'

Chris tucked a sheaf of papers into his file folder. 'For the moment, yes,' he replied. 'I'll let you know when you're needed next.'

'Hang on,' Sara interrupted. 'You said *for the moment.*'

'That's right,' Chris said.

'No, it isn't,' Sara countered. 'I've done enough. I'm finished now.'

Chris looked to Mir, who brushed a hand against Sara's arm. She meant it to be reassuring, but Sara flinched. 'You're just tired,' Mir said.

'I've done my bit,' Sara repeated. 'I'm going to go to my new house now, to see what the builders are up to. If you schedule more interviews, your Senior Investigating

Officer can do them.' She looked down and stared at Mir. 'And what I'm *tired* of, Detective Sergeant Mir, is having to dodge questions about my past.' She waved a hand angrily in Chris's direction. 'Questions this young lad seems to have encouraged.'

'Wait a minute–' Chris said.

'Let's not argue on the street,' Mir cut in. 'Why don't we pop in here for a moment?'

She led them into the lobby of a hotel next to the church. Mir held up her badge to the two people on reception. 'The street's so noisy,' she explained. 'We just need a moment to hear ourselves speak.'

The receptionists smiled politely and made a show of looking away.

'I haven't had to encourage questions about your past,' Chris told Sara. He had hushed his voice, but its tone was marbled thickly with irritation. 'Everyone already knows who you are. The whole of the media was excited to hear you've finally accepted some interviews. They said they've been trying to get you on air for years.'

'I am not accepting interviews,' Sara stated. 'I'm representing this investigation, and that's all. Anyone who asks me about anything else is behaving irresponsibly.

Frankly, I'm annoyed you let them think it was OK.'

Mir held out her hands. 'I'm sure that wasn't the DMC's intention.'

Chris smiled with all the condescension of the young go-getter. 'Dr Jones,' he explained, 'my job is to get our message across. Your rarity as a guest has helped us with that.'

'Well, there you go,' Sara said. 'I'm no longer rare, so it can stop now. Everyone should have enough sound bites from me.'

Chris stepped backwards. 'Please keep an open mind,' he said. 'This investigation is fast developing.' He tucked his file folder under an arm and nodded cordially. 'I'll be in touch,' he said, and left the lobby.

Sara watched him stride out. 'What did he mean, *fast developing*?' she asked Mir.

Mir glanced at the reception staff, who were pointedly ignoring their conversation. 'This hasn't been made public,' she cautioned in a near-whisper. 'One of our teams found Gregory Blackadar's van this morning. It was in the car park by College Green.'

'That's right across from Victoria Tower Gardens,' Sara whispered back. 'Do you know for sure it was parked there by the girl?'

Mir grimaced. 'A car seat was found in the back. And there were baby clothes inside the van's cabin – sitting right next to stacks of banknotes.'

'What?'

'Stolen from Blackadar.'

'She thought she could get back to the van,' Sara noted. 'Once she'd…'

'Killed the minister, yes,' Mir agreed. 'We haven't got DNA or fingerprints back yet, but they're likely to match the cricket bat used in that assault.'

'So, the young mother is our killer,' Sara said. It was a conclusion she had been resisting; Sara felt only pity for the bedraggled waif who'd stood on her pavement. Knowing the girl was capable of such gruesome acts suggested she should alter her opinion, but Sara didn't know if she could.

'House-to-house teams are still flooding Brixton,' Mir continued. 'As far as I know, they found nothing on the streets immediately surrounding your house. Now they're looking farther afield.'

'They'll find her,' Sara said. 'They've got to. She's pushing around a baby, for heaven's sake.'

Sara steadied herself on a rack of pamphlets advertising London attractions. The pathos of the situation was overwhelming. Something awful must have happened to this young girl to make her take a young child from murder scene to murder scene. Sara's mind worked quickly as she sorted the connections. Mother Edwina had admitted that Blackadar and Sawyer were members of her order. But she had also claimed not to know the identity of the killer. Now there was a photo, and proof that its subject, the girl, was the killer.

Two tourists with enough baggage for four entered the small lobby and squeezed past Sara and Mir towards the desk. Their conversation with the receptionists allowed Sara to speak at a more normal volume. 'Where do we stand with Edwina Koch?' she asked.

'Mrs Koch will be interviewed today,' Mir replied. 'We'll see how she responds once we confront her with the photo.'

Sara wagged her head. 'She could still lie. She has no need to cooperate with us – and she might have plenty of reasons to keep quiet.'

Mir shrugged in a way that suggested this was likely. 'The Superintendent is sending DCs from the Met to that farm in Dorset, as well. Most of the residents will turn into mutes, I'm sure. But not all of them. The larger a conspiracy of silence gets, the easier it is to find its cracks.'

Sara repressed a chortle. That sounded like the kind of thing Ceri would say. No wonder the two women got along.

Mir gestured to the hotel's front door. 'I'll keep you posted,' she promised. 'If you're going to your new house, I may see you later.'

Sara offered a perfunctory smile – she suspected she could count on it. 'Before you go, there's one more thing,' Sara said. 'What are you doing about Bennett?'

Mir cocked her head. 'Sorry?'

'We now have a direct link between Bennett's attacker and the murders.'

'So?'

Sara groped for the right words. She was still unwilling to reveal that Bennett had asked about the girl the day before his assault. First, it would raise the question of why she had not shared this information before. Second, it would require Bennett to be informed of Sara's claims, and that might open up a rich seam of disputes and denials that could harm the trajectory of the investigation. And, a tentative third reason, it might also be unnecessary to reveal that fact. Sara's argument was persuasive enough without it.

'The girl who murdered Blackadar and Sawyer,' Sara explained, 'had personal reasons to kill. The level of violence tells us that. It's possible she had a similar connection to Joseph Bennett.'

Mir frowned. 'The Minister has already explained this,' she said. 'The girl saw him on television.'

'That's one possibility,' Sara admitted.

Mir sighed heavily. 'Look,' it's as plausible as any,' she reminded Sara. 'You can't accuse a government minister of lying without some pretty conclusive evidence.'

Sara swallowed, then nodded. The tourists at the reception desk now dragged their luggage sideways, towards the elevators. One of the lifts emitted a low bong, and the doors swished open. The couple waited for a guest to exit, then began tugging their cases inside.

'And yet,' Sara reminded Mir, 'the girl saw me on television, too. I wasn't attacked.'

The DS raised a finger as though Sara had had just proved the point. 'But she did turn up at your house.'

A woman who had just left the lift squeezed past Sara,

but Mir was between her and the glass doors. The woman waited as Mir added, 'That's why teams of police are going door to door in Brixton.'

Mir turned; the sliding doors whooshed open, then shut behind her. The woman from the lift blocked Sara's path to the exit. Instead of getting out of the way, she turned. 'They won't do anything about Bennett,' the woman told Sara.

Sara looked up. The frosted blue tips of the woman's afro sparkled in the hotel lobby's soft lighting. 'Oh, good God,' she said.

'And you won't do anything, either,' Daniela Atta went on. 'At least, not immediately.'

'I'm getting awfully tired of playing games with you,' Sara said.

'You know this isn't a game,' Daniela replied softly. 'It's all very serious.'

'Look,' Sara hissed. 'Whatever point you've been trying to prove, you've proved it, OK? You're psychic. More than I am, obviously. So, you must know what I've been struggling with, and how little I want to have to deal with it – or you. Please, just go away.'

Daniela Atta stepped back, away from Sara and closer

to the door. 'The reason you won't do anything about Bennett is, you're going to have your hands full with other fun and games.' She smiled. 'I'm just telling you something you need to know. Things are going to get a lot more interesting,' Daniela said in parting. 'And pretty fast, too.'

SEVENTEEN

Morven stood in front of the front door to Sara's house. Behind her, Cherub sat in his shiny new pushchair; Morven had spent the trip from Wimbledon saying goodbye to him. She'd suppressed the urge to cry; there was no point in drawing attention to herself. Now, she was prepared to put Cherub in the hands of a far better parent. Next to his chair were his nappy bag, a case holding his new clothes, and a small bag containing Morven's few possessions. She would leave with that small bag alone.

There was only one snag – Morven was on the wrong side of the door. She had tried knocking, of course. Her plan had been simple: if someone had answered, she would have pushed Cherub towards the door and run away. But there had been no answer, and Morven did not think it was safe simply to leave the baby here alone, near the street, until Dr Jones arrived. Up to now, Morven had always trusted in the angels to provide her with last-minute instructions on how to handle situations like this. But lately, the angels had increasingly little to say to her.

Then, as if some higher power had overheard her plea, a woman appeared on the path leading to the door. She was middle-aged and dressed in a business suit. 'Good afternoon,' she said to Morven. 'Are you looking for someone?'

'I'm here for Dr Jones,' Morven said. 'Sara, I mean.'

'Are you staying?' the neighbour asked.

Morven nodded.

'Another guest!' the woman exclaimed. 'Is Ceri still at the house in Marylebone, then?'

'Err, yes,' Morven busked. 'That's why I'm here. The other house is full.'

The neighbour pulled out a key ring. 'I imagine it is, with all that construction.' She opened the front door. 'Well, come in,' she said. 'Do you have a key to their flat?'

Morven shook her head. 'I just got here,' she said.

In the hallway, the woman picked up post from the carpet. She sorted it into piles and placed them side-by-side on a small shelf under a mirror. Morven decided the hallway looked almost as comfortable as the hotel room they'd left. If she parked Cherub next to Dr Jones's door, maybe he'd be all right until his new mummy got home.

'Well,' the neighbour said, 'I keep a key for Sara and Jamie upstairs. I don't imagine they'd mind if I let the two of you in.'

To Morven, Sara Jones's flat was simply awesome. The air smelled like a thousand cinnamon candles. By the door, holding a spare set of keys, was the most beautiful bowl Morven had ever seen. It was mottled brown ceramic with olive green streaks, and it was amazing. There was a wall covered in wooden masks that were unlike anything Morven had ever seen. They all had such stern faces, as if they'd risen from the underworld itself. Some of the masks were plain wood, while others had been painted in beautiful reds, yellows and greens. Interspersed between them were some astonishing paintings, even more colourful than the masks. They were all made of fine dots that came together in swirls and geometric shapes. Every now and again, the dots would form some kind of living creature. Morven spotted a lizard, and a dolphin, and a tree. Everything was burnt reds and oranges, or else vibrant purples and greens.

After making Cherub a fresh bottle, Morven leapt to a bookshelf crammed with hardbacks and paperbacks of all kinds. There were more novels than Morven thought she could read in a lifetime – and Morven could read novels quite quickly. She still had her new paperback stuffed in her bag, and as soon as things calmed down, she planned to read it. Morven thought about how much Mother Edwina would love some of the books in Dr Jones's collection. They were about gods and heroes and myths and magic. There was even an encyclopaedia of angels and demons. And there, jammed between a couple of textbooks, was a volume called *Magical Thinking in the Secular World,* written by Dr Sara Jones! Morven trembled proudly.

'Cherub,' she said, 'we've picked the right home for you.'

Cherub gurgled. The bottle Morven had made in Dr Jones's own kitchen lay untasted at his side. Maybe he was amazed by his surroundings, too, Morven thought.

Morven spent time moving through the flat. She walked reverently, as though on sacred ground. Morven touched Dr Jones's things like they were holy relics. She smoothed her hand on the bedspread. She fixed her hair with Dr Jones's own brush. She used the toilet.

On a Welsh dresser next to the small dining room table, Morven noticed Dr Jones's landline. She picked up the receiver, imagining all the words Dr Jones must have spoken into that mouthpiece. The telephone's number was written on a small sticker above the keypad. Morven thought it couldn't hurt to write it down. One day – if she were still alive, and not in prison – Morven may have the urge to ring Dr Jones and ask how the baby was doing. If Cherub were old enough, Morven might even be able to have a conversation with him. She would like to give him some wise advice, like about all the people he should avoid in life. Morven found a pen and opened the tray of Dr Jones's printer for a sheet of paper. She was about to write down Dr Jones's number when she realised she could simply punch it into the pay-as-you-go phone Mother had given her.

Still, Morven realised she could make use of the paper she'd taken. She should introduce Cherub to Dr Jones. She sat at the dining room table and, in her best penmanship, wrote a quick note. When she had finished, she folded it in half and rose, returning for one more look at the wall of masks and art. Morven had noticed a couple of books about these masks on the shelf. If she'd had time, Morven would have loved to thumb through them and find out where they were from. Kneeling on the sofa, Morven spotted a picture she hadn't noticed before. It hung low on the wall near the sofa back. She leant in close and squinted. The picture was a framed woodcut, featuring a winged figure surrounded by locusts. In ornate type at the bottom was a caption reading *Abaddon*. To Morven, the figure looked familiar, like a fallen angel. Yet, she couldn't remember Mother ever mentioning one named Abaddon.

A thought occurred to her. She returned to Sara's books, and located the encyclopaedia of angels and demons. Morven found that Abaddon had an entry between Abachta, an angel of confusion, and Albagtha, which turned out to be another name for Abachta. The write-up said Abaddon was a figure from the Book of Revelation, who was known as *The Destroyer* and *The Angel of the Abyss*. To Morven, those titles had a ring as familiar as the alphabet itself. As early as the 1700s, she read, Abaddon was being equated with the Devil.

The Devil! Morven thought. She had read all about him in the books of Genesis and Isaiah and Ezekiel. She knew the common story of how he'd been an angel cast from heaven for rebelling against God. And yet, Morven also understood that *rebellion* was the wrong word. Fallen angels descended to lower levels of the Kingdom to do jobs they couldn't have accomplished on higher planes. The Devil and God were friends, too – the book of Job made that clear. It was strange that Mother had never mentioned him. She was concerned with fallen angels, but it occurred to Morven that Mother had always ignored *the* fallen angel.

But there he was, right on Dr Sara Jones's wall. It was like a message from the Kingdom itself, straight to Morven's brain.

The message told Morven, *do not kill yourself. There are things for you to do*.

Morven gave Cherub a final embrace. Tears welled in her eyes for the first time since... since she could remember. She sniffed and said, 'This isn't goodbye. I'm not going to die now. Dr Jones will be your new mummy, and I will be your old one. We will see each other again.'

Just in case she ever needed to make sure of that, Morven swept up the spare keys that sat in the beautiful ceramic bowl.

Morven closed Dr Jones's door and left the baby in his new home. This act required her to stifle her sniffles and bury whole strata of emotions. She promised herself she would unearth them at a later time. Right now, she wandered down Dr Jones's street trying not to feel anything; circumstances required her to proceed in this emotionally-diminished state. Morven knew she would need to plan her next moves carefully. Any action she chose to take, she decided, would be part and parcel of her whole new way of looking at the Kingdom. Questions Morven had never asked herself were now the most important thoughts in her mind. None of these questions challenged the order's teachings, specifically. Rather, they exposed gaps within them. For example, every Supplicant knew light and darkness were separate paths to the same divine end. Different angels performed different tasks, and most people on earth were drawn to the prettier angels who did gentle things. That was just human nature. But Supplicants had been steeped in a stronger brew – they knew the power that came from fallen angels and all their grim works. But if that were true, why had Mother never mentioned the *first* angel to fall like lightning from heaven? Why had Supplicants excluded the Devil himself from their dark catechisms? Morven knew many people were spooked by the very mention of the Devil. Then again, those timid folks would fear the other fallen angels, too. That was because they didn't understand how the Kingdom really worked. If all angels laboured for the highest good of the Kingdom, then the Devil should be most-exalted of all the fallen angels. It didn't matter what you called him – Satan, Lucifer, or Abaddon. He was the most important one, and he could be petitioned like the rest of them.

Morven heard a thin electric tune piping in her bag. Her breath caught in her throat… the only person who had this number was the who who'd given her the phone in the first place. It must be Mother calling! Morven dropped the bag, bent and rummaged through her clothing. 'Hello?' she answered hastily.

'Thank the angels,' Mother replied. 'I was so fearful you'd already carried out your final orders.'

'You mean, killing myself?' Morven said. 'No, Mother, I haven't done that.'

And, Mother, I've reached a new understanding that means I won't have to.

'That's good, my dear. Is Cherub still with you?'

'No, Mother. I've… just put him up for adoption.'

Mother made a pleased sound. 'How?' she asked. 'Did you leave him at Social Services?'

'I did indeed,' Morven said. It was easier than explaining how hard it was to get rid of a baby, and how she had found a much better an option. 'It was simpler than I expected.'

'That's wonderful news,' Mother said. 'And it comes at the perfect moment. I have received a new message from the Kingdom. It involves you.'

Morven gasped. 'Is it about Abaddon?' she asked.

'Who?'

'The Bright One, Mother. Lucifer. Satan. Beelzebub. Mephistopheles. Moloch. Abaddon. The first fallen angel. Was your revelation about him?'

'Err –'

'Did he speak to you?'

Mother maintained a puzzled silence, so Morven pressed on. 'I'm not sure what the Kingdom has told you, but I do understand,' she said. 'Whatever new revelation you've had, I've had it, too.' Her heart thudded wildly, and her breath came in sharp bursts. 'This is a sign, Mother. You and I have been called to recognise the true holy order. The angels we revere have a leader, and in our blindness, we have ignored him. We must tell all Supplicants about Abaddon!'

For a moment, Morven received no answer. Then, Mother said, 'I think all this is best discussed in person, don't you?'

'Of course,' Morven agreed. 'Do you want me to come to The Retreat? I can get a bus to Waterloo right now.'

'That won't be necessary,' Mother said. 'As it happens, I will be coming to London.'

Morven tingled with such excitement she found it hard to breathe. This must be proof that she was on the right track. Mother, too, had a revelation about Abaddon – Morven was sure of it. Now, Mother was coming to see her. Together, they would forge a new path for the order!

'When, Mother?' she asked.

'Monday. I'll leave at dawn and see you in London for breakfast.'

Breakfast with Mother! Morven thought. That was an honour indeed. 'Where will we meet?' she asked.

'Stewart's house,' Mother said.

'Stewart Delaney?' In a flash, Morven's breathing became even more laboured. Did Mother know what had happened between herself and Stewie?

'Mother–' Morven began.

'Hush,' Mother said. 'I know all about the two of you, and what you've been up to – and it doesn't matter. There are far more important things in this world than sins of the flesh. The three of us have important business to discuss – *angelic* business.'

Morven forced her quivering body to sober up. *Angelic business!* That was important indeed. But when she'd last left Chiswick, she had been swimming in choppy emotional waters. 'What about Stewart?' she asked. 'Will he mind my being there?'

Morven imagined she could hear Mother chuckle. 'Stewart,' Mother said, 'won't mind in the least.'

'Well, Andreas, that's the worst thing we've ever done for the Kingdom.'

Edwina Koch put away her pay-as-you-go phone and wandered into the conservatory. She looked across the garden to the boat moored in the Thames. Usually, when she needed to talk to her late husband, she'd do it out there. But today the narrow boat on that bend of river seemed far too isolating. At this chilling moment in her life, Edwina needed to feel protected. Of course, Cara was in the house – Edwina could hear her pottering about – but that slip of a girl did little to make her feel safe. Raymond had always made Edwina feel that nothing could go wrong, but he was in London. Edwina realised how much she had come to rely on his unflappable presence for peace of mind. Raymond was a loyal Supplicant – perhaps the most loyal in the order. He'd certainly proved that today. He had calmly agreed to do away with Stewart Delaney before Edwina had even rung Morven, and he'd do the same to the girl without complaint.

Once he had, of course, Edwina would be complicit in two separate homicides. The thought made her body feel brittle, as though it were made of paper. One more ill wind was liable to blow her away.

'Stewart always was a bit of a shit,' she told long-dead Andreas, 'but I never disliked the girl. She was troubled, of course. Crazy, even. She probably needed psychiatric attention. But none of that matters now. What's important is, she's a danger to us all.'

Edwina looked at a clock. She wouldn't have had time to sit in the boat, anyway. Soon, unwelcome visitors would be knocking at her front door. They wouldn't know about Stewart and Morven yet... but even so, their questions would be a lot more probing this time. Edwina's only hope was to stick to the script – *I didn't really know the girl* – and hope her denials proved to be enough.

And even then – even dead – Morven might pose a

threat. Edwina knew she would never be safe. There were too many links between the murders the girl had committed and the Supplicants of Dusk. Scandal was a certainty: there would be salacious stories of slavery, rape, and revenge. The tabloids would have a field day. Edwina only hoped she could keep her problems at the level of scandal, rather than arrest. If Raymond did an effective job in Chiswick, the police would conclude Morven had killed Stewart and then taken her own life.

Would that mean the case was closed? Not likely. Surely, there would be an inquiry into… well, into all of it.

I didn't really know the girl, she would say.

I had no idea what Greg was up to on that farm.

I don't know who the baby's father is.

The doorbell sounded through the house, followed by firm knocking. She heard Cara flutter down the staircase to answer it. 'Well, Dre,' Edwina said, 'wish me luck.'

Cara leaned into the conservatory. 'Mother?'

'Yes?'

'There are police at the front door,' she said. 'They've come from London. They said you were expecting them.'

'That's right,' Edwina confirmed pleasantly. 'Please, show them in.'

EIGHTEEN

As Sara entered the house's communal hallway, she could hear the cries of a baby. The noise sounded as though it were coming through – no, it definitely *was* coming through – the door to her own flat. It was such an impossible circumstance that, for a moment, Sara's brain would not allow her to process the information. She stood in the hall, her mind growing increasingly fuzzy from the buzz of cognitive dissonance.

How could a baby have got into her flat?

It couldn't have. That was impossible. Hence, there was no baby in her flat.

But there's a baby crying in my flat.

Something prevented Sara from putting the key in the lock. She caught a glimpse of her reflection in the hallway mirror. Her own eyes told her what she was hiding from herself. If there was a baby in her flat, it meant that, somehow, the girl–

Just then, the door on the first floor opened and Sara's neighbour appeared. 'Ah, you're home,' the woman said from the top of the stairs.

'Oh – Noel,' Sara replied.

'I was about to come down and knock,' Noel went on. 'I wondered if your young friend needed some help.'

'My young friend?'

'Your guest,' Noel replied. 'I hope you don't mind – I let her in about an hour ago. The baby was happy then, but he's been fussy for the last twenty minutes.'

Sara felt her muscles sinking.

Noel angled her head towards Sara's door. 'She's so young, that one. She's taken on an awfully big responsibility. She probably doesn't know how to look after him yet.'

Sara tried a carefree laugh. 'No, it's something all young mothers have to learn,' she said. Swiftly, she slid her key in the lock. 'Please excuse me.'

Sara waited for Noel to retreat behind her own door. She groped in her medical bag for the syringe of barbiturate she kept there, then slid the key into her lock. She flung open the door, brandishing the syringe, and scanned the living room and kitchen. The crying baby had been marooned in a pushchair in the middle of the living room floor. Sara ignored him and moved cautiously, checking the bathroom and bedroom. Finally, she dropped the syringe back into her medical bag, let her coat fall from her shoulders, and unsnapped the pushchair's restraints. Sara took the baby into her arms. 'Shhh,' she said.

The girl had been here – the killer. Not out on the pavement this time, but here, inside. The first time the young mother had come, she must have been sizing up Sara. Auditioning her for just this moment. The presence of a baby seemed to be evidence that she'd passed the test; the girl had left her child with Sara. Sara's mobile was in the pocket of the coat she'd dropped to the floor. She knew she should ring DS Mir immediately.

Well – almost immediately. There were things she had to do first. Next to the baby's chair sat a bag. Holding the baby in her arms, Sara squatted and looked inside. It held two outfits, nappies, wipes, formula, and a few jars of baby food. A plastic formula bottle nestled in the chair. Sara had been hoping for a dummy to quieten the squalls and stop Noel from coming back downstairs. Instead, Sara straightened herself and began to sway rhythmically. She sung the first childhood song that popped into her mind –

‘London Bridge is Falling Down’. In moments, the infant had stopped sobbing. Sara felt a tingle of satisfaction. The powers of a mother were equal to those of any psychic.

Sara noticed that on the kitchen table there sat a pen and a folded sheet of paper. She rushed over, and with one hand unfolded the note. *This is Cherub*, the note began.

‘Hello, Cherub,’ Sara whispered, her heart thumping. Her eyes flitted over the scrawled words to the bottom of the letter. Yes – the killer had signed it.

Her name was Morven.

The baby – Cherub – squirmed. Sara set the note on the arm of Jamie’s chair and cradled him tightly. Her landline was behind her, near the Welsh dresser, and her mobile was in her coat pocket. ‘Shhh,’ she said to Cherub. ‘Shhh.’

Mir could wait, Sara thought.

Sara had little experience with infants. Save for the kids on the playground, her own youth had been completely child free. There hadn’t even been cousins around: Sara’s father was an only child, and her mother’s sister Issy had remained single her whole life. Added to that, Sara’s family had kept largely to themselves. In medical school, Sara had learned basic paediatrics during a clinical sciences course, and had taken one dedicated module. After that, her only training had been an antenatal class she and Jamie had taken during the weeks of her own ill-fated pregnancy. That wasn't a lot of preparation for having a live baby in her flat right now.

Once I ring Sergeant Mir, Sara thought, *I won't have to worry*. Social Services would take the baby and Sara's part would be over. And yet, it wasn't that simple. The boy's mother would still be out there, trying her best to cope with whatever burden she carried. And Sara would still be working to catch her so she could be put on trial for murder, or locked up as insane. *At least I should make sure Cherub isn't hungry before subjecting him to the police*. Sara took a jar of baby food from his bag. She warmed it in the microwave and got a spoon and a square of paper towel. Sara sat the baby in her lap, tucked the paper towel into his collar, and began to feed him pureed carrots and cauliflower. Cherub ate hungrily. When the jar was empty, his hands and face were mucky. It wouldn't hurt to wash him before ringing Mir.

Sara laid the baby on a blanket and filled the bath shallowly with tepid water. She had no hypoallergenic soap, and so decided not to use any at all. She simply lowered Cherub into the water and rinsed him. He splashed joyously, soaking the tiles and Sara's blouse. When bath-time was over, Sara changed into a dry T-shirt and made Cherub a fresh bottle. She eased into a chair and watched him devour the formula.

In the unfamiliar mother-and-baby calm, Sara found deeply-buried memories opening, in the same way new wounds could split old scars. Unbidden images seeped into her consciousness and spread like fluids through gauze. Looking down at this baby, Sara found herself transported back to a large room in a hospital basement. It was a place and event she had unearthed from deep memory several times before. In these re-imaginings of long-gone moments, that hospital room was always an all-purpose space. There was never any medical equipment, nor filing cabinets, nor even a kettle. The original room must have had some particular function, but in memory it was a non-specific setting in which the reconstructed past could play out.

Sara recalled maybe six couples arranged in a circle. She remembered she and Jamie sitting with their backs to the door. In this reconstructed scenario, they were all on the floor, cross-legged like kids in reception class… but that couldn't be right. Surely the hospital would have offered chairs to pregnant women. This particular memory had reeled through Sara's thoughts so many times, most of its authentic details had been worn away.

But a few seemed as fresh as they'd been five years ago. Sara knew this event had taken place at the end of her first and only trimester. She and Jamie were a new couple, tentatively finding small bonds to weave their lives together. Antenatal classes had become one of those ties, a once-weekly commitment to their shared future. Sara recalled that, on that evening, the midwife had discussed foetal development. Near the end of the session, she'd said that, this late in the trimester, they should be able to hear their baby's heartbeat. She produced a Doppler device and asked for volunteers.

Neither Sara or Jamie were the types to push forward. They sat back and smiled with everyone else as a teenage couple heard their baby's heart for the first time. Sara recalled the young lad squeezing his girlfriend's wrist, and how sweetly she'd smiled. Next, a couple in their twenties heard their own child's rapid-fire heartbeat. Finally, the midwife settled her gaze on Sara. 'You want a go?' she had

asked.

Sara declined with a smile, but Jamie rested a hand on her knee. 'Go on,' he'd whispered to her. 'I want to hear.'

Self-consciously, Sara had approached the midwife and sat. Once again, she could picture herself on the floor. Had she really been? This part of the memory was more fragmented, less reliable than the young lad squeezing his partner's wrist. Sara seemed to recall a blue-grey carpet, fraying. She definitely remembered exposing her belly enough to apply gel. The midwife had slid the foetal stethoscope against Sara's skin. The other couples waited in expectation of the rapid tapping of the foetal heart. Instead, the only sound to emerge from the monitor was a small hiss of white noise. The midwife moved the stethoscope upwards. 'This isn't unusual,' she reassured Sara. 'Heartbeats can be hard to hear in the first trimester.'

'I heard it last week,' Sara said. 'At an antenatal appointment.'

'Well, there you go,' the midwife said with a smile.

'Keep trying, please,' Sara urged.

The midwife shifted the stethoscope, but could conjure no sound. 'So many things can cause this,' she explained. She offered the group an insincere chuckle. 'Sometimes, the baby's so active it's like a game of chase, trying to catch the heartbeat.'

'It hasn't been active since yesterday morning,' Sara said. She could feel her throat tightening as she spoke, her voice turning thin. Across the room, Jamie stared, his eyes blank.

'I didn't mean your baby is active right now,' the woman said. 'Our ability to hear a heartbeat can depend on so many things. For example, the baby's–'

'Position in the uterus, I know,' Sara interrupted. 'Do you have a Pinard horn?'

'Err – no,' the midwife said. 'We tend to use ultrasound.' She held up the monitor and smiled at the group. 'So everyone can hear.'

'A fetoscope, then,' Sara said. 'You must have a fetoscope somewhere in this hospital.'

'Not to hand.'

'Find one, please?' She phrased it as a strained question.

The midwife set down the probe and wiped Sara's bump with paper towel. 'Dr Jones, you mustn't get–'

Sara felt herself twitch like someone jolting under restraints. Without meaning to, she released a frustrated bark. The rest of the group watched helplessly as Sara fought down a surge of panic. She swallowed, and struggled to keep her emotions in check.

'I'd like you to find a fetoscope, please,' she said quietly. 'I'd like you to do that *right now*.'

Even as she'd asked for the equipment, Sara had known it was too late. For the past day, possibly more, she had suppressed the worry that the baby's activity was diminishing. Like the midwife, Sara had tried to play down the potential severity of the problem. She'd reminded herself that foetal movement could be unpredictable even into the second trimester. Had she been advising a friend, Sara would have recommended a far more active approach. She would have told the friend to call her doctor immediately. She would have explained the benefits of having a Non-Stress Test, which monitored the baby's heartbeat as it went from rest to movement. But this hadn't been about a friend, it had been about Sara – so she had shoved her worries to the back of her mind and carried on seeing clients at her Harley Street practice.

Sara glanced down at the baby now sleeping in her arms. Five years ago, she would have expected this vignette to have been a constant in her life. Sara had worn her pregnancy like a badge of approval on her new relationship with the copper-fringed police inspector. She could not have imagined that little life slipping away before its time. And here, years on but just as unexpectedly, she had been entrusted with the care of a new life. Once again, Sara looked at the note she had found on the table:

This is Cherub, the letter read. *You saw him before, when we were outside. You were so kind to us that day. I wish I'd let you help us like you wanted to. I'm asking for your help now. Cherub needs a new mummy. You can probably figure out why! I love him and have tried to be good to him, even with all the things we've been through lately. I didn't get many lessons about how to be a mummy when I was growing up. My own mum died when I was little, and my dad passed away a few years ago. I've had to work it out for myself. I know you don't have any babies, but you're a doctor and you're very smart. Thank you for taking Cherub into your home.*

The letter was signed, *Morven*.

Morven. Sara could picture the girl: bedraggled, with dirty red hair, a thin face and a haunted expression. Suddenly, Sara felt a welling rage for whatever had happened to this young woman to so unhinge her. It wasn't the girl's fault. Without Aunt Issy, or an inheritance, or the regular attention of a social worker, Sara herself might have stumbled down an equally fraught route. It seemed that Morven's acts were crimes of passion, brought on by years of deep hurt. What that pain had been, Sara did not know.

She remembered how Daniela Atta had encouraged her to use her psychic abilities to delve into Morven's life. One thing Sara's years as a psychic had taught her was, her past visions had led only to limited success. Four years ago, serial killer Eldon Carson had envisioned a man named Edmond Haney murdering a young girl. Carson killed Haney before he could carry out that awful crime. And yet, when Sara had psychically witnessed the same time period – and ostensibly the same event – her vision had contradicted Carson's, and proved Haney innocent. This discrepancy suggested that fortune-telling wasn't all it was cracked up to be.

It was true that, last year, Sara had acted on her visions regarding Tim Wilson. But that had only been after the young man's actions validated her darkest fears. And that experience had left Sara shattered. After becoming a murderer herself, Dr Sara Jones had resolved not to use her shaky psychic powers to go looking for any more fights.

Cherub twitched in Sara's arms. His own arms flailed in reaction to a vivid baby dream. This child was as much a victim as the girl who called herself Morven, Sara thought. And he was far more innocent, too. Sara looked down at Cherub. For a crazy moment, she wondered what life would be like if she were to do what Morven had asked – if she kept the baby as her own. Was that even possible? Could she pull strings to adopt? The very thought replaced her anger with something like yearning.

The door opened. Jamie stood before her. 'Good evening,' he said. Sara watched his gaze as he clocked her coat sprawled on the floor, then looked to the pushchair and upwards towards Sara. His eyes widened. 'Holy shit,' he said. 'That's not hers… is it?'

'You're quicker than I was,' Sara replied. 'My first reaction was to believe I was imagining a baby in our flat.'

'When did…?' Jamie began. 'I mean, how…?'

Briefly, Sara described the events of the past hour. Jamie read Morven's note. 'The poor kid,' he said. 'She's bonkers.'

'We don't know what she is,' Sara said sharply.

Jamie caught the edge in her voice. 'Troubled,' he

corrected. 'What I meant was, she needs help.'

'It's this baby I feel for,' Sara said.

Jamie made a noise in agreement. 'When are they coming?' he asked.

'Who?'

'Social Services, the police – whoever you've called.'

Sara remained silent. She stroked Cherub's head.

'You have rung the police, haven't you?' Jamie asked warily.

'He was hungry,' Sara explained. 'Then he needed a bath and a bottle…'

'You've had this letter for over an hour and you haven't rung the police?' Jamie cried. 'Sara, what were you thinking?'

'I was thinking,' she snapped, 'that I had a baby to look after. I'm going to ring Mir now, okay?'

Her sudden anger softened Jamie's expression. Sara watched understanding, and then compassion, seep into his eyes. It made her nauseous. 'I'm fine,' she muttered pointedly.

'Good,' Jamie replied mildly. 'I know.'

'Good,' she said sullenly. She glanced again at Cherub, asleep in her arms, and grimaced. 'My mobile's in my coat pocket,' she told Jamie. 'Get it for me, will you?'

Sara had called the police late in the day. As she did, Jamie had held the baby. The sight of Jamie in his chair, with Cherub swaddled in a blanket, made her chest feel like it was being squeezed by a warm hand. Jamie looked so natural as a father. Sara had watched him bending his head low, whispering nonsense to Cherub in a soothing voice, as if he'd been doing it for years.

Social Services said they would be along in the morning. This meant both their parenting skills would be tested overnight. They had no cot – only the pushchair that Morven had left with the child. Sara fashioned a nest on the floor next to her side of the bed. She had started by vacuuming Ego's old cat bed and placing blankets over it, with pillows around its edge. Despite the relative comfort of Sara's makeshift cot, Cherub had fussed in the night. Sara ended up taking him into the bed between herself and Jamie. Then, Cherub had fallen asleep almost immediately; it seemed he was unused to sleeping without an adult body next to him.

Sara had slept little. She found herself lying on her side, gazing out the window as the sky lightened to silver. She let her fingers gently brush the slumbering baby's forehead.

The following morning, Sara had not yet changed from her dressing gown before a representative from Social Services was at her door. She was a woman named Kate, in early middle age with a chestnut-dyed perm. 'From what the Met told me,' Kate told Sara, 'it's clearly a case of child abandonment.'

'What does that mean legally?' Sara asked.

'Child abandonment occurs any time a parent discontinues a parenting role, without an intention to resume it,' Kate said. 'It's been an offense since the 1860s.'

'So, what will happen to Cherub?'

'Under normal circumstances, we try to reunite the child with the parents – but from what I understand, that would not be advisable in this case.'

Jamie entered the room with three cups of coffee. 'That's an understatement,' he said.

'After that, we tend to look for relatives,' Kate continued. Pressing on before either Sara or Jamie could interject, she added, 'In this case, he'll go to a foster family. If it works out, I hope there'll be a view towards establishing a permanent relationship.'

'You mean, the foster family may adopt,' Sara said.

'That would be the ideal,' Kate agreed.

'Good,' Sara said, nodding in satisfaction. 'It's what Morven would want.'

As soon as she'd said the words, Sara regretted them. Jamie took Cherub for a final cuddle and, handing him back to Sara, helped Kate to pack together his things. To Sara's relief, neither asked why she would concern herself with what an adolescent killer might want.

NINETEEN

All conflicts were resolved. The squalls of emotion between herself and Stewie had been quelled – Mother had virtually said as much. That left only calm for the holy work that lay ahead. Morven bounded up the stairs to Stewie's front door two at a time. The last time she'd been there, she'd had to lug a pram, bumping it up step by step. Now she felt light and free. Mother was here, or else she would be soon. They would discuss angelic business, and Morven would share her new understanding of the Kingdom. Maybe the angels had told Mother the same facts, or maybe they hadn't… but one thing was sure. What Morven knew would shake up the Supplicants of Dusk. It was likely to change everyone in a way that would resonate through the dark halls of the underworld.

When her feet hit the landing, Morven stopped to catch her breath. She adjusted her leather jacket and ran her hand over the stubble on her head. She tried smiling from her heart to heighten the frequency of her body of light.

Then Morven felt ready. She knocked on the door.

It was answered by a tall man with bulging muscles. The man's hair was wet, as though he had just emerged from the shower. Yet, he must have got back into his old clothing, because it was stained.

'Morven,' he said, taking in her shaved head and leather jacket. 'Come in.'

Then Morven placed him: he was Raymond, Mother's houseboy. *Of course*, she thought, *he probably drove Mother here today.* Morven thanked him and nearly leapt into the hallway. It had only been a short time since she'd been here last. So much had happened, though, that this visit felt not only exciting, but also nostalgic. Morven glanced around the hallway. That wall was where she'd rested the cricket bat. There were the stairs where she'd laid her clothes and stood naked, poised to murder Stewie. And through here, in the living room, was the carpet on which she and Stewart had–

Morven passed into the room and froze.

She looked down; Stewie was on the floor. But, unlike last time, he wasn't breathing. He was just sprawled there, as though he'd been posed like a still life. One of his eyes was so bloody Morven couldn't tell whether it was open or closed. Above it, a deep gash dented his head. One of Stewie's shiny television awards lay broken at his side.

So many thoughts swarmed through Morven, each one contradicting the last. She wondered what she should be feeling right now. Morven liked Stewart, after all – that was why she'd been relieved when she hadn't had to kill him. And yet, here he was – just as bloody and exactly as dead. Morven's eyes drifted to the wall above the mantle, where the painting of the angel hung. She hadn't recognised the figure the first time but now, with a gasp, she understood who it was depicting. With its dark wings and buzzing insects – locusts! – the figure was of Abaddon.

The Devil.

Behind her, Morven heard the snick of a sliding bolt. Raymond stood at the front door. Besides the bolt, Stewart's door had two locks, and Raymond turned them both. He strode forwards and, without warning, thrust his hands between Morven's shoulder blades and shoved her forwards. She stumbled into the living room. She had to skip to avoid tripping over Stewart's body.

'Where's Mother?' she yelped.

'Mother couldn't make it,' Raymond said, deadpan.

‘Why is Stewart dead?’ she demanded. Morven examined Raymond with narrow eyes. ‘Did the angels order this?’

Raymond pursed his lips. ‘I’d say yes,’ he told her. ‘The angels want you both dead.’

‘That’s impossible!’ Morven gasped. She pointed to the painting. ‘I know about Abaddon now. I was going to explain everything to Mother.’

Raymond grasped Morven by the shoulders and spun her around, pushing her into Stewart’s chair. Her back impacted with a thud. The air left her lungs. Raymond smiled – a look that did not come naturally to him. ‘Here’s what the world’s going to know,’ he said. ‘You came back today to make a second attempt on Mr Delaney’s life.’

‘That’s not true!’ Morven said.

‘And you succeeded,’ Raymond went on. ‘You came here and killed him,’ He flicked his hand towards Stewart Delaney’s body. ‘See? You bashed in his head with that trophy.’

Raymond produced one of Mother’s cards, and held it high between a thumb and forefinger. He let go and it fluttered end-over-end, settling near Stewart. ‘Then you left one of these,’ he said.

Morven peered down at the card. It depicted the angel Rogziel. She wrinkled her nose – *how stupid.* She would *never* assign Rogziel to take Stewie to the underworld. Stewie was too gentle a soul for such a wrathful angel. He'd be a trembling wreck before the journey was half-over.

'But,' Raymond went on, 'after you committed murder, the weight of all the things you'd done bore down on you. You felt such great remorse that you pulled out a knife–'

From his pocket he withdrew a small blade.

'And took your own life.'

Raymond leapt so quickly he was behind Morven's chair before she'd known he was planning to move. She felt the blade, warm from Raymond's thigh, press against her throat. Raymond's free hand slid down the sleeve of Morven's jacket and grasped her right hand. He forced it up to Morven's neck, and clasped her first around the handle of his knife. He wrapped his own hand firmly around her fingers. Her eyes began to tear up. Above the mantle, Abaddon melted into watery swirls.

Abaddon is the Devil, Morven thought,

and the Devil is

the king of the fallen angels. He

has revealed himself to me and so

no harm can come–

Raymond wrenched Morven's blade hand to the fleshy spot just under her ear. She felt the knife's point needle her skin. 'The carotid artery,' Raymond said, 'is where you decided to cut.'

because Abaddon knows

I will be his new messenger–

Suddenly, Morven felt Raymond jerk. He flailed backwards and she heard him yelp, then scream.

Finally, he gurgled.

Morven turned. In the small space between the chair and the kitchen, she saw an unfamiliar woman. The woman was hunched over, with Raymond on her back. Raymond twisted spasmodically, as though dancing to harsh music only he could hear. Morven noticed the woman's gloved hands grasped the ends of a garrotte. She held it taught behind her head, its thin wire slicing deep into Raymond's throat. Blood ran freely down his shirt.

Morven cleared her own throat violently and wiped the tears from her eyes. She looked from the woman garrotting Raymond to the painting of Abaddon with his bible-black wings. Right now, the two figures seemed one and the same.

Once Raymond's flailing had turned to twitching, the woman shrugged off his body and let it slump to the floor. Morven rose from the chair. The woman wiped her garrotte carefully on Raymond's motionless trouser leg. When she righted herself, Morven noticed how tall she was. She was dressed like an athlete, too, all stretchy polyester and sporting logos. What was coolest about her was her frizzy hair. Its ends were a shocking shade of blue.

The woman's eyes locked on Morven. 'Hello,' she said calmly.

Remaining placid in these circumstances must take a whole lot of skill, Morven thought. When *she* killed someone, Morven always stayed really twitchy for hours afterwards.

'Hey,' Morven said back. She flicked her hand towards the painting. 'You wouldn't be the Devil, would you?'

The woman blinked. 'No one's ever asked me that before,' she said.

Morven waited. 'Well, are you?'

The woman smirked. 'Do I look like the Devil?'

'Maybe,' Morven said. 'He takes many forms.' She indicated the painting. 'See?'

The woman considered this. 'What would you do if I said I was?' she asked.

Without hesitation, Morven replied, 'I would worship you.'

'Eugh.' The woman gave an exaggerated shudder. 'Now you've gone and spoiled it. Only a creep wants to be worshipped.' Unexpectedly, she laughed merrily. 'So I will confirm that I am not the Devil.'

'Then who are you?'

The woman sucked in her cheeks and considered this. 'Think of me as your older sister,' she said.

Morven nodded earnestly. She had always wanted a sister. 'OK.'

'And as your older sister,' the woman went on, 'I am here to offer you some advice. Would you like to hear it?'

'I would – please.'

'Mother Edwina,' the woman said, 'is not your friend. She wasn't even civil to you when you saw her in Weybridge.'

'How did you know about that?'

The woman looked up to the ceiling. 'I have ways of keeping tabs on people I'm interested in,' she said. 'That charlatan you call Mother has relied on your ingrained loyalty. Now she wants to distance herself from you.' She cast her eyes over the bodies. 'And look how she's chosen to do it.'

Morven shook her head. 'Mother doesn't understand. Maybe she knows about Abaddon but hadn't told me yet. When I see her, I'll…'

The woman's blue-tipped afro shook ever so slightly. She looked at Morven with all the compassion in the world.

Instantly, Morven knew it was true. Raymond wouldn't have come here unless Mother told him to. Such an understanding was a seismic shift in her thinking. Even when Mother had instructed her to kill herself, Morven would not have dared to ascribe bad motives to her. But now, as she looked at Stewart's caved-in skull, Morven understood that her perspective had been extremely limited.

'So, she sent Raymond to kill me, too. Is that it?' Morven asked her blue-tipped saviour-sister.

The woman nudged Raymond's blood-soaked body with her trainer. 'She absolutely did.'

'Why?'

'Why do you think?'

Morven considered. 'Because I wouldn't kill myself?' she ventured. 'Mother wanted me to.'

The woman's blue-frosted afro shook again. 'Not exactly,' she said. 'She wants you dead because you're out of control.'

Before Morven could protest, the woman held up her hand and said, 'Look... personally, I don't give a shit. It's all the same to me.'

She clocked Morven's crestfallen expression and sighed. 'I mean, I don't condemn you for anything you've done,' she said. 'I'm just telling you how your Mother Edwina sees you. You've brought the police to her door and she's scared of what you'll do next. That's why she wants you dead. It's just more convenient that way.'

Morven could feel the tension in her face as she puzzled out these strange dynamics. 'But now *you've* come,' she said finally. 'You saved me.'

'I did.'

'Is that because you're a... Supplicant?' Morven asked hesitantly.

The woman chuckled. 'You were closer when you thought I was the Devil,' she said. 'I'm pretty fucking far from being a Supplicant.'

'So why did you kill Raymond for me?' Morven asked.

The woman reached out and gently cradled Morven's

chin. She radiated a warm energy that made Morven feel calm. 'Maybe I do give a shit after all,' she said. 'Maybe I just have a soft spot for messed-up little waifs.'

The woman bent next to Raymond's body and picked up the small, sharp knife that he'd held to Morven's throat. She offered it to Morven. 'Or maybe I know there's stuff left for you to do before you can rest,' she said.

Morven accepted the knife. She put it in her bag.

'I'll watch out for you,' the woman said. 'But we both know there are things you're going to have to do for yourself.'

Morven felt herself trembling. Maybe this woman wasn't the Devil, but she sure was *something*. 'What things?' Morven asked.

'I think you know,' the woman said.

Morven released a deep breath and looked again at the painting. 'Did… did Abaddon *send* you, at least?' she asked.

The woman stared as well. 'Who is he?'

'Abaddon's one of the names for the Devil,' Morven replied. 'I told you, he takes many forms.'

The woman shrugged. 'You know what?' she said. 'Maybe the Devil did send me. Hell, I don't know.' She looked down at Raymond's body. 'Either way, we got ourselves a result.'

The woman wound up the freshly-wiped strip of wire and slipped it into a pocket of her tracksuit bottoms. 'Listen, babe,' she said to Morven, 'we've got to leave. Lingering at a crime scene is never a good idea.'

'Yeah,' Morven said softly. 'I've realised that, too.'

Morven was staring again at the painting of Abaddon. Obviously, he was not Stewie's angel, or he would have done more to protect the poor guy. As for Morven herself, she couldn't imagine anything really bad happening to her when she was in Abaddon's presence. She looked to the woman, then down to Raymond's body. If this woman wasn't an actual manifestation of the Devil, then maybe the Devil had sent her here today.

'Wow – you really like that picture, don't you?' the woman asked.

'I've pledged myself to him,' Morven told her.

The woman studied Morven for several seconds, then relaxed into a *why-the-hell-not* posture. 'First things first,' she said. 'My name's Daniela.'

Morven nodded. 'I'm Morven.'

'I know,' Daniela said. 'So, listen, Morven – if you like that picture so much, why don't you just take it?' She looked down at the bodies on the floor. 'It's not like your friend Stewart needs it now.'

'I have nowhere to live,' Morven explained. 'I couldn't keep it anywhere nice.' She bit her lip, trying to find the right words. 'When you accept a painting of the Devil,' she said, 'you have an obligation to it.'

Daniela released a soft peal of laughter. 'I think you know the perfect house for this painting,' she said.

'Where?'

'Think.'

Morven thought, then said, 'Ah.'

'You have a key to her flat, don't you?' Daniela asked. 'You took it from that ceramic bowl.'

Morven felt her lips part. 'How did you know that?'

'I have a car,' Daniela continued. 'I borrowed it from a friend. But it'll get you and the painting to Brixton if you'd like.'

Morven's eyes widened. 'I would like to see Cherub,' she said. 'But Dr Jones knows the police are looking for me. What would she do when she saw me at her door?'

Daniela reached out and gently cradled Morven's arm.

'Nobody's there, babe,' she said.

'They've gone out?'

'The only thing you'll do is drop off the painting.' She gave Morven's arm a squeeze. 'It's better that way. Less complicated.'

Morven stared once more at the painting before shifting her glance to Daniela. 'You know a lot,' she said.

Daniela nodded matter-of-factly. 'I also know you'll be boarding a train at Waterloo this evening,' she said. 'So, if you want to give Dr Jones this painting, we'd better get moving.'

Sara parked her Mini in her favourite spot outside the house. It was only mid-afternoon, but already she trembled with exhaustion. It was hard to believe it was only a week ago that Morven had tried to murder Joseph Bennett. Since then, Sara had endured a blitz of interviews. She had to admit, though, they'd led to some success. Members of the public had rung the police with claims of sightings. A hotel manager claimed Morven had stayed in two of his hotels at the same time. Hertfordshire police were going through security images for both premises.

It wasn't just Sara who had been busy. Ceri complained

that her new friend Adeela had been working night and day. At least that had freed Ceri to join Sara and Jamie yesterday to watch the Six Nations final. To the delight of all of them – even England-supporting Jamie – Wales had won the series. Celebrations stopped abruptly this morning, when Sara had to attend the investigation's morning briefing. Now, she wanted nothing more than to slip back into her pyjamas and return to bed.

As soon as she entered the flat, Sara knew things weren't going to work out that way. Propped up on the sofa was an oil painting of an angel with dark wings. Immediately, Sara jerked open her medical bag and withdrew her syringe of barbiturate. She edged from the living room into the small foyer leading to the bathroom and bedroom. She burst into the bathroom brandishing the syringe like a knife. The only living creature there was a spider in the bath. She crept into the bedroom. It was empty as well. Sara allowed herself to relax enough to tuck away the syringe, pull off her coat and withdraw her mobile phone.

She braced herself, and then dialled DS Mir. She needed to report that, once again, her flat had become a crime scene.

TWENTY

Along one side of The Retreat's garden was a copse of poplar trees. That was where Morven had slept the previous night. It hadn't been as comfortable as a hotel room, but the February weather was mild enough. Morven had not planned to stay out of doors all night; she'd intended to sleep in Mother's canal boat. She had taken a late train to Weybridge Station, then a taxi to a golf club not far from The Retreat. Morven didn't want anyone tipped off that a young girl had journeyed to the headquarters of the Supplicants of Dusk. From the golf club, she had followed the towpath all the way around to Mother's boat. There, she'd been badly disappointed. Mother had locked the cabin.

Now, it was early morning, and Morven sat with her back against a gnarled tree trunk. Her joints ached from hours of exposure to the damp ground. Every few minutes, Morven would notice that Cherub was not with her, and pulse with panic. It wasn't until she recalled that he was now with a more suitable mummy that her angst would subside.

At the moment, the dawning sun was a shade of deep amber. Its rays filtered through the barren tree branches in shafts. The mist rising off the Thames glowed yellow. Mother's lawn looked orange. Morven savoured one of the sandwiches she'd bought last night at Waterloo Station, thinking about how these fire shades made the garden look pretty. Despite enjoying the view, she wondered how long she'd have to sit in this cluster of trees. When would Mother make her way down the lawn and towards her boat? Morven could have rung her, of course, and announced her presence right there and then. That certainly would have sent Mother down here rather sharpish. But then, Morven would lose the element of surprise. And who knew who else would accompany Mother, or what Mother would order them to do?

Morven popped the last crust of sandwich into her mouth and chewed pensively. She may have to wait here all day. Mother may not come down until tomorrow. That would entail another achy night in these trees.

I should ration these sandwiches, Morven thought as

she opened another one.

Morven had been keeping an eye on the two back doors – one from the conservatory, and one from the kitchen. She had not imagined someone would round the house from the front. That was why she was late in seeing the motion on the other side of the trees, just up the lawn. Worse, she heard her name being whispered.

'Morven?' someone said. 'Is that you?'

Morven had never heard Mother whisper, so she couldn't be certain what she would sound like if she did. To be safe, Morven pulled up her knees and tried to crouch into as small a ball as possible. She kept her head down; she'd read somewhere that eyes are the first thing the predator sees.

Morven looked at the ground until she heard the rustle of feet on dead leaves. When that sound was only feet away from her, she jerked her head upwards. The figure loomed over her and placed a hand on her shoulder. 'Morven, what are you doing here?'

Morven focused… 'Cara,' she said.

'You're dirty,' Mother Edwina's house girl observed. 'Did you sleep out here?'

‘Where’s Mother?’

Cara twitched her head back towards The Retreat. ‘She doesn’t know you’re here.’

‘How do you?’

‘Saw you from the upstairs window.’ Cara took off her coat and laid it on the ground before sitting. ‘I don’t imagine your being here points to anything good,’ she said.

‘What it points to is rectification,’ Morven said. When Cara’s brows knitted, she explained, ‘It means making things right again.’

‘What are you trying to make right?’ Cara asked. ‘And how, exactly?’

Morven grinned at her understandingly. ‘What you’re really asking is, are all those rumours about me true?’ she said.

Cara sucked her bottom lip. ‘Are they? What they said you did to Greg. And that other one, too.’

Morven nodded soberly.

‘And you hurt that politician. The one Mother’s close to. I know that for a fact.’ She snorted at the irony. ‘But then, the whole of Britain knows it, too. Everyone’s seen that photo.’

‘I’m the most famous Supplicant alive,’ Morven said

with sad whimsy. She picked up a leaf and fiddled with it dejectedly. 'I was trying to kill him, you know. I just got unlucky.'

'Tell me about it,' Cara said. 'Tell me everything.'

'I just did,' Morven replied.

'You're a better storyteller than that,' Cara admonished. 'Back at the farm, you told me some amazing things. Things you read in books, or what your papa had told you that morning. Or else you'd just make something up.'

Morven smiled at the memory.

'And you said you'd tell me everything when you had the time.' Cara gestured to the absence of anything but trees around them. 'Looks like right now you've got nothing but.'

So Morven told her. She told her how she'd finally realised the feelings she was having towards Greg – feelings that surged through her like petrol running close to flame – were messages from angels. It had been angels who'd told Morven to do what she did. Not just to Greg, but to Jeff as well. And she talked about giving Cherub to Dr Sara Jones, and how finding the perfect mummy had turned a time of hurt into one of joy. Morven explained how she'd seen a picture of Abaddon on Dr Jones's wall, and how, in a flash, she had finally understood the first fallen angel. She told Cara how excited she had been when she'd anticipated sharing this information about the Devil with Mother.

And then she described how Mother had sent Raymond to kill Stewart, and how Raymond had done just that. And how Raymond had tried to kill her, too – again on Mother's orders.

Then she talked about how Raymond had died. That caused a range of emotions to cross Cara's face all at once.

'You're the only person alive who knows all that,' Morven said. She chuckled sardonically. 'Well, you and Cherub – but he's not going to tell anyone!'

'Neither will I,' Cara promised.

'I believe you,' Morven said. She looked furtively around the garden. 'You know what you should do? You should run away.'

Cara looked shocked. 'What? Where?'

Morven waved her hand. 'Anywhere.'

'I don't have any money,' Cara told her. 'I only have what Mother gives me. And that's not a lot.'

'You'd find a job,' Morven said.

'It takes money just to leave,' Cara noted.

Morven considered this. Cara was right – in the last couple of months, Morven had grown so used to having cash, she'd forgotten what life was like without it. She raised a finger – *wait a moment*.

Morven dug into her bag and withdrew a thick bundle of notes. 'I can't spare everything,' she explained. 'At one point, I would've given you this whole wad. I literally had a truckload of the stuff. But I went and lost most of it.'

'I didn't mean you should give me money,' Cara insisted.

'Don't worry about it.' Morven divided the bundle in half. 'You can take this. I reckon there's a couple thousand there. Probably more. If you're careful, that'll last you till you get to somewhere you want to be.'

Cara held up her hand. 'I can't take all that,' she protested. 'It's too much.'

'That's not the last of it,' Morven informed her. 'I've got a couple more bundles in the bag. There's still something I've got to do.'

For a moment, the two women sat together silently. Cara's forehead was creased in thought. In the shade-dappled bushes nearby, a chaffinch chirruped and took flight. Its swift movement pierced her reverie. She said,

'But then what? If I did go away, I mean. What would I do when that money ran out?'

'You'd focus on making a life, like most everyone else,' Morven replied. 'You'd find yourself a job. You could even do what you're doing for Mother, but be paid way more for it. Think about that!'

Cara hung her head. 'I'm not like you,' she said. 'I don't know if I could ever just run away.'

Morven thrust the banknotes towards her. 'Take the money anyway,' she said. 'Just in case you need it.'

Cara hesitated, then mouthed a silent *thank you*. She nestled the stack of notes between her crossed legs on the sag of her skirt.

Morven nodded in approval. 'Trust me,' she assured Cara, 'having money is a whole lot better than not having money.'

'I tried to ring you last night,' Edwina snapped into the mouthpiece of a cheap mobile phone. 'Several times.'

'I noticed,' said Joseph Bennett.

'You should have called me back.'

'I haven't been quite myself in the last week,' he replied tartly. 'You know that.'

Edwina tried to soften her tone. 'When did you get out of hospital?'

'The weekend,' he said. 'I have stitches in my head and a couple of broken ribs. So, please forgive my tardiness in returning your call.'

Edwina swallowed bile. Bastards like this were happy enough to snap to attention when times were good. They liked being bribed with all the little delights of life – money, drugs, girls. But when things turned sour…

'I assume you've had another visit?' Bennett said.

'From the police?' Edwina asked. 'Naturally. It was the Met this time, not the locals.'

'What did you tell them?'

'What do you think?'

He grunted, satisfied.

'I'm not senile yet,' Edwina went on. 'And besides, that's not why I've been ringing you. I need to know something.'

'Go on,' he said cautiously.

'Were there any significant reports of police activity last night?'

Bennett snorted. 'There's significant activity every night.'

'In Chiswick,' she clarified. 'If you'd heard anything, you would know what I'm talking about.'

Edwina heard a heavy sigh on the line. 'Is this about Stewart Delaney?'

'Morven went back to Stewart's.'

Edwina listened to silence as he came up with the obvious question. 'Did she kill him?'

'I believe so.'

'Oh, Christ,' he whispered. 'Where is she now?'

'That's what I'm trying to find out,' Edwina said. She didn't want to tell this bastard any more than was necessary. Certainly, Edwina was not going to admit to having dispatched Raymond to Chiswick, or confess what she'd told him to do there. Nor would she reveal that Raymond had yet to return home, and wasn't answering her calls. But if this man knew anything about Raymond – or simply what the scene at Stewart's looked like – she needed him to tell her.

'Listen,' she said. 'I know for a fact Morven is unstable.'

Bennett released a sarcastic bark. 'There's a newsflash.'

'More so than usual, I mean. I have reason to believe she was feeling suicidal when she went to Chiswick.'

Edwina could feel hope swelling on the other end of the line. 'You think she might have…?'

'Killed him, then taken her own life? There's a good possibility.'

Edwina would have sworn she heard a giggle. 'That's wonderful news,' Bennett said.

At the front of the house, a door closed. 'Hang on,' she told him, and scurried into the hallway. There, Cara stood in her coat, eyes wide.

'Why were you outside?' Edwina demanded.

Cara shrugged. 'I took out the recycling,' she said.

'Well, go upstairs,' Edwina snapped. The girl hung up her coat and sprang silently up the steps. Edwina moved towards the conservatory, lowering her voice to say, 'Don't count on anything, though. Until we know something for sure, it's all just speculation.'

'I'll find out what I can,' Bennett reassured her. 'When I know anything, you will, too. Until then, we can only hope.'

Edwina snorted. *Hope!* she thought. *What a simpleton.*

They said their goodbyes and Edwina rang off. How someone like that ever wormed his way into a position of authority, she'd never know. The best Morven's death could do would be to prevent their immediate arrests. Whatever happened, there would still be continued investigations, inquests, and very likely charges. Still, Mother's man in London was right about one thing – until they knew more, there was nothing else to do. Nothing but to crochet. Edwina placed the mobile back in the desk with the others, then picked up her bag of yarn and stepped into the garden.

When Morven saw Mother's thin figure leaving her house from the conservatory, she felt less bad about having eaten three of her sandwiches. She wouldn't be needing the remaining one after all. She could go back to London soon.

Morven sensed her breathing growing shallow, her muscles tensing, and most of her thoughts disappearing. It was how she imagined actors felt before going on stage. The only thing left streaming through her mind was a series of random images, stray sentences and old memories that rose and fell unbidden. She had been in this state of blank readiness when she'd killed Greg, too. Morven had asked the angels no logistical questions. She'd simply let Greg do what he wanted to her, then did whatever came to mind. In that case, it had been scissors to the eye. *Pump, pump,*

pump, stab. But now, with Mother, the situation was even more confusing. As Daniela had said, Mother was no longer her friend. She'd had Stewart killed, and wanted Morven dead, too. If her blue-tipped saviour hadn't intervened, Morven wouldn't be here right now – she'd be traversing some narrow canyon in the underworld.

But was sending Mother there in her place the right thing to do? Morven wasn't sure. She did know one thing – if previously she'd been guided by messages from angels, the guidance she received now would be even more accurate. Now, it came from the very top of the fallen angel hierarchy – Abaddon himself. Fallen angel of fallen angels. Devil of devils.

Morven watched the boat bob gently as Mother stepped aboard. Mother opened the hatch and descended into the cabin. Morven braced herself, and left her copse of trees for the towpath.

Edwina's latest piece was almost finished. Crocheted blankets were her favourite things to make. Last year she'd given Raymond a bobbled blanket in black and grey. Now, in the quiet of her boat, Edwina worked the hooks and yarn and tried to feel Andreas's presence. These were the moments when she took most comfort in speaking to her husband. Yet today, Andreas was hazy at best, and Edwina's words would not come. She was uncertain what to say to him. Would he want her to justify having ordered the murders of two of her followers? Would he simply listen as she told him her fears?

Andreas was so much in the forefront of Edwina's mind that, when a shadow appeared at the top of the stairs, part of her thought it might be him – his spirit turning corporeal to be with her at this time of need. But as the figure descended the steps, she saw it was a ghost of another kind.

'Why, Morven,' she said in what she hoped was an unflustered lilt. 'You should have called.' She smiled sweetly. 'It's what I gave you the phone for, dear.'

'We spoke yesterday,' Morven said.

'Yes,' Edwina said. She wished desperately she was aware of how much Morven knew. Did the girl turn up at the house in Chiswick yesterday? How much had she seen? And if she'd been there, why was she still alive? 'So, tell me, dear – what happened?'

'What you had planned,' Morven said. 'That's what happened. At least, some of it. Stewart's dead.'

'Oh, my goodness,' Edwina began, but was silenced by

Morven's pained expression.

'That much you knew already,' Morven said. 'But Raymond is dead too. I'm betting you didn't know that.'

Morven was now fully in the boat, and settling onto the bench across from Mother.

Raymond! Edwina could feel her face flush, her sense of balance skew. It was as though a lifeline had been cut, or a rudder lost. Edwina had come to depend on that solid, silent man for so much. The voice in her head started immediately with recriminations. *If you hadn't given him that dangerous task...* Edwina stilled it in mid-harangue. She would deal with its accusations later. 'Did you kill him?' she asked.

'No,' Morven replied. 'The Devil did.'

'The Devil.'

'He was in the form of a tall woman with blue tips in her hair,' Morven elaborated. 'She denied being the Devil, of course, and it's possible she wasn't. Or maybe she really was, but doesn't know it.'

Edwina nodded understandingly and wondered whether she could stab the girl in the eye with one of her crochet hooks. Unlike Morven, she was not physically strong, and the angle was poor, but these sticks of plastic were the only weapons she had. Edwina was unsure what Morven intended, but she was astute enough to realise this might not end well for her. It was likely that Morven had managed to kill Raymond herself, and had fabricated the story of the devil-woman for no better reason than straightforward insanity. It could be that trying to stab Morven as she delivered a crazy monologue was Edwina's only hope.

'But all angels work to one divine end,' Morven was saying, 'so if she *were* the Devil, then killing Raymond was what the Celestial Kingdom wanted.' Morven put her elbows on the table and leaned forward. That made her an easier target, Edwina thought.

'But there's a problem, Mother,' Morven went on. 'You sent Raymond to kill me, and the Devil herself came to stop him. That puts you on the wrong side of the Celestial Kingdom, don't you think?'

Unobtrusively, Edwina slid her blanket onto her lap and detached the hooks. She let the blanket and a single hook drop to the floor, and gripped the other tightly in her right hand. 'I have allied myself to the Kingdom for many years,' she told Morven. 'I have every single fallen angel on my side.'

'Not quite,' Morven countered. 'I have the best fallen angel of all. You see, I had a revelation, Mother. We Supplicants have been doing things wrong.' She reached out and grasped Mother's right wrist – the one clasping the crochet hook. 'We trust the angels, sure, but we've been ignoring their number one poster boy.'

'Poster boy?'

'The Devil himself,' she said. 'He goes by many names, but he wants me to call him Abaddon. If things had been different, I would have come here today to explain it all. After that, I would have done whatever you needed to put the order on the right track. We could have followed the true will of the Celestial Kingdom.' Morven shook her head sadly. 'But you had other ideas.'

Edwina took a moment to ensure she was ready. She placed her left palm on the table top and pressed herself upwards and forwards. Edwina slid across the laminated surface, bringing the crochet hook down towards Morven's eye. Morven managed to jerk backwards in time to save her sight. Instead, the hook grazed her left cheek. As Morven cried out, Edwina saw blood gushing down the girl's face.

That wasn't enough, Edwina thought. *I had one shot! I blew it – and now I'm dead*. She hoped with all her might that the Celestial Kingdom was real. She prayed that, in a matter of moments, she would find Andreas waiting on the underworld's murky shores. She felt Morven reach out and grasp her bony shoulder. Morven slammed her to the table and pressed down with surprising strength. Strangely, Edwina thought she could hear the girl crying.

'Why, Mother?' Morven asked through phlegmy sobs.

'It was necessary,' Mother Edwina gasped. 'Couldn't be helped. It wasn't your fault. They made you this way. We did – all of us.' She coughed, then sputtered. 'I'm sorry, dear,' she whispered.

'I'm sorry too, Mother,' Morven said.

Edwina felt the press of a blade against her neck. There was a single, sharp flash of pain, followed by the sparkling of fading consciousness. Then Mother Edwina Koch felt no more.

Morven had Mother's tea towel pressed to her left cheek. The blood had soaked through, turning the towel red and wet, but she thought she'd staunched most of the bleeding. She didn't dare pull away the towel to find out, though.

Morven stood at the stern of the boat, leaning on the tiller. Her free hand toyed with the card she'd kept back from Mother the last time she'd been at The Retreat. This was the one she'd intended to leave next to Stewart, but hadn't. Leaving the card down in the cabin with Mother would have felt wrong, too. It wasn't that kind of killing, and Mother didn't need Morven to assign her an angel for the underworld. She would have all of them, every single angel in the kingdom, lining up to greet her. Maybe even Abaddon himself. Wouldn't Mother be surprised then! *Morven was right*, she would have to admit.

Mother's unfinished blanket rested on the cabin top in front of Morven. She slid the card into a pocket and tossed the blanket carefully onto the towpath. There might be room for it in her bag, she thought. It would be a memento that Morven would treasure when… well, whenever she ended up wherever it was she was going. Morven would find out whether it fit in her bag when she retrieved her things from the copse of trees beside the garden.

But first, she needed to do something about Mother's body. It would feel wrong just to leave it all bloody like that, sprawled down there in the boat's cabin. It had felt OK to leave Greg and Jeff to rot, but not Mother. Morven wished she could bury her. That would be the right thing to do – the *respectful* thing. But a proper burial was out of the question. Still, Morven had another idea – it was second best, but it was a burial nonetheless. The blanket was not the only thing that Morven had salvaged from Mother; she also had the boat's keys in her pocket. She withdrew them now and inserted one into the ignition. She realised she needed to tug open the metal box just under the tiller, and that would require both hands. Morven had been holding the tea towel against her face with one of them. Now, she let it drop. For the moment at least, no fresh blood cascaded down her face.

After opening the box, Morven unscrewed the bar that protected the boat's weed hatch. She pulled out the hatch's metal seal and righted herself. With a last glance at the open hatch, Morven turned over the engine. Immediately, the propeller began churning water. It splashed over the edges of the lidless metal box and slopped into the boat. Morven was surprised at how quickly the vessel started to fill. She wasted no more time in leaping to the towpath.

By the time she'd made it back to her copse of trees, the boat was already sinking.

TWENTY-ONE

Stewart's and Raymond's bodies were not discovered for over a week. Over those arid days, the police made little progress on the investigation. Ceri spent more time with Sara and Jamie, but only when Adeela Mir was otherwise engaged. Jamie passed a couple of pleasant nights with his mother in Kent, and when he got back, Sara reopened the kitten discussion. It had not yet reached a conclusion. At the Marylebone property, plasterers coated drywall.

On the day when things finally got busy again, it was Ceri who called Sara. DS Mir was busy driving, she said. They were driving fast, too – Ceri's voice competed with the car's siren. She told Sara they were on their way to Chiswick. There had been a double homicide… and one of the Supplicants' cards had been found next to a body. Sara said she'd meet them there.

When she pulled up on the tranquil Chiswick street, Sara saw the police had already taped off the house. Scenes of Crime officers busied themselves around the property. As she passed through the barrier, Sara was overwhelmed by the feeling she was being watched. It was the first time she had sensed Daniela Atta's presence since their conversation in Brixton. *Go away*, she said mentally, and felt a pulse of something like amusement.

The first person Sara met was Ceri, who stood just outside the door, smoking a cigarette. As soon as Sara laid eyes on her, Ceri offered a heavy-lidded stare. 'Don't you start,' she said.

'I wasn't going to,' Sara said. 'You want another heart attack, that's your business.' Even to Sara, the faux-innocent lilt in her voice dripped with passive-aggression.

'It's temporary,' Ceri said flatly. 'This has been a hell of a time.' Ceri took a deep pull on her Marlboro and spoke again as the smoke leaked from her lips. 'I'll just finish this.' She grinned sardonically. 'Then maybe I'll have another. You go in and look around.'

Sara nodded and moved through the open front door. Behind her, Ceri asked, 'D'you ever watch soap operas?'

'No. Why?'

Ceri returned the cigarette to her lips. 'Doesn't matter.'

In the small living room, Sara found Mir speaking in

hushed tones to the Superintendent. At the moment, they were the only officers in the room. They broke off their conversation as Sara entered and offered sombre greetings. On the floor between the police and Sara lay two bodies.

Mir gestured to the one closest to Sara. 'That,' she said, 'was Mr Stewart Delaney. A television actor. He owned the property.'

Sara crouched near Delaney.

'As Ceri would say,' Mir added, 'deceased.'

'Just as well,' Sara said. 'He'd have severe traumatic brain injury if he weren't.' She surveyed the area around the floor. 'I'm told there was a card?'

'It's been bagged,' said the Superintendent.

'I'd like to see it.'

'Of course.'

Without warning, a thought popped into Sara's mind: *You could see anything you want. You could crack this case wide-open. And you know how to do it.*

The thought had not been Sara's own. She sent a pulse of irritation at her psychic stalker.

'So far, the second victim is unknown to us. There's no ID on the body.'

Sara stepped over Delaney, moved around a black-upholstered chair and kneeled next to the second man. 'He was garrotted,' she said. After closely examining the wound, Sara stood. 'This isn't Morven's work,' she said. 'It's possible she bludgeoned Mr Delaney over there, but she certainly did not do this.'

'Why do you say that?' the Superintendent asked.

'Whoever killed this man ruptured the internal carotids,' Sara explained. 'That takes size and strength. You don't need a lot of force to cut off blood flow and kill someone. But the more force used, the more trauma there'll be.' She indicated the man's body. 'To collapse two jugular veins, two carotid arteries, and then make an impact on the trachea itself – that takes someone bigger than the girl we saw in the photo.'

Inside Sara's mind, a voice said, *Look at him.*

'We don't think Morven killed either man,' Mir said. 'Scenes of Crime suggest that this one bludgeoned Delaney and was subsequently killed by a third party.'

'A third party who wasn't Morven,' Sara said.

'Who is unlikely to have been Morven.'

Look at him.

Reluctantly, Sara crouched again. Suddenly, she understood what Daniela was telling her. 'I know this man,' she said abruptly.

'What?' the Superintendent said.

'His name is Raymond,' Sara said. 'I'm not sure of his surname – but I do know he works for Edwina Koch.'

'The lady who runs The Supplicants of Dusk?' the Superintendent asked.

'He's her bodyguard and general dogsbody,' Sara said. 'Lives in her house.'

'What are we saying?' the Superintendent asked. 'That this man's been the killer all along?'

'Not likely,' sounded a voice from the hallway. All three of them looked to the door, where Ceri now stood. Sara could smell the fresh cigarette smoke that radiated from her like an aura. It competed with the lingering aroma of Stewart Delaney's incense.

'Why do you say that?' the Superintendent said.

'Well, he sure didn't have vaginal sex with Gregory Blackadar.'

Sara suppressed a grin, then nodded in agreement. 'She's right,' she said. 'Remember the angle of the scissors. They indicated Blackadar's sexual partner was also his killer.'

The Superintendent grunted. 'Maybe,' he said. 'But we

also place Raymond at the headboard of the bed. If he'd brought the scissors down from there, they would have entered Blackadar's eye at the same angle.' He turned to Mir. 'We shouldn't jump to hasty conclusions. What fingerprints were found on the scissors?'

'Blackadar's and one other set,' Mir replied. 'There were no matches on the database, but now we know they're Morven's. They match with the prints in the stolen van.'

'Check to make sure nothing's been missed,' the Superintendent said.

'When I went to Edwina Koch's house,' Sara said, 'Raymond was there. The place was his permanent residence. Personally, I find it unlikely he's been hanging about London helping Morven to kill people.'

'Which means he came here specially for this,' Ceri observed. 'We may not yet know who murdered this man, but we sure as hell know who sent him.'

A deep chuckle sounded in Sara's mind. She searched her sensations and felt again the unwelcome presence of Daniela Atta. From that moment, Sara was overwhelmed by the queasy feeling she knew exactly who killed Edwina Koch's servant.

It was you, wasn't it? she asked silently, and was

rewarded by a pulse of emotion that felt like confirmation.

'There's not enough evidence to arrest Mrs Koch for anything,' the Superintendent said. He looked down at Raymond's body. 'Knowing someone isn't a crime.'

'Shall I get in touch with the Surrey constabulary, at least?' Mir asked. 'I'd like them to request an interview under caution.'

The Superintendent wagged his head speculatively. 'Do you think she'd attend voluntarily?'

'We'll have to see,' Mir said.

'Go ahead, then.'

Mir withdrew her phone and left the room. As she passed through the door, Ceri followed.

The Superintendent watched them go. 'Can I have a word?' he said quietly to Sara. Sara looked up attentively, trying to mask any expression of wariness. She knew what the Superintendent was going to say, and had anticipated it ever since Ceri accompanied her to Mir's first briefing at West End Central.

'I'm told Inspector Lloyd is your friend,' the Superintendent said.

'She is,' Sara confirmed.

'DS Mir said you'd requested her presence as emotional

support.'

Sara did not answer. She waited.

'Yet,' the Superintendent went on, 'the Sergeant seems to be spending more time with your friend than you are.'

'I believe Ceri is proving useful to the investigation,' Sara said carefully.

'That's not her role,' said the Superintendent. 'We have every possible rank involved, each working to his or her own brief. Even if Inspector Lloyd were allowed to contribute, what could she do that one of the Met's officers couldn't?'

Sara could not think of a helpful response. She settled for, 'I couldn't speculate, sir.'

The conversation was interrupted by Mir re-entering the room with Ceri in her wake. The Superintendent lowered his voice. 'She is here as emotional support for you – and that's all.'

Sara smiled agreeably and looked to Mir with eyebrows raised.

'Surrey Police will contact Mrs Koch,' Mir said. She turned to the Superintendent. 'If she agrees to arrange a date for an interview under caution, I'd like to be there.'

The Superintendent nodded. 'That'll be at the discretion

of the Surrey force,' he said 'but I can't imagine they'd refuse.'

'There might be some value in speaking to the staff at Mr Blackadar's farm, as well,' Sara suggested. 'Dorset Police took statements at the time of his murder, but…'

'You're right,' Mir said. 'Especially the one called Lorna.' Mir looked at the Superintendent and explained, 'She was Blackadar's right-hand woman.'

'Is there any reason to interview her under caution?' asked the Superintendent. 'Maybe book an interview room at Bournemouth?'

Mir considered. 'Probably not. We're investigating Morven's murders, and there's no suggestion that Lorna or anyone else at the farm had a direct connection to them.'

'But a chat will be useful,' Sara said, 'before speaking to Mrs Koch.'

Ceri clapped her hands with vigour. 'I can be ready whenever you are,' she said. 'Just let me know when.'

The Superintendent shot a glance at the Welsh Inspector. Sara wondered whether he'd intended to look as irritated as he did. Soon, his frown softened and he cleared his throat. 'DS Mir?' he said. 'You and Dr Jones should be able to conduct these interviews yourselves, don't you think?'

When Mir looked puzzled, he added, 'I mean, without additional support from the Dyfed-Powys force.'

They had agreed that Mir would contact Gregory Blackadar's farm. She would try to arrange a date and time for an informal interview with Lorna. From what Sara knew of the woman, it was possible she would refuse, at least at first. However, once Lorna understood a chat would be less hassle than a formal interview, and far better than arrest as an accessory to murder, it was likely she'd comply.

Mir remained at the scene in Chiswick. Sara convinced Ceri to let her drive them both back to Marylebone. For Sara, it was an uncomfortable ride, filled with turbulent thoughts. The woman who called herself Daniela not only was stalking her, but had cemented their bond with a rather intrusive murder. It was a crime that Sara, knowing full well who the culprit was, could never explain to the Metropolitan Police. Had Daniela done it to get Sara's attention? It may have been part of the motivation, but it wasn't all. Clearly, Daniela was a trained psychic who had moved past her moral compunctions about murder, just as

Eldon Carson had done in Aberystwyth.

And Sara Jones in London, Sara thought.

But that wasn't entirely true. Sara had not got passed any of her moral compunctions. But she knew how dangerous someone who'd done so could be. That was why Sara had been working to avoid any more special cases, and trying to cope with this disease called psychic ability. This new assassin's introduction into Sara's life – whatever it was she actually wanted – only made that more difficult.

The other reason Sara was troubled was Ceri herself. It was obvious the Superintendent had noticed her unwarranted presence, and had started to balk. Sara knew Ceri's moods better than anyone, and had been expecting a ride home filled with outrage. Possibly even derision aimed at the Superintendent's competence. Yet, as they crawled around the Hogarth Roundabout towards Hammersmith, Ceri was the very image of reason. 'He was right,' she said. 'If the situation had been reversed, and some London cop were mooching around one of my investigations, I'd feel just the same way he does.'

Sara couldn't resist saying, 'Remember how you reacted to Jamie in Aberystwyth? And *he* was on the investigation officially.'

‘There you go,’ Ceri said, keeping her professionalism intact. ‘It’s just human nature.’

‘And who knows what other factors might be in play?’ Sara speculated. ‘This may be as much about the Superintendent’s relationship with Adeela as it is about you.’

Sara caught her friend’s reflection in the rear-view mirror. It shifted into a kind of studied concern. ‘I hope not,’ Ceri said. ‘I don’t know what he thinks of Adeela – she’s never mentioned it. But I wouldn’t want to think I was causing her any trouble.’

‘Of course not,’ Sara said. ‘You like her.’

‘Yes, I bloody like her. These last few weeks, she’s added something to my life, you know?’ Ceri furrowed her brow. ‘Don’t get me wrong, things were OK before. My life’s actually quite good. I like my work, and when I retire I’ll enjoy that too. I volunteer politically and I’ve made plenty of good friends that way.’ Suddenly, Ceri huffed angrily. ‘But this damned heart attack… it’s made me realise a thing or two. I’m not getting any younger. So, I’m going to do whatever I want while I still can.’

Sara suppressed a grin. When had Ceri Lloyd ever done what she *didn’t* want to do? On other occasions, that observation might have been a wonderful way to get a rise out of her oldest friend. But not today. Today, all Sara said was, ‘You should.’

TWENTY-TWO

Mir and Sara drove along the M3 towards Dorset. This time, Sara was the passenger. Gregory Blackadar's farm administrator, Lorna, had agreed to meet them late that afternoon. Mir had been unable to get hold of Edwina Koch, either on her mobile or landline. She had asked the Surrey police to visit the property.

'Will it bother you if I smoke?' Mir asked.

'No, of course not,' Sara lied. She wondered whether Mir was even allowed to smoke in a CID car – but she didn't know, and it was Mir's CID car.

Mir lit her cigarette and lowered the window halfway. She took her first drag and blew smoke from the side of her mouth. Some of it was sucked through the window and across the M3. What remained inside made Sara's nostrils sting. She hoped she could continue to breathe without coughing. Last year, Sara had fractured several ribs, and later, her car crash had exacerbated the injury. A bone fragment had healed crookedly, and now Sara suffered sharp pains in her side whenever she took a deep breath. It also hurt to cough.

They had passed Eastleigh and were heading towards the New Forest. Sara had not been the most personable travelling companion; she had been silent for most of the trip. If they'd been allowed to bring Ceri, Sara could have sat in the back seat and fretted, while the other two fell into their routine pattern of chat. With no Ceri, the car was quiet. The psychic appearance of Daniela Atta back at the crime scene had changed so much. For the first time in years someone had been able to break into Sara's mind and force a conversation. Sara recalled a dinner in her old farmhouse near Aberystwyth: Ceri had been there, and Jamie, and Rhodri... and in Sara's mind, her psychic mentor, Eldon Carson. That was at a point when Carson was training her, and Sara was keeping his identity secret. It wasn't long after that Carson had given Sara the original papier-mâché Eye-in-the-Pyramid pendant – the one whose likeness she now wore in silver around her neck. After offering his gift, Eldon had fled Aberystwyth and tried to murder Rhodri.

But it was that dinner Sara recalled so vividly right now.

They had been discussing the investigation when Eldon's mocking laughter had rung through Sara's mind. She could recall how violated she'd felt then. Today, when Sara sensed Daniela's intrusive attention, she'd experienced a shadow of that same feeling.

Mir switched on the radio and scanned the stations. She listened to a fragment of a song, rejected it, then moved on. By the time she had repeated this process several times, Sara felt like she was listening to an incredibly discordant medley.

One thing, Sara reflected, was worse than the feeling of violation, and that was Daniela's psychic admission she had killed Edwina Koch's thug, Raymond. Sara had long doubted her own psychic senses, but she was dead certain about this one. Daniela Atta had not only spied on her psychically, but now she'd murdered someone, too. Sara had the feeling this problem wouldn't go away quickly.

Mir stabbed off the radio and wondered aloud why stations never played any good music. She lit another cigarette, and Sara suppressed her gag reflex. 'How many of those does Ceri smoke in a day?' Sara asked Mir.

Mir glanced sideways. Her eyes were fixed with a look of appraisal. 'Ceri misses her Marlboros,' she answered finally. 'But at least this brand has lower tar.'

Sara released a frustrated *ugh.* 'There's a reason the government no longer allows tobacco to be advertised that way,' she said. 'Low tar doesn't make them any better for you. There have been studies.'

'She doesn't smoke much,' Mir said.

'She shouldn't smoke at all. She had a heart attack, for goodness' sake.'

Mir nodded contritely. Then, mid-nod, she shook her head and frowned. 'No,' she said, 'I'm not taking the rap for this.'

Sara mimed surprise. 'Does Ceri have some other smoking companion?'

'She doesn't need one. Ceri Lloyd can make her own decisions.'

'I saw you give her a cigarette at the Sawyer murder scene,' Sara said, her voice rising.

'She wanted one.'

Sara splayed her hands helplessly. 'And that's all it took?'

'You try saying no to Ceri,' Mir retorted. 'She is the most stubborn, obstinate woman I have ever known.'

All of a sudden, Sara's irritation dissolved into the

familiarity of their shared experience. She snorted. 'Welcome to my world,' she said. 'Remember, I've dealt with Ceri since I was fourteen.'

'There you are,' Mir said. 'You understand.'

Sara sank back in her seat. 'I suppose I do.'

'I'd rather have a contented Ceri than an annoyed one.'

Sara chuckled softly. 'Me, too. When Ceri's cranky, she can summon a thunderstorm indoors. But please, just don't encourage her smoking.'

'I promise,' Mir said. She threw her cigarette out the window. 'She loves you, you know. You're the most important person in the world to her.'

Sara smiled. She knew that, and there was no point in denying it. 'I'm very glad you've become her friend,' she told Mir.

Whenever Sara thought of the word *farmhouse*, she always pictured the home she had once owned in Penweddig, Wales. She would envision a white-painted stone cottage with red trim, a ramshackle place that had been renovated many times in its long history. By contrast, the late Greg Blackadar's farmhouse was a large, modern property. Its grey stone cladding nodded to the expected rural aesthetic, but the structure would not have looked out of place on a suburban estate. Mir parked on the gravel drive that fronted the house. Sara rapped on the wooden front door with a wrought-iron knocker, and soon after, a lanky, shirtless man holding a tin of beer answered.

'Yeah?' he said.

'We're here to see Lorna,' Mir said.

He sized them up as though he found the concept unlikely. 'You sure?' he asked.

Mir showed him her credentials and replied, 'I'm positive.'

The man wiped his nose with the back of his hand. 'Come in.'

As they entered, Sara raised her eyebrow at Mir. Obviously, standards had slipped since Blackadar's death. Sara couldn't imagine Mother Edwina countenancing such slovenly behaviour. He led them to the ground floor's main room, and indicated they should stay there. When they were alone, Sara and Mir surveyed their surroundings; the bland decor gave away little about anyone's life on this farm. Most of its walls were eggshell white and its furniture pine, save for a beige floral-patterned sofa and matching chair. A freestanding cast-iron fireplace stood next to a wall of exposed brick. On that same wall hung the one piece of decoration that displayed any personality. It was a pastel caricature of Gregory Blackadar – the kind sketch artists sell at carnivals.

The farm employee known as Lorna did not enter quietly. Both women looked up as they heard a shrill voice ringing above them, overhead on the first floor. It contrasted with the beer-drinking man's lower monotone. Soon, there were footsteps thudding down the stairs, and Lorna loped into the room. Sara thought the best word to describe her was *stringy* – Lorna was lanky and gaunt, her black hair pulled back into a no-nonsense ponytail. Her cheekbones were high and pronounced, her mouth small. She curled in her lips as though protecting her teeth.

The three women made perfunctory introductions and sat without formality. The Detective Sergeant began with some gentle probing to discover how much the staff knew about their situation. Lorna said everyone was aware the Supplicants now owned Greg's property. She also revealed that Edwina Koch herself had been in touch by telephone; Mother had told everyone to keep to their routines until the reading of Blackadar's will.

'And what is your responsibility here?' Mir asked.

'Now? I kind of run the place,' Lorna replied. 'I mean, by default, because nobody else knows how everything's supposed to happen, and I do.'

'And before?'

'I worked, just like everyone else,' Lorna said.

'The Dorset police referred to you as a kind of gang-master,' Mir said. 'They got the impression from interviewing the staff that you kept order for Mr Blackadar.'

'You make me sound like a criminal,' Lorna said.

Mir pursed her lips thoughtfully. 'We know cannabis is grown commercially on this property, and that there are undocumented labourers here.' She smiled sweetly. 'So, yes, there's a suspicion you've been involved in illegal activities.'

Lorna's stare grew hard. 'You going to arrest me?'

'Not my business,' Mir said. 'I'm investigating a series of murders. Investigating your crimes would be up to the Dorset force.'

'I don't know anything about the drugs,' Lorna insisted. 'And if any worker here's *undocumented*, I don't know about that, either.'

'What about Morven?' Sara asked.

'What about her?'

'She's as undocumented as they come. From what I understand, she doesn't even have a birth certificate.'

Lorna released a sigh of frustration. 'Morven grew up here,' she said. 'I think she might have been born right on the property. How would I know whether she has a birth certificate or not? She was just Cuddy's kid.'

'Whose?'

'Cuddy,' Lorna repeated. 'Her dad. Died of a heart attack a couple years ago.'

Mir poised her pen. 'Could you give me the family name?'

Lorna frowned as though she were being horribly inconvenienced. 'Glasson – that was his last name. I don't know that Morven ever used it.'

In their notebooks, Sara and Mir wrote *Cuddy Glasson*.

'Surely she must have used her full name at school,' Sara said.

'She was home-educated,' Lorna told her.

'What about when she visited the doctor, or went to the dentist?' Mir asked.

'Don't remember her ever going to the dentist,' Lorna said. 'As for doctors, when anyone got sick, Greg brought in a friend. I mean, the guy was a qualified doctor, but he'd treat us right here.'

'Do you know his name?' Mir said.

Lorna shook her head. 'Just a mate of Greg's. He died last year.' Anticipating Sara's next question, she emphasised, 'Of natural causes. Just after Morven delivered. Since then, I don't think anyone's had medical attention.'

Sara leaned forwards. 'Was he a member of the Supplicants of Dusk?'

Lorna snorted. 'No.'

'But you are – is that correct?'

'Kind of,' Lorna said. She swept an arm to include everyone in the house. 'Greg made people who worked for him swallow that stuff. We're all Supplicants, whether we believe in angels or not.' She sucked her lower lip thoughtfully. 'It's not all bad, mind you. To be fair, the order has given an odd crowd of people something to believe in together. Or, at least, pretend to believe. And Mother Edwina's a smart lady.'

'If the doctor wasn't a Supplicant,' Mir pressed, 'how did Mr Blackadar get him to make regular visits, and keep quiet about things?'

Lorna tutted as though the question were naïve. 'People will live up to some dodgy expectations if cash is on offer,' she said. 'Not everyone Greg dealt with was a Supplicant. There were plenty of civilians around – people he just needed. He didn't care what they believed, so long as they helped him.'

'These were people he hired?' Mir asked. 'People he paid?'

'He paid them all in one way or another,' Lorna replied. 'He'd give gifts to some of them.'

'Marijuana?'

'Or other things. Just so long as they could do something for him.'

Lorna watched Mir scribble notes. Her eyes followed the pen greedily, as though she wanted to read – to possess – every word Mir wrote.

Sara fixed Lorna with a hard stare. 'Was sex one of those things?'

Lorna shifted her attention to Sara. 'What do you mean?'

'Did Mr Blackadar offer his friends sex with girls on the farm?'

Lorna's eyes flashed. She looked outraged that Sara

would even dare to ask the question. Quickly, the spark of angry defiance died and she lowered her gaze. 'I wouldn't know anything about that,' she muttered.

'Really? Are you saying Blackadar never offered *you* to anyone?' Sara asked.

Lorna looked up again. In a second, her expression had switched back to fierce. 'Don't be stupid,' she said forcefully.

Sara and Mir exchanged brief glances. Lorna had a combative nature, but who knew what terrible experiences had formed it? Mir's very posture softened, and she leaned forwards towards the woman. 'He can't hurt you anymore,' she said. 'You can tell us.'

'What I can do is look after myself,' Lorna snarled. 'Greg knew enough to leave me to my work and stay the fuck away.'

Sara looked at Mir, and raised an eyebrow slightly – just enough to say, *it's possible*.

'We can see you know how to defend yourself,' Mir said. 'I'm sure you had Mr Blackadar well trained. But not everyone here is as emotionally strong as you.'

Lorna pondered this, then accepted it as a compliment. She nodded, then sat back with her arms folded.

As she did, Mir sat back. 'Morven, for example,' she went on. 'What about her?'

There were plenty of places to camp on Hampstead Heath. Morven wasn't sure whether it was legal or not, but on a couple of nights the Heath constabulary rode past her on mountain bikes and hadn't stopped. That was even though her tent was visible through the trees. Anyone could have seen it, even now, in the darkness of a new moon. It was a good tent. Morven had bought it at an outdoor shop in Highgate just last week. It was roomy – family-sized – and had cost nearly five hundred pounds, although it was marked down from its original seven. The sales person at the shop had actually tried to down-sell her – he'd said a large tent with one person would stay too cold. She should consider a smaller model. But if Morven couldn't have a hotel room, at least she wanted space in her tent. She'd decided she could create warmth in other ways. Morven had also purchased a thick, top-of-the-line camping mattress – another hundred-and-fifty pounds – a feather pillow, and a sleeping bag with down insulation. She had thrown in some disposable heat packs, too, just in case she still felt a chill in the night. Altogether, it had been a costly set of purchases – but Morven still had enough of Greg's cash, and these were likely to be the last big expenditures she would need to make. There was only one more thing Morven had to do, and that would happen right here on the Heath. After that… well, then Morven's fate would rest in the talons of Abaddon, who was the Devil.

Somehow, Morven had become a celebrity. Staying in another hotel was out of the question now – celebrities tended to get noticed. Even camping was a risk. The moment the Heath constabulary did decide to inspect Morven's tent, they were bound to recognise her, despite her changed appearance. That was the reason Morven had fought her desires so fiercely when her train had arrived at Waterloo. Every instinct had screamed for her to visit Dr Jones's house. All she would have to do was get on the Northern Line to Stockwell, then the Victoria line to Brixton. She wouldn't have knocked on the door, of course – she would have been content to stand on the street, staring at Dr Jones's bay window and knowing Cherub was inside. But even such maternal yearning was too risky. Instead, Morven had to rest in the knowledge that her baby was being cared for, safe and happy with Dr Jones.

Morven was strolling a path next to one of the bathing

ponds when her pay-as-you-go phone rang. She started. Since Mother's death, there was only one person it could have been – her friend Cara. After sinking Mother's boat, Morven had returned to her copse of trees to collect her things. She had planned to walk the towpath back to the golf club, and ring a cab to take her to the station. However, as she trekked across the lawn, Morven had noticed Cara watching from an upstairs window. She hadn't had the heart to leave her friend without an explanation and a final goodbye. And since Cara was the only person left in the house, there was nothing to stop her.

After Cara had cleaned up Morven's cheek and applied a large plaster, Morven had retrieved one of Mother's phones from the roll-top desk where she kept them. She chose one at random and entered its number in her own phone. Then she had given it to Cara.

'If you have troubles – or just want to talk – call me,' she'd said. Cara had not asked about Mother; presumably, she had watched the boat sink and drawn her own conclusions. Morven had spent her time with Cara trying to convince the girl to flee. Even knowing that Mother rested at the bottom of the Thames, Cara refused. She couldn't imagine where she would go, or what she would do. Like a deer in headlights, Cara had frozen, and was waiting for some unknown but inevitable impact.

But now Cara was calling. Morven had to admit she had been lonely. She picked up the handset with joy. 'Guess it's pretty quiet down there,' she said.

'No, it's really not,' Cara hissed. 'The police are here.'

Morven felt herself flush with concern. 'Right now?'

'Yes! They're ringing the doorbell.' Morven heard the girl give an audible shudder. 'Morven,' she said, 'tell me what to do.'

Morven had noticed that about people. They seldom did the sensible thing until they'd exhausted all the stupider possibilities. She had already told Cara what to do. She'd told her to get out of town. But she'd said it when the act would have been simple. That had been too early – too *easy* – for Cara, just like it would have been for most people on the planet. 'You should have left,' Morven sighed. 'You should have done it when I said to.'

'Well, I didn't,' Cara replied sulkily. That was another thing people did – they stated the obvious a lot.

'You've got money,' Morven reminded her. 'You could still escape.'

'No,' Cara stammered. 'I can't.'

Morven saw a bench and plunked herself down. Suddenly, her legs had grown heavy. She had to remember that Cara wasn't made for things like this. 'Then I guess you should answer the door,' she suggested.

'But they'll find her!' Cara squealed softly. 'They'll see the boat you sunk – you still can, right there in the water – and then they'll find Mother, and after that–'

'Cara!' Morven barked. 'What you need to do is untwist your knickers.'

'Huh?'

'Take a breath.'

Morven could hear Cara doing just that.

'Are you calmer now?'

'Uh-huh,' Cara whimpered.

'OK then, here's what you've got to do…' Morven felt as though there should be a drum roll. Or maybe one of those musical stings film makers used to highlight something important. But despite knowing how significant what she was about to say would sound, it was simply the next thing that had to be done. 'Are you listening?' she asked.

'Just tell me!' Cara squealed.

'OK, here it is,' Morven said. 'You've got to turn me

in.'

'Morven, no!' Cara cried. 'I couldn't do that.'

'They're going to know it was me, anyway,' Morven told her. 'Do you want to be an accessory to murder?'

'No.'

'Then this is the only way to play it. Just tell them Mother's been missing for a week. Say that Raymond left just before she did, and you assumed they'd met up somewhere but didn't bother to tell you.'

A thought occurred to Morven. If the police were knocking on Mother's door, the chances were good they had also discovered the bodies in Chiswick. And if that were so, they may also have realised Raymond had killed Stewart. Morven didn't know much about police work, but she'd been given to understand their scientist boffins were pretty clever. So, who was to say Raymond hadn't killed Mother, too? It would be an easy thing for the police to conclude. Morven wondered whether she should suggest to Cara subtly steering the interview that way. Certainly, if Morven were being questioned, she could have led them to such a suspicion easily. But was Cara as convincing a liar?

Probably not. Best not to confuse the girl.

'So, I just say they both left and I stayed here alone?'

Cara asked. 'Do you think they'll believe that?'

'You're nobody,' Morven told her. 'A frightened little maid. The police will buy it.'

'What about you?' Cara asked. 'How do I…?'

'Turn me in?' Morven said. 'First, you need to stash the phone and the money I gave you. Hide them well, mind, because if they find them, you'll be on the naughty step. Then tell the police you saw someone in the garden that day. You only caught a brief glimpse, but you think the woman you saw had a shaved head.'

'Do they know you cut off all your hair?'

'They will when you tell them. It doesn't matter, Cara. I only have one more thing to do, and after that – well, whatever happens will happen.'

Morven could hear Mother's doorbell ring repeatedly through her phone. 'You'd better get that,' she told Cara. 'Just say what I told you.'

'What'll they do to me?'

'I don't know,' Morven said. It was a horrible shame Cara had to be tangled up in all this, she thought. Then again, Cara had lived at the farm before working at The Retreat. In a way, she'd been caught up in it her whole life. It occurred to Morven how little she really knew about her friend. They'd been comrades-in-arms at Greg's, of course, but they'd never really shared intimacies. The culture at the farm had not allowed for it. For the first time, Morven wondered whether Cara had been through the same sort of things she herself had suffered. If Morven managed to live through the next few days, she decided she'd find Cara and, for the first time, they would compare notes about their lives.

Of course, that required Cara to be free, rather than in prison.

'Cara?' Morven said.

'I'm still here.'

'Promise me something,' Morven went on. 'After the police leave, dig out that money and scarper. Just run away and never look back… OK?'

On the Dorset farm, Lorna uncrossed her arms slowly and slid her hand to the back of her neck. Slowly, she adjusted her ponytail. She ran her tongue over her front teeth contemplatively. 'Morven?' she asked finally. 'What do you need to know about Morven?'

'Did Greg ever offer her to any of his friends?' Mir asked. 'Sexually, I mean.'

Lorna's eyes flashed, but she said nothing. For that brief moment, all Sara could hear was the clacking of a wall clock in another room. The silence offered all the confirmation Sara and Mir needed. They exchanged glances and Lorna caught their knowing look.

'I'll tell you something,' she spat impatiently. 'Whatever that girl did, she did for herself.'

'Hang on a minute,' Sara said. 'For herself?'

'Yes – for personal gain,' Lorna confirmed. 'She was always a selfish girl. Greedy.'

'That girl,' Sara shouted, 'was raped!'

Mir peered at Lorna with a furrowed brow. 'Are you saying she *chose* to have sex with men who came to this farm?'

'Of course,' Lorna insisted. She looked at Sara contemptuously. 'It was never rape. They'd give her things. You don't know how much she liked that.' Her expression shifted to sour disgust. 'Morven was no victim, I'll tell you that much.'

Sara fought the urge to argue with this bitter bully of a woman; there were further things they needed to know. 'Can you name the men who'd come regularly for Morven?'

Lorna looked at her with narrow eyes. 'You know who they were,' she said. 'There was Stewart. And I've mentioned the doctor…'

'What about Jeffrey Sawyer?'

She nodded. 'Him, too.'

Sara had expected as much. Perhaps Morven was considered a perk of their business relationship. However Gregory Blackadar had rationalised the abuse, it still meant the only people Morven had killed were men who had hurt her. Where, Sara wondered, did that leave the man Morven had *tried* to kill?

'I want to know about people you haven't mentioned,' Sara probed. 'Mother Edwina had some powerful friends. Did any of them ever visit Morven?'

Lorna huffed air from her lungs helplessly. 'I can only tell you what I know,' she said.

Before Sara could pursue the question further, Mir cut in. 'Let's get back to the special gifts,' she said. 'Did Mr Blackadar give her things, too?'

'Greg? Not that I know of.' Lorna shrugged. 'But maybe.' Her expression said, *I couldn't care less*.

The look made Sara wince. After her parents died, and she and Rhoddo had been placed in Aunt Issy's care in

Machynlleth, Sara had felt like a pariah. Their tragedy was big news in Mid Wales, and sometimes people in town would stare openly. Many had compassion in their eyes, but a few revealed an unfathomable hostility, as though Sara herself had been tainted by the tragedy she'd suffered. She would feel breathless, smothered by that blanket of judgement thrown over her so unfairly and with no chance of removal. Now, Sara could see all this misplaced hatred once again in Lorna's fierce, unfair bitterness towards Morven.

Sara learned forwards. 'Was Mr Blackadar the father of Morven's baby?'

Lorna recoiled. 'I already told you,' she said gruffly. 'Pretty much *any*one could've been Cherub's daddy.'

'But Greg did have a relationship with her?' Mir asked.

The muscles of Lorna's cheeks twitched as she worked out what to say. Finally, she settled for a partial confirmation. 'It's not like I watched them do it or anything,' she said, 'but, yeah, I guess so.'

'You *guess* so?'

'That girl acted all smug, like she had something I didn't. I assume it was because she'd been screwing the boss.'

'So, you're confirming your personal knowledge that Morven and Blackadar had a relationship,' Mir clarified, and she made a note in her book.

Lorna's expression suggested a number of things at once. It asked what she could have done to stop it. It spoke of her contempt for Morven as a conspirator in her own abuse. It hinted at a jealousy Lorna would never admit. And, somehow, what it conveyed most was the sense that Lorna was the real victim in all of this.

'Did Morven think the baby was Greg's?' Mir asked.

'Maybe she did,' Lorna said, 'but I never thought it was so damned obvious. Like I said, Cherub could've been anyone's. Long as someone was friends with Greg, that girl was up for it.' Her frown tightened as though she'd smelled something bad. 'And Greg just went along with it, you know? These were people he wanted to keep happy, and Morven was really good at that. That girl got away with murder.'

Lorna realised what she'd just said and snorted. 'I didn't mean that literally, by the way.'

'Whose baby do you think Cherub was?' Sara asked.

'I told you. It could have been–'

'Speculate,' Sara suggested. 'Anyone you haven't

mentioned who might be a good candidate?'

Lorna stared at the ground. She shook her head.

'I'm sorry,' Sara interrupted, 'but I don't believe you.'

Mir shot Sara a questioning glance.

'What?'

'I think there are things you're not telling us,' she said. 'You're far too quick to blame Morven – a girl who was raised on this farm, kept isolated, denied medical care, and who was obviously the victim of terrible physical abuse. You knew the staff here intimately. I cannot believe you didn't see and know more than you've admitted to.'

'How do you respond to that?' Mir asked.

'Did you have anything to do with it?' Sara pressed on.

'With what?'

'With arranging Morven's…' Sara searched for a diplomatic word. 'Exploits,' she said finally. 'Her exploits with men.'

'Wait a minute,' Lorna cried. 'You think I'm some sort of a pimp?'

'I presume you did whatever Greg asked you to do. You said you oversaw workers on the farm.'

'That's different.'

'You kept people in line,' Sara said.

'That's my job,' Lorna agreed.

'So, just to be clear,' Mir cut in, 'if Mr Blackadar needed Morven in a particular place at a particular time, he may well have asked you to ensure she got there.'

Lorna shook her head stubbornly. 'No.'

'You wouldn't? You would have defied him?'

'I never did that.'

'Are you claiming he never asked you to? That you never had to force Morven to go with a particular man?'

Lorna looked between her two interviewers with a hunted expression. It appeared as though she might spring forward and try to bite them. 'I'm finished talking to you,' she snapped. 'If you want to speak to me again, it's going to be with a lawyer next to me.'

Mir angled her head. 'That's your choice,' she said.

'You can leave now,' Lorna said. 'And as soon as you do, I'm ringing Mother Edwina.'

For Lorna, this seemed the biggest threat she could make.

Mir gathered her things. 'Tell her I look forward to speaking to her next week,' she said. Standing, she added, 'in a police interview room.'

TWENTY-THREE

'That Lorna girl is guilty as hell,' Mir said. 'She knew Morven was kept as a slave.'

'There may have been others she's helped to enslave, too,' Sara agreed. 'She knew all about the rapes, the drugs…'

'She was Greg's right hand,' Mir agreed. 'His enforcer. There's no way she could have been as ignorant as she claims.'

They were driving along the wide expanse of the M3 motorway, heading towards London. Mir's satnav told Sara they were just north of Farnborough airport, but the landscape could have been anywhere. Nothing in front but tarmac and bridges, nothing to the sides but trees and shrubbery.

'What will you do?' Sara asked.

'Modern-day slavery is a big concern for all police forces,' Mir said. 'I'll pass along my notes to the Dorset force, and they can decide whether to take action. Let's hope when all of this comes together, Lorna will end up behind bars.'

Prison might be the safest place for Lorna, Sara thought. So far, Morven had only killed a couple of her rapists. If she were still on the loose once that mission had been completed, there was a strong possibility she'd widen her net. Then Lorna would not be safe – unless Morven was caught.

Sara feared what would happen to Morven in the criminal justice system. The girl needed psychiatric care, not incarceration. Sara was certain of this not just as a mental health professional, but as someone who had considered crime and retribution from a rather rarefied perspective. Over the past four years, Sara had thought about justice within the prism of what Eldon Carson had told her – that one day, her psychic gifts would make her a killer, just like him. Carson had been right, of course: she had killed. She had also suffered from months of stomach-churning worry and – worse – shame. Shame for a murder that, even by Carson's strictest standards, had been necessary. Sara had done it to save a life. Maybe two lives, including her own.

Sara's thoughts were interrupted by the ringing of Mir's phone. Mir was edging into the lane that led to the M25. 'Could you answer?' she asked.

Sara thumbed the icon and said hello. Mir's superintendent was on the other end. 'Who is it?' Mir asked quietly. Sara told her in a whisper and Mir frowned. 'I only spoke to him ninety minutes ago,' she sighed.

'Dr Jones,' the Superintendent said. 'Have you left Dorset?'

'We're approaching London now, sir,' Sara confirmed.

'How long would it take you to get to Weybridge?'

'Edwina Koch's house?' Sara asked, and Mir looked at her sharply. 'From here, I'd say twenty minutes.'

'Then I suggest you get there,' he said. 'Surrey police will brief you at the scene.'

'What's happened?' Mir whispered.

'Sir?' Sara said. 'DS Mir has asked what we should–'

'Just get there as soon as you can. We believe our suspect has paid another visit to the property.'

Sara must have gasped, because Mir turned to her sharply and said, 'What?'

Sara shushed her with a raised finger. 'What's happened, sir?' she asked.

'Mrs Koch,' the Superintendent told her, 'has been murdered.'

Sara and Mir were directed around the side of The Retreat and into the garden. Blue-and-white police tape formed a border around the entire property; Sara was becoming reacquainted with the stuff in a way she had hoped she'd never be again. The garden crawled with police teams carrying out their various specialties. Mir excused herself to find the officer in charge. Sara made her way down the long strip of grass she and Mother Edwina had walked only recently, and introduced herself to a constable guarding the tow path. He pointed out where the submerged boat lay barely visible in the muddy tide.

'Where are Mrs Koch's remains?' Sara asked.

'The body recovery team has already left,' he said. 'So has the hearse. I think they've taken her to the morgue at the East Surrey Hospital.'

Sara recalled the tent in Hertfordshire that had kept Jeff Sawyer's bloated corpse hidden from public view. She said, 'That happened quickly.'

'When a person's submerged, it does,' he confirmed. 'They scramble a police diving team within minutes, in case someone's alive down there.'

'Is that likely?' Sara asked.

'A person could be trapped in an air pocket,' the constable said. 'In this case, it appears the victim was deceased prior to submersion, though. They say she'd been down there for a week or so.'

Sara knew the Surrey police would have jurisdiction over the crime, at least for the moment. It was likely that, in time, the Met and Surrey would amalgamate the investigation under a single coordinator. Given that the Met was already searching for Morven, it was likely to be Mir's superintendent. But, for now, Surrey was in charge. Sara looked up the garden for Mir, but could see no sign of her. She asked the constable where the Detective Sergeant was likely to have been directed.

'Not sure,' the constable said, 'but she could be in the house, talking to the witness.'

'Witness?' Sara said.

Mir was in the front parlour, speaking to Edwina Koch's maid. The Surrey police had already taken the girl's statement, and the conversation she was having with Mir would not be considered an official interview. Still, Sara suspected Mir's questions stood a better chance of finding Morven than the Surrey force's would have done.

The parlour had an underused air, as though it only came to life on special occasions. Perhaps it had seen more action in days gone by, maybe when Andreas Koch was alive. The parlour's long-sealed airlessness made it feel like a crypt, and the ghostly young woman trembling in a wing chair did little to relieve the gloom.

'You can positively identify her?' Mir was asking. 'You're sure of it?'

'Well, I mean, she was in the trees and I was at the window,' Cara said hesitantly. 'But it seemed like her.'

Mir gestured for Sara to join them. 'This is Cara,' she said quietly, and Sara nodded. Quickly, Mir picked up the thread of their conversation. 'When you say the woman you saw seemed like Morven,' she prompted, 'how exactly do you mean that?'

The girl twirled her hair until it was coiled around her index finger. 'The way she moved, I guess.' Cara pulled her finger from the twisted clump of hair, leaving an untidy ringlet. 'The shape of her, maybe.' She looked uncertainly from Mir to Sara. 'Does that make sense?'

Sara eased into a chair next to the girl. 'It makes perfect

sense,' she told her. 'We don't just recognise people from their facial features. We can identify them by their gait – that means the way they walk – or their choice of clothing, or hair style…'

'She'd changed a bit,' Cara said.

'How?' Mir asked.

'She'd shaved her head, for one thing,' Cara said. 'And her jacket was new. Black leather.'

Mir scribbled in her notebook. 'And did she have the baby with her?' she asked casually.

Sara looked at Mir and raised her eyebrows. They both knew that was not possible.

'I didn't see him,' Cara said. 'I'm pretty sure she was alone.'

Mir returned Sara's glance and made a gesture of approval. Cara had offered a small morsel of proof as to her honesty. The girl was looking down, staring at the floral rug. Her lips were parted. 'I didn't even think about Cherub,' she said. 'You don't imagine something's happened to him, do you?'

'Cherub is fine,' Mir assured her. 'We know that.'

'But,' Sara interjected, 'we also need to know you're certain that the woman you saw was Morven.'

Cara nodded resolutely. 'It was her.'

'If you had to testify in court,' Mir pressed, 'would you still be as sure?'

Cara hesitated, then nodded again.

'OK – that's all for now.' Mir slipped her notebook into her pocket. 'If you want to go to your room, you can. I know this has been very upsetting.'

Before Mir could rise, Cara said, 'Wait.' Mir looked at her questioningly. 'Am I under arrest?' the girl asked.

Mir smiled kindly. 'You have nothing to worry about,' she said. 'My advice would be to sit tight. I gather this house is owned by the Supplicants of Dusk rather than Mrs Koch directly, and, frankly, I'm not sure who will end up owning what. But for the time being, nobody's going to mind if you keep living in your room. But if you choose to move to another residence, please make sure we know about it.'

Mir stood. 'I'll be in the garden,' she said to Sara.

Sara did not follow. There were things she wanted to ask Cara – but they were based on hunches she did not want to explain to DS Mir. Cara must have sensed that Sara was not finished with her; she looked wary. 'Can I go?' she

asked.

'In a moment,' Sara said. 'I'm just curious about a few things.'

'OK,' Cara said. Sara thought she could detect a waver in her voice.

'The gentlemen outside tell me Mother Edwina's body has been in the water for over a week. Do you think that's about right?'

'I guess so,' Cara said. 'That's how long it's been since I saw Morven.'

'A week is a long time to stay here alone – especially if you're uncertain about where someone has gone. Why didn't you report Mother Edwina missing?'

Cara bit her cheek. 'Because of Raymond, I guess,' she said.

'Raymond?'

'He went on a trip without telling me he was leaving. When Mother went away, too, I thought maybe she'd joined him.'

'It didn't seem strange, staying here for a week all by yourself?'

'It's my job,' Cara said, an edge creeping into her voice. 'I clean, that's what I do. I get groceries.'

Sara nodded slowly. 'I could believe that,' she said, 'except, you just described seeing Morven on the day Mother disappeared.'

Cara's eyes widened as though she'd just seen a trap Sara had laid for her. 'I saw *some*one in the garden,' Cara insisted. 'At the time, I didn't think it was Morven. And I sure didn't know she'd killed Mother.'

Sara held out a hand and took a slow, deep breath – an indication for Cara to do the same. 'And what about the boat?' she asked calmly. 'What did you think when you noticed it was missing?'

'I didn't think about it at all!'

Sara leaned forwards. She smiled gently. 'Cara, I'm not a police officer,' she said. 'I'm a psychiatrist. That means I can tell when people are lying.'

Tears began to well in Cara's eyes. 'I'm not,' she protested. 'I'm telling you the truth.'

Sara nodded slowly and did her best to look thoughtful. She pressed her pen against her chin contemplatively, holding the silence for as long as she thought Cara could stand it. Finally, she said, 'You've spoken to Morven since Mother disappeared, haven't you?'

Cara's face contorted into a look of shock and fear. The

tears in her eyes dribbled down her cheeks. 'No!' she cried.

'Where is she, Cara?'

'I don't know.' The young woman's breath grew laboured. She started to sob. Sara sat back again and waited for the emotional storm to blow itself out. Cara bit her lower lip and held her breath.

Slowly, she regained composure. Cara's muscles slackened. Sara lowered her voice to a near-whisper. 'Where is she?'

In a voice even quieter than Sara's, Cara said, 'She wouldn't tell me.'

Sara released a breath. She looked at Cara calmly. 'When you spoke to her, what sort of things *did* she tell you?'

'She – she said to turn her in,' Cara cried. 'That's all she told me – that I shouldn't get myself in trouble.' She clenched her eyes shut. 'She just doesn't care anymore. She said she only has one more thing to do, then she doesn't mind what happens to her.'

'One more thing?' Sara asked sharply. 'Did she say what it was?'

Cara shook her head softly, once again studying the carpet.

'You need to tell this to the police,' Sara said.

The girl looked frightened. 'What'll happen to me if I do?'

Sara reached out and touched the girl's fingers. She flinched. 'As I say,' Sara told her in a reassuring tone, 'I'm not a police officer. But nobody's suggesting you're anything other than a witness. My guess is, if you tell DS Mir, she'll inform the Surrey police that you want to amend your statement.'

'That's all?'

'I'd think so.'

'Oh.' Cara squirmed in her chair. *She's still troubled*, Sara thought. She suspected she knew why. 'And Morven won't mind, either,' she said. 'I promise you that.'

In a flash, Cara's mood turned from troubled to contemptuous. She snorted. 'You promise, do you? How do you know? You don't know Morven at all.'

Sara nodded understandingly. 'I can see why you'd think that.'

She stood and walked to the door. Before passing into the hallway, she added, 'There's no time to explain it to you, Cara, but you should trust me on this – I know Morven a lot better than most people do.'

Sara went through the conservatory and into the back garden to summon Mir. 'You should go back inside,' she told her. 'Cara has more to say.'

Mir looked at her keenly. 'What?'

'Contact with Morven.'

The detective sergeant's eyes widened, and she moved hastily towards the house. Sara followed, but stopped at the parlour door. She decided it was best not to intrude. Instead, Sara stepped out the front door. There, she paused for a moment, recalling how she had stood on that very spot not long ago, looking into Raymond's slack face as he said, 'You're a doctor?'

Sara walked down the pathway towards the street, where Mir's nondescript CID car was parked. If the police tape, teams of specialist officers and a hearse had aroused neighbourhood suspicion, it was no longer evident. Whatever gawping the neighbours had done had ceased to amuse them. Sara leaned on the car's bonnet and pulled out her phone. She selected a contact, and in her mind scripted a short message for the inevitable voicemail.

As she did, the press of Daniela Atta's bodiless presence bore down on her. It was like a balloon swelling in her chest. *Finally, you've understood,* Daniela's voice sounded within her thoughts.

Leave me alone, Sara thought back.

Despite Sara expecting to leave a message, the Right Honourable Joseph Bennett answered on the third ring. 'Dr Jones,' the Minister for Policing said. 'What a pleasure.'

'Minister,' Sara said. 'How are you coping?'

'I'm battered and sore,' Bennett said, 'but I'll heal.'

'I'm sorry to bother you,' Sara went on, 'but you asked for updates.'

'I thought you'd forgotten about me.'

'No, sir,' she said, 'I have a lot to tell you. You've heard today's news, I assume?'

'Actually, I haven't,' Bennett said. 'I don't know if you follow politics, Dr Jones, but the government's been rather busy these days. I've been in the chamber all morning.'

'You're back working so soon?' Sara asked.

Bennett snorted – *of course.*

'Well… this news isn't public yet,' Sara told him, 'but Edwina Koch is dead.'

Bennett paused, then cleared his throat. Inside Sara's mind, Daniela shimmered with silent laughter.

'Minister?'

‘I’m here,’ Bennett said. ‘Was she…?’

‘Murdered? Yes, sir.’

Sara thought she heard the minister’s breath catch. He managed to say, ‘By…?’

In Sara’s mind, Daniela pulsed with joy. *By our girl!*

Sara did not wait for Bennett to complete the sentence. ‘We believe so, yes,’ she answered. ‘She was likely murdered by Morven.’

‘How close are you to apprehending this young woman?’

‘We do have a witness,’ Sara told him, ‘who places Morven at the scene prior to the murder. She has given us an updated description.’

Bennett cleared his throat again; it turned into a hollow bark as he stifled a coughing jag. ‘How soon can you meet me?’ he asked, his voice clotted in phlegm. ‘I want to know everything – just from you. I don’t want any police to come along.’ Sara listened as he swallowed noisily. ‘What I mean is,’ he explained, ‘I need your unbiased point of view.’

‘It can’t be this evening,’ Sara said. ‘I’m in Surrey. Tomorrow?’

Bennett huffed. ‘Ring me first thing in the morning,’ he

commanded. 'I'm not sure where I'll be, but I'll need you to come, wherever it is.'

Sara had no problem with that. Bennett thought she was offering answers to his questions. As it happened, she had some queries of her own. 'Wherever you say,' Sara said. 'I'll be there.'

A voice inside her head cackled.

Me too, it said.

Morven had spent some of the previous week trying to find Joseph Bennett. The day after she had purchased her supplies and pitched her tent on the Heath, she'd walked down to Regent's Park, and from there to Westminster. She knew this particular politician spent a lot of time at the Home Office – a huge glass-and-steel bunker of a building – and in the past Morven had also spied him across the street in a coffee shop. And, of course, old Joe also liked to lunch in the gardens next to the Palace of Westminster. Morven wondered whether he still did that, or if those benches now triggered too many unpleasant memories. Such caution would be justifiable. Morven had already decided that, if she saw him, she wouldn't waste the opportunity. She would stick her knife straight into his neck and be done with it. Morven knew such an act, especially in Central London, would be even more dangerous for her now. She should be more cautious of cameras than ever before. And yet, there were gazillions of them in London anyway, and she could only be so careful. She would have to rely on her changed appearance, and the guiding hand of Abaddon.

As it happened, Morven hadn't seen old Joe anywhere in Westminster. That hadn't surprised her; she wasn't sure how extensive his injuries were. But there was one place she knew he'd turn up eventually – and her tent was pitched very nearby…

When Sara got home, she discovered Ego's cat bed sitting in the middle of the living room. It was the same one she had fashioned as a makeshift cot for Cherub. Now, it held a new blanket Sara didn't recognise. Next to it was one of Ego's old bowls, filled with milk.

'Jamie?' she called.

'On the bed,' he sang.

Her excitement mounting, Sara shucked off her coat and bustled into the bedroom. Jamie lay propped against the headboard, a small dove-grey kitten stretched over his chest. Sara stopped and released a hard breath; her skin tingled with excitement.

'Jamie!' she gasped. 'You didn't!'

'What choice did I have?' he asked with a grin, and shook his wrist. The Rolex gleamed. 'I mean, after Valentine's Day.'

Not wanting to scare the kitten, Sara moved slowly to the bed and lay gently next to Jamie. She held out a finger and stroked its tiny head.

'Burmese,' Jamie said. 'I tried to get a brown one like Ego, but it's not easy to find Burmese kittens exactly when you want one. You've got to take what's available.'

'He's perfect,' Sara whispered. 'Is he a boy?'

'He is,' Jamie confirmed. He ran a hand gently over the kitten's fur. 'This colour's known as lilac. In the right light, the little guy looks almost pink.'

'When did you get him?'

'Today,' Jamie said. 'Had to drive to a breeder's place in Reading.'

The kitten yawned and stretched. Sara whispered hello, and began lavishing her new pet with heaps of unearned praise. He was the most beautiful, most clever, most wonderful cat in the world, she told him. 'Have you given him a name?' Sara asked.

'I wouldn't dare.' He smiled. 'After all, you're his mummy.'

Sara edged closer and rested her head on Jamie's shoulder. 'Would it be too awfully Freudian if I called him Id?'

Jamie chuckled, and the kitten rode the shuddering of his chest. 'What else would you call the successor to Ego?' he asked.

Sara nuzzled Jamie's cheek. He hadn't shaved. 'Thank you,' she said, and they kissed.

Jamie looked down at Id. The kitten stretched again and flexed his claws into his shirt. The sight was almost as amazing to her as when she'd seen her partner cuddle Cherub – perhaps more so. Jamie didn't dislike babies the way he did cats. Maybe he was maturing. Or maybe Id was just so adorable, he could melt the heart of even a cat-hating ex-police inspector.

Sara thought how surprising it always was, the way a pet could reduce the world to a comfortable pocket of intimate concerns. She had been staggering through the last few weeks, punch-drunk from a series of swift and sudden blows. She'd had contact with a killer for whom she could only feel kinship. She'd been manipulated by a politician from whom she needed to seek distance. And, perhaps worst of all, she had repeatedly suffered the violation of her own thoughts by… yes, by a psychic whom she could not begin to understand.

Little wonder she'd wanted a kitten.

'Since we seem to be taking big life decisions today,' Jamie said, 'I've thought of another.'

'Intriguing,' Sara said, stroking the dove-grey fur and causing Id to dig his claws deeper into Jamie's skin.

He shifted uncomfortably. 'I was just wondering… do you want to try for a baby?'

Sara's hand fell away from the kitten. She suddenness of the question, its sheer unexpectedness, left her uncertain of what to say. She decided upon, 'You'll need to put Id in his basket first.'

'I'm serious,' he said. 'You seemed to enjoy your time with Cherub, such as it was, and I thought…'

Sara moved up her hand and placed a finger on Jamie's lips. His offer was sweet, if not entirely unselfish. Sara had seen the way Jamie looked at Cherub. 'That's sweet,' she said, 'but no.'

'You don't want a baby?'

'It's the wrong time.'

'Is there a right time?' Jamie asked. Sara sensed she could see him deflate a little. 'If it's the investigation you're thinking about, remember – that won't last. By the time we–'

'That's not it,' Sara said. 'I'm opening a new practice. You know how draining that is. It's going to take all my time and energy.'

'OK, sure,' Jamie said, as though his suggestion was no big deal.

'And,' Sara went on, 'I've got to be honest – I don't know how I'd cope if I lost another one.'

'That was a fluke,' Jamie assured her.

Sara laughed in exasperation. 'I had no idea you were a doctor, too,' she said.

'All I'm saying is, we're still young enough,' he said. 'If you don't want a baby right now, fine. We'll wait. Just remember, there's still time.'

'I'm in my late thirties,' Sara pointed out. 'Once, that would have been considered over the hill, mothering-wise.'

Jamie shifted the kitten. It mewled unhappily. 'Not these days,' he said. 'You're still a spring chicken.'

Sara shuffled into a sitting position and relieved him of

Id. She cuddled the cat close to her neck. 'We'll revisit it,' she said, 'at some point in the future.'

'Sure,' Jamie said with a sad smile.

'In the meantime,' Sara concluded, 'I have this little man to look after.'

TWENTY-FOUR

It was late afternoon, and Morven sat in her tent, reading a magazine she'd bought at a newsagent's shop in Hampstead. She had the tent's flap open, and her legs protruding onto the small patch of lawn before her. She liked the way the grass tickled her bare feet.

From outside, Morven heard a voice. 'I see you solved your problem with Mother Edwina.'

Morven set the book aside and reached for the blade that lay next to her.

'No need for that, girl,' the voice said. 'It's only me.'

The woman with the blue-tipped afro appeared next to Morven's legs. She was on her hands and knees. 'Budge over.'

'Abaddon?' Morven said. She set aside the blade.

'Daniela will do,' she said as she crawled into the tent and sat beside Morven. 'How's your face?'

Morven's fingers brushed against the livid cut on her

cheek. 'Oh, yeah,' she said. 'This is just a scratch I got when–'

'I know exactly how you got it,' Daniela said. 'I asked how it was.'

Morven considered this, then poked the wound and winced. 'Healing,' she said.

'You putting anything on it?'

Morven smiled. 'Forest air,' she said.

Daniela grinned. For a moment, the two women sat silently together, gazing out of the tent flap at the bushes and heath pathways that spread before them. Morven was glad of the company. She wasn't sure why, but being with this woman felt awfully comfortable. Finally, Daniela spoke. 'What are you planning to do after you kill Bennett?' she asked.

Morven looked at her sharply, then shrugged. 'I guess it won't matter.'

'Of course it'll matter,' Daniela admonished. 'Because you matter. Hasn't anyone ever told you that before?'

As far as Morven could tell, her own expression had not changed. Still, somehow, Daniela seemed to have caught her pulse of irritation at the question. Daniela leaned away even before Morven said, 'I'm not some unloved little waif. My papa used to tell me how much I mattered all the time.'

'He was right,' Daniela said. She reached out and adjusted the errant collar of Morven's blouse. 'And because you matter, you can't let them catch you. You understand that, right?'

After a moment, Morven nodded.

'Are you clever enough to get away?'

Morven's forehead puckered uncertainly. 'Probably.'

'You'll need to decide on that very soon,' Daniela said. 'I've come to tell you that your wait is over.'

'What do you mean?'

'Your friend old Joe is going bird-watching this evening.'

'Here?'

Daniela nodded.

Morven shifted eagerly. 'Now?'

'Soon.'

'I didn't think he'd do anything till the weekend,' Morven said. 'I guessed he'd be recuperating. Or maybe in Parliament, or at the Home Office or something.'

'Normally, that would be true,' Daniela said. 'But this evening, he's going to need to let off some steam.'

Morven's knife lay beside her. She picked it up and ran her finger along the short blade. 'Why?'

Daniela's laughter chimed in the tent. 'Because in a moment,' she said, 'old Joe is going to have an experience that will upset him very, very much.'

Bennett had arranged to meet Sara in a pub near Parliament, on a site that had hosted a tavern since the thirteenth century. Its most recent incarnation – a landmark on that spot for over a hundred years – was a political watering hole in which Prime Ministers Churchill, Attlee, and Heath had all been regulars, as well as generations of journalists thirsty for beer and insider gossip. Sara had arrived before Bennett, ordered a Chardonnay, and taken a seat in a brown leather bucket chair. The chair, and everything that surrounded it, wouldn't have been out of place in a gentleman's club on Pall Mall. The place had an air of old-dufferdom: etched-glass windows, dark wood, green walls, chandeliers, and decades of political cartoons festooning the walls.

When Bennett arrived, Sara was surprised to see he was alone. He bought Sara another glass of wine as he ordered for himself, and joined her at the table. 'I thought you'd be with a security detail,' Sara said.

Bennett snorted long-sufferingly. 'When I was attacked, they gave me one,' he said. 'They insisted it was for my own protection. That lasted all of a few hours. Then I sent them away.'

'For heaven's sake, why?'

He waved a hand airily. 'Have you ever had a security detail?'

In fact, Sara had. She didn't bother to say that.

'It's so restrictive. They tell you what you can and can't do,' Bennett went on. 'When I have a moment to myself, I want to go where I want – and without being shadowed.'

'Like when you watch birds,' Sara suggested.

'Exactly,' Bennett agreed. At the mention of his favourite pastime, Bennett's lined face lit up. 'The weather has been incredible. I haven't had nearly enough opportunities to exploit it.'

After the chit-chat had run its course, Bennett drained his beer. His posture shifted and his tone became business-like. 'Now,' he said, 'tell me what happened at Edwina Koch's house.'

Sara offered Bennett an overview of her meeting with Lorna, and a description of the murder scene at The

Retreat. He listened with a dark countenance. When Sara had finished, he said soberly, 'And you're certain this Morven girl killed her?'

Sara grimaced in acknowledgement. 'There was a witness.'

'At one point,' Bennett said, 'I received unofficial intelligence that Morven had been killed herself.'

Sara's brows knitted. 'Where did you hear that?'

He waved his hand airily. 'Channels.'

Sara ignored his vagary. 'Was this information connected to the murders of Stewart Delaney and Edwina Koch's right-hand-man, Raymond Rojek?' she asked.

Bennett frowned. 'Not directly,' he said. His tone suggested he could say no more.

'Because there's no evidence Morven was ever at Mr Delaney's house.'

'I've read the reports,' he said in agreement.

Sara offered to get the next round, and used her time at the bar to put her thoughts in order. She had been dancing with this man for quite a while now. She decided to come to the point.

Once Sara had set his pint on the beer mat and sat down, she said, 'Here's what's puzzling me, Mr Bennett. Morven has attacked four people that we know of. She killed three of them. One of those was Edwina Koch, whose religious order she grew up in. We do not know her precise motives for doing this, but we can assume Morven blamed Mrs Koch for certain perceived injustices that have taken place in her life. We know that the other two fatalities – Mr Blackadar and Mr Sawyer – had both raped the girl on numerous occasions, and that this abuse began after the death of Morven's father. We have confirmation on all that from a witness at the farm.'

Sara sat back and stared directly at Bennett. 'That leaves only one victim with no explanation for the assault,' she said. 'And that's you.'

For a moment, Sara sensed a pulse of panic shoot through Joseph Bennett. Just as quickly, he stifled it. 'Surely, Dr Jones, we've solved that puzzle,' he said. 'Morven assaulted me after seeing me on television. As I'm the minister responsible for policing, she probably viewed me as the leader of an investigation that was going to apprehend her.'

Sara nodded as if his explanation were plausible. 'Had you ever met Morven before that?'

'Of course not.'

‘And what about Mother Edwina? Had you had any dealings with her?’

Bennett raised a single eyebrow as he took a pull on his beer. ‘You sound like a policewoman, Dr Jones,’ he said. ‘You’ve missed your calling.’ He set down the pint glass. ‘I believe I may have met Edwina Koch once when I was in the Department for the Environment, Food, and Rural Affairs. She was close to Mr Blackadar, a poultry producer in Dorset with whom I’d had several encounters. I believe I shook Mrs Koch’s hand at some function.’

‘And that’s all?’

His smile looked self-satisfied. ‘That’s all she wrote, I’m afraid.’

Sara looked at Joseph Bennett’s eyes, which gleamed both warily and smugly at the same time. Despite the potential danger he was in, Bennett seemed to be enjoying the game. He knew Sara had no solid evidence against him. Sara and Mir had spoken to Lorna, and Lorna had not incriminated him. From Bennett’s perspective, he was home and dry. Sara could question him all she wanted, but the Right Honourable Joseph Bennett MP would never admit to anything.

But Sara needed to know. She sensed strongly that

Bennett was the missing piece of Morven's story. The suspicion had grown forcefully for days. Now, it had built to an intolerable urge. Countermanding every rule she had set for herself over the last several months, Sara shot out her hand. She wrapped her fingers around Bennett's wrist.

'What are you doing?' Bennett cried.

Sara began to feel hazy. Her senses were being overwhelmed by wispy tendrils of Bennett's past.

'Let go of me,' he cried, and Sara tightened her grip. See saw a vague flash of a casually-dressed Bennett sitting with… with whom?

The Bennett from here-and-now began to sway. He, too, was overcome by the psychic blanket Sara had covered them with. 'Let… let go of me,' he repeated thickly. 'You can't…'

Before Bennett finished the sentence, Sara could no longer feel his presence – or indeed her own – in the pub. She was in Dorset, a disembodied visitor, hovering over a scene that had taken place one warm evening, a few years before.

Joe's spending the weekend on the farm. He and his new acquaintance Greg are on the back deck, drinking beer and sharing a joint. It's the first time the MP has been here to Dorset to pass time with his newest friend. They'd met over a shared concern for poultry exports – right now, Joe's a Parliamentary Under-Secretary in the Department for the Environment, Food, and Rural Affairs. As for Greg, he sells a lot of broilers to the Netherlands. Some to Ireland, too. But tonight, there's not a whit of business talk. And Joe doesn't look much like a minister, either – not like when he's roaming the halls of power. Joe's off-duty now, barefoot, wearing a chain store polo shirt and short trousers. Truth be told, Joe is feeling rather magnificent; the weed – grown a few hundred yards away, right here on the farm – makes him feel like he's blasting through hyperspace. Another beer arrives every quarter-hour, served by a pretty girl in her mid-to-late teens. She has red hair and a slight Scottish accent, even though Greg says she's never been to Scotland. She learned to talk that way by copying her father.

'Where's the padre now?' Joe asks.

'Died,' Greg says. 'A month or so ago, poor bugger.'

Joe's watching Morven's arse as she takes the empty tins back into the house. 'Sad,' he mutters.

Greg agrees – it is sad. He sizes up Joe and asks slyly,

'You want to go console her?'

Sara fluttered open her eyes. She noticed her hand still gripping Bennett's wrist. Bennett himself looked like any punter who'd had one-too-many – blurry, wavering, red-faced angry. He tried to speak – his lips moved, but a thick slurring was all Sara could hear.

Her own head grew heavy again.

It pitched forward – and the location shifted.

It is the same night, and Sara finds herself in a boxy bedroom at the top of the farmhouse. She hovers over Morven, who reads a book, snatching time away from Greg and his brunette-dyed buddy before she needs to go to the kitchen and fetch more beer. Without notice, her door opens, and Sara's perspective changes. She sees the room through Morven's eyes. She is Morven. And at the door, it's Greg, telling her she should be a good girl. Greg tugs the book from her fingers, and picks up the bookmark. He saves her page before setting the book on the dresser. The older man with the dye job eases in, smiling. Greg makes a gesture – somewhere between 'there she is' *and* 'ta-dah!' *Then he leaves. Dye-job, his voice husky, tells Morven they're going to become very good friends. 'What do you mean?' Morven asks, and Bennett begins to remove his clothing...*

No! Sara thought. She would not experience this. She did not want to feel Morven being raped by this man. That gruesome re-visitation would not provide any answers. Her head swam as she tried to levitate from Morven's body, to rise above this situation. Sara could not tell what her actual body was doing back in the bar, but here, in this bodiless space, she could feel herself lurch, like a seasick sailor on the roiling waves.

And suddenly, she was in another time.

It's a few weeks later, and Joe's back in Dorset. Greg jokes that he must like the air down here. But Greg's no fool – he knows what's what, and he's made certain Morven's ready. No beer this time. No joint. That can all come later. Joe's directed to a guest bedroom and that black-haired scarecrow of a woman delivers the teen in nothing but a thin cotton dressing gown. One of her small breasts pokes from the parting. Joe really likes this girl. The first time they were together, she'd played the blushing virgin. The girl had told him only Greg had ever done that to her before. That may or may not have been true – but she was funny and good-natured and really not a bad fuck at all. Worth coming back for. And Joe knows Greg's got this kid wrapped around his little finger. She's pliable, and available, and she's not going anywhere...

In a shifting kaleidoscope of visions, Sara sensed other moments, other moods. She witnessed the time Joe found out Greg had been giving Morven to a couple of his other guests as well. That hadn't sat well with an important man like Joe, and for a time Sara watched the men argue. But soon they'd made up over a beer and a joint and the ministrations of Morven – both of them, together. Sara saw a time, perhaps a year on, when Bennett had become Minister for Policing. Greg was paying him even more attention than before. Bennett lapped up all that fawning, but Sara could feel his even-deeper emotions. If the shit ever hit the fan, Bennett thought, there would be little he'd actually be able to do for this chicken farmer. Indeed, even at a distance, Bennett was well aware how far that shit might fling – Greg was a drug supplier, albeit a small-time one, and they made dangerous contacts. But Joe understood how deep in he already was. Far, far too deep. Greg's guru, that old crone cult leader, knew all about him and his clandestine visits to Dorset. The one they called Mother carried such knowledge with shrewd menace, knowing that a Minister of State with a secret might just be a useful ally. But, for Bennett, the perks of the relationship remained as alluring as the most addictive drug. And they were still on tap, whenever he had the time. Occasionally, Greg would even bring Morven to London with him. Sometimes, Bennett had her right there inside the fellow's Kensington pied-a-terre. Bennett assured himself that he tried to be a considerate lover. He was never cruel, and once in a while, Sara could hear him think, Morven even liked it.

Plunging so deeply she could no longer remember the pub in which she sat, Sara finally found the decisive moment – the memory that explained everything. She saw Bennett once more – but now he was in his full politician's suit, behind a desk and hissing into his phone.

'I've only got your word for it,' Joe whispers violently into the landline's mouthpiece. 'The way you whore that girl out, it could be anyone's. Lorna tells me everything, you know. It could be that actor's. You've let him fuck her

enough. It could belong to that other fellow you do business with. Most probably, the child is yours.'

'The calendar doesn't lie, mate,' Greg says calmly. 'I know when you saw her last.'

'I've only got your word,' Joe repeats.

'Don't worry, Minister' Greg says. The word minister *comes out like a threat. 'Nobody wants anything from you.'*

'I'm not saying you're lying about the child,' Joe replies, his tone more ingratiating now, 'but you could be mistaken, that's all.'

Greg hums with equanimity – I could be, but it's not likely. *'When she delivers, my doctor friend could do a paternity test if you'd like,' Greg offers. 'Then you'd know for sure.'*

'Jesus!' Joe hisses. 'Your doctor friend. Is he fucking her, too?'

Greg laughs merrily. 'No, mate,' he says, 'not recently.'

And suddenly, lights spangled. The conversation before Sara dimmed, and was replaced by a tear-clouded, skew-whiff vision of the pub. Sara's head lolled on the small round table. Her cheek pressed against a patch sticky with beer. She could feel her heart palpating wildly. Her breath came in short gasps, and her lungs juddered.

Sara experimented with moving her hands, and noticed she'd let go of Bennett's wrist. She lifted her head and leaned back until she was upright. She groped for a napkin. Sara tried to speak, but couldn't direct breath through her larynx. Frustration pulsed inside her – she needed to tell Bennett what tremendous danger he was in. As Sara wiped her face, she saw a few drinkers looking her way, concerned. Bennett was making facial gestures their way. *What can I do? She's drunk.*

Once Sara had righted herself, Bennett adopted a look of pleasant condescension. It was a smokescreen for anyone still observing them; his voice was less controlled as he whispered, 'Jesus, what was that? Are you an epileptic? A diabetic? What are you, for fuck's sake?'

'You're the father,' she said.

'What?'

'You raped the girl, just like all the others.'

Sara watched Bennett's expression shift quickly to fear – and from there, to fury. 'What the hell are you talking about?' he demanded.

'Blackadar, Sawyer, Delaney, that doctor – God knows if there were others – they all had her,' Sara said. 'But only you managed to get her pregnant.'

'Keep your voice down,' Bennett hissed.

'But you can't admit that,' she continued, 'because then, you'd have to admit to rape. That's why you've been following the investigation so closely.' Sara glanced around the pub. 'I'm guessing it's why you don't have a security detail with you, either. You'd rather Morven kill you than see her arrested. Because, then, the truth would come out.' She smiled woozily at him. 'Everyone would know.'

'You're a fantasist,' Bennett said. 'This is a story you've made up. If you had any evidence, you'd be showing it to me.'

Sara forced herself to breathe deeply. 'We have Cherub,' she said. 'He's the best evidence we could present to a court of law. I wonder what a DNA test would reveal?'

'That's it,' Bennett said. He stood so quickly his leather chair shrieked on the wooden floorboards. 'I'm not indulging your fantasies any longer. Don't ever try to speak to me again.'

'She's going to kill you,' Sara said. 'You know that.'

'Leave me alone,' Bennett said, and walked with undignified haste from the pub.

TWENTY-FIVE

'What's the matter?' Jamie asked. Their new kitten, Id, stretched in his lap. He lay a reassuring hand on his elongated body. 'You haven't been yourself since you got home.'

Sara had been back in Brixton for less than half an hour. She had spent those few minutes bustling through the flat, absent-mindedly doing household chores: angrily sweeping the kitchen counter with a dishcloth, shunting objects from tables to drawers, energetically plumping pillows. All the while, she'd been thinking about Joseph Bennett. She'd cycled through the usual tropes about abuse of power, sexual violence, and especially the banality of evil. For years, the Minister for Policing had worn his power suits and hand-shaken his way through the upper reaches of British privilege. Then, when he needed a bit of me-time stronger than ornithology, he would drive to Dorset. There, he'd get high with a mate and rape an enslaved teenager.

Afterwards, he would return to Westminster with bland confidence in his own untouchability.

'I've been thinking about Morven,' Sara replied. 'I'm so worried she'll be caught and sent to prison.'

'Isn't that what you're doing this for?' Jamie asked. 'To catch her?'

'Yes, to catch her,' Sara agreed pointedly. 'But this girl needs treatment, not punishment. A prison sentence is not the same as justice. She's done what she's done because of a lifetime of abuse.'

Jamie pursed his lips. 'Let's be fair,' he said. 'You've suffered throughout your life, too, and you didn't go around killing people.'

Sara snorted. Somewhere at the back of her mind, she knew she should find the statement ironic. Either she was too upset for that, or too used to living a double life. 'If I had been through what Morven's been through,' she said, 'I'd probably go after the bastards as well. Maybe it's because I've led the life I have that I can empathise with the girl.'

She swept up the previous day's copy of *The Guardian* and dumped it into a waste bin. 'Besides,' she added, 'I know what waits for her in the criminal justice system, and it's not going to be fair. Not by a long shot.'

It wasn't just the knowledge of Bennett's misdeeds that had shaken Sara. It was fact that she'd experienced the assaults from both perspectives – from Bennett's point of view and from Morven's. For those brief moments, she had become both the abuser and the abused. As for Sara's mistrust of her own psychic visions, Bennett's reaction had all-but-confirmed the reality of what she'd seen.

Jamie nodded placatingly and glanced noncommittally at his phone. He knew better than to engage Sara when she was in a mood like this.

She moved into the bedroom. She'd been meaning to wash the bedsheets for a week. Sara unbuttoned the bottom of the duvet cover and began angrily stripping it off. What had the use of her psychic powers brought her? Was she able to help the girl in any way? Using her powers was exactly what that new wrinkle in her life, Daniela Atta, had urged her to do. Had Sara envisioned all that Daniela had intended? And why had she wanted it?

Suddenly, in her mind, Sara heard Daniela's voice.

You can't let them catch you.

Sara stopped, duvet cover in hand. She tilted her head, focused, and heard Daniela again.

Are you clever enough to get away? she said.

Slowly, images started to form. At first, they were just a series of shapes – a plane of green, brown lines jutting perpendicular to it. Sara's head grew heavy. She shook it rapidly to avoid succumbing twice in a single day. The tactic proved to be of little use. She set down the linen and leaned forward until her knees rested on the mattress. The shapes solidified – into grass, barren trees, pathways. Immediately, Sara knew where she was. This was Hampstead Heath – not far from the area where she'd met Bennett. She felt herself collapse forwards until her body had sprawled across the bed. Sara's mind, however, was hovering above a camping tent set back from one of the paths near the Heath's bathing ponds. In a flash, she was inside its vinyl interior, inches away from Morven. Sara could feel herself – the self on the bed – gasp. This had happened recently! She was witnessing the events of earlier today. Sara watched Morven shrug in response to Daniela's question about escape.

That was when Sara realised Daniela was inside the tent, too. As soon as she understood that, she could see the woman clearly.

I've come to tell you that your wait is over, Daniela

said. *Your friend old Joe is going bird-watching this evening.*

Gasping, Sara awoke in a swirl of thought-storms. When had Daniela first contacted Morven? Had she been guiding her in these murders all the time? And Bennett – Sara had just been with him in the pub. Was it likely he'd go bird-watching *now*? *Possibly*, Sara thought. Tramping through the Heath was Bennett's release, after all – a way to take his mind off whatever troubles plagued him. And Sara's words had plagued him with a lot of troubles.

Even as she had these thoughts, Sara got an image of Bennett in his olive waxed jacket and boonie hat, scouting for woodcocks. Then, Sara saw Morven appear from a thicket with a knife in her hand. Sara began to hyperventilate. Her mouth grew dry, her vision sparkled. She shoved herself to a sitting position. What she'd just seen was new. That part hadn't happened yet… but it was about to. Sara forced herself to stand. She had to get to Hampstead Heath. Morven was there right now – and Bennett would be soon. She lurched into the living room and grabbed her Burberry coat from the rack.

'Where are you going?' Jamie asked.

'Morven,' Sara said. 'The Heath – she's there. And

Bennett, he's going to–' She searched for her medical bag and picked it up. 'Going to – never mind. I've got to go.' Sara picked up her car keys and flung open the door.

Jamie leapt up. 'Whoa,' he said, 'wait a moment.' He moved to her and lay a firm hand on her arm. 'How do you know this? What's happening?'

Sara jerked her arm, flinging away his hand. 'I've got to stop her,' she said.

'Do you want me to call Ceri and Adeela?' Jamie asked. Sara hustled into the hallway, Jamie watching her from behind. As she raced for her car, he leapt back into the living room to find his phone.

Sara passed the rail station on South End Road where she'd met Bennett only a few weeks ago. Cars lined both sides of the street. There were no parking spaces. On the wide expanse where South End met Keats Grove, Sara jerked the wheel and mounted the pavement, abandoning the car next to a low brick wall. She dashed across the street to the paved path on the edge of the Heath. Sara stopped, steadying herself with a hand on the trunk of a tree. She focused and tried to tune in to Morven. Immediately, she was assailed by a rush of fear that told her she was almost too late. Sara turned to the left instinctively and ran.

This part of the Heath was wide and barren, with grassy leas and broad walkways of crumbling tarmac. With her medical bag bouncing against her thigh, Sara dashed past several clusters of people. They strolled in the opposite direction, moving towards Hampstead from the smaller paths that cut through woodier groves. If Morven were pursuing Bennett, those thickets of trees were where they'd both be. But which area specifically?

Her vision blurred by speed and bounce, Sara searched to find a landmark common to the scenes she'd witnessed only an hour before in Brixton. She recalled glimpsing a woody area where paths converged. Sara knew she could simply head towards the place Bennett had taken her last, but there was no guarantee that was where he'd be.

Sara forced herself to slow. She came to a large car park at a trot. Gasping, she stopped and let her back press against a post and rail fence. *A car park*, she thought with a mental snort… part of her mind admonished her for not having thought to drive the car here. *I'll remember next time I chase a teenage killer through Hampstead Heath*, she told herself grimly.

Sara's lungs burned and her face pounded. A bird's eye

view – that's what she needed. She fought to control her breathing. Commanded herself to focus. Mumbling a set of random coordinates, Sara focused on Joseph Bennett. In her mind's eye, she rose from her body and hovered above the car park.

From that vantage, she could see two bathing ponds. They lay immediately to her right, bisected by a bridge. The trees were thicker on the bridge's other side. Mentally, Sara swooped down to one of the paths – and witnessed Bennett wandering leisurely, binoculars in hand. It was an image identical to the one she'd been assailed by in her bedroom. The one addition was that now, Sara could sense Bennett's thoughts – and they did not match the idyllic image he projected. He was fretting about Sara. The more he tried to drive her accusations from his mind, the more anxious he grew. Sara had used the word *rape*, he thought. She'd accused him of fathering Cherub. Bennett searched his every stray experience to find a way to stop a DNA test.

Bennett was interrupted by footsteps advancing behind him. He turned to see Morven approaching.

In her hand, she brandished a knife.

This is happening now, Sara thought. *I'm too late*.

Bennett began to speak, but halted mid-word as Morven

slapped the binoculars from his hand. They fell to the path with a small thud. *Heya, Joe*, she said with a wide grin. Morven grasped his arm. *Cherub sends his love*, she went on. *Did you know he's got a new mummy and daddy now? You'd like them.*

Bennett tried to jerk away, but the girl was strong. Her grip on his arm tightened. *In fact, I'm pretty sure you know the mummy…*

Morven kept speaking, all friendly and chatty, as she tugged him into the trees. Bennett squirmed and fought.

Sara shook herself awake and gasped a deep lung-full of breath. She got her bearings. The bridge was up and to the right. Forcing her reluctant body to move again at speed, she ran.

Once Sara had crossed the bridge, it became obvious which way to turn. She'd been here in her mind only moments before. She went left, and came upon a pair of pricey binoculars lying in the dirt. To Sara's right was a small thicket of trees, dividing the path from a grassy camping area.

Pressed against one of the trees was Bennett. Morven nestled against his body, entwined as close as a lover.

'Just like old times, don't you think, Joe?' Sara heard

her ask.

Morven had her knife pressed against his jugular vein.

Sara froze. She crouched low and eased open her medical bag. As quietly as possible, she groped inside and withdrew the syringe of pentobarbital. It was a strong barbiturate, guaranteed to sedate even the largest assailant. Morven might have been strong for her size, but she wasn't all that big. If Sara couldn't stop the girl with words alone, she could drop her with this ampoule of liquid sleep. She set aside her bag and rose, stepping through foliage, silently towards Morven.

Bennett saw her first. 'Dr Jones!' he screamed. 'Stop this crazy bitch!'

Sara grimaced at the man's stupidity. Morven kept the knife pressed against Bennett's throat, but swivelled her head to see Sara. 'Well, look at you,' she said. 'You're like a visit from the angels themselves.'

'It's good to see you again,' Sara said. She had meant to sound soothing, but her voice was thin and strained. 'Why don't you take away the knife so there are no accidents? Then we'll talk, OK?'

Morven's leather jacket rose and fell as she shrugged her bony shoulders. 'I can talk like this,' she said. 'How's

Cherub?'

'You have the baby?' croaked Bennett.

'He's good,' Sara said.

'Is he still eating like a pig?' Morven chortled.

Sara forced a laugh. 'He certainly does like his food.'

'He sure does,' Morven agreed. 'Have you offered him a Hob Nob yet?'

Bennett seized the opportunity to jerk sideways and try to roll to the ground. Morven's knee rose swiftly and struck between his legs. At the same time, the knife bit into his neck and he shrieked. Blood tricked onto the collar of his waxed jacket. 'Naughty!' Morven cried.

'Morven, look at me,' Sara commanded. 'Focus over here.'

'In a minute,' the girl said distractedly. 'I've got to punish old Joe first. He was bad.' She looked up at Bennett's bleeding neck. 'What'll it be, Joe?' she asked. 'Think I should take out one of your eyes?'

Before Morven could act, Sara strode forwards and pressed the syringe against the girl's neck.

'Ow!' Morven yelped. 'What's that?'

'It's a sleeping potion,' Sara told her. 'I don't want to inject you with it. It doesn't feel nice when you wake up.

But, Morven, listen to me – I'll do it if I have to. Please, just drop the knife.'

'I've got a better idea,' Morven said. 'Let's make this into a game. See if you can put me to sleep before I cut old Joe's jugular vein.' She chortled. 'I'm betting you can't.'

She pressed the blade more forcefully against Bennett's neck.

'I'll show you pictures of Cherub,' Sara fibbed. 'I have some on my phone. He looks so cute.'

'I would like to see them,' said Morven with genuine yearning. 'Hold your phone in front of me.'

'Not until you drop the knife,' Sara said.

'Please,' Morven said.

'If you drop the knife, I'll take away the syringe,' Sara said. 'We'll let Mr Bennett go. Then I'll show you photos of your baby. In fact, my car is just down the road. We could even go see Cherub.'

Morven looked behind her, directly into Sara's eyes. Her own gaze revealed confusion as she negotiated her conflicting desires.

'You'd like that, wouldn't you, Morven?'

'Yes,' the girl breathed. Tears formed at the corners of her eyes.

Suddenly, a voice sounded from the grassy camp site. 'Dr Jones is lying,' it called.

Both Sara and Morven looked over. Walking towards them, her bright athletic wear darkened by the setting sun, was Daniela Atta. 'Dr Jones doesn't even have Cherub anymore,' Daniela told Morven languidly. 'She's given him up to Social Services.'

Morven waivered. 'Is that true?' she asked Sara.

Bennett's resilience had run dry. He started to blubber. 'Oh, God, please,' he said, 'just let me go. Morven, I apologise if I've hurt you, but please–'

'You shut up,' Daniela told him, and his words dissolved into wracking sobs.

'Is it true?' Morven repeated.

'Yes,' Sara said. 'I don't have your baby anymore. It was best for him.'

'But...' the girl stammered, 'but you lied to me.'

'To stop you from doing something awful,' Sara said. 'You've killed enough people, Morven. It's time to end this.'

Daniela was right beside them now. The four of them stood clustered next to the tree, a tableau of intersecting threats.

'If you drop the knife,' Sara continued, 'I'll work for you, I promise. You need psychiatric care. Everyone will understand what you've been through. They'll let me help you.' Sara hardened her tone. 'But if you kill Mr Bennett,' she went on, 'they'll stop me from ever seeing you again. You'll go to prison, and I won't be able to intervene. Do you understand?'

Morven's breath wavered. She looked at Daniela. Daniela held her gaze firmly. 'Dr Jones is right,' she told Morven. 'If you get yourself into the hands of the authorities, you're toast.' She looked at Sara and grinned mirthlessly. 'After all, a prison sentence is not the same as justice… is it, Dr Jones?'

Sara ignored the provocation and waited expectantly.

'Here's what we're going to do,' Daniela said to Morven. 'Dr Jones is going to take away that nasty needle from your neck, and you're going to give me the knife.'

Sara could feel the breath of psychic calm that Daniela blew gently into Morven's mind. Sara saw the girl soften. 'That's right,' Daniela cooed. 'Nice and gentle now.'

Daniela looked to Sara and said, 'Throw that syringe into the bushes. You don't need it anymore.'

Sara hesitated. She did not trust her fellow psychic, and

would not surrender her only weapon. Instead, she ostentatiously pulled the needle away from Morven's neck and took a small step backwards.

'That'll do,' Daniela said. 'Now, Morven… I'm going to take the blade from you, OK?' Morven's head twitched uncertainly. 'Do you trust me?' Daniela asked.

The girl nodded shallowly. Daniela reached a hand slowly to the knife's handle. 'I'll hold it in place,' she said. 'You step over there.' She angled her head towards a clearing at the entrance to the camp site.

Morven relinquished the knife and eased between Daniela and Sara, moving to the patch of grass.

'Good,' said Daniela. 'Now, here's what's going to happen next. I'm taking charge of Morven.' With the knife still pressed to Bennett's throat, Daniela called out, 'Did you hear that, babe? You're coming with me. I won't let them arrest you. I'll take care of you.'

'Please,' Bennett rasped. 'Can you release me now?'

'I believe,' Daniela replied, 'I told you to shut up.'

In the distance, Sara heard the wail of police sirens. It was almost certainly an armed response vehicle. That meant Jamie had rung Mir.

Daniela shifted so she could see Sara. 'In a minute,

Morven and I will leave,' she said. 'Tell your police friends they won't find us. I guarantee it. But *you'll* see me again. You and I have interests in common.'

'OK,' Sara said in as steady a voice as she could summon. She found she was almost pleased that Daniela wanted to spirit away Morven. The sirens were getting closer, and Sara did not trust an armed response unit to understand that the girl posed them no threat. 'Just go.'

Daniela bit her lip thoughtfully. 'You know the one big mistake you made?' she asked.

'No,' Sara said.

'You identified with this girl too much. You heard the story of her troubled life and thought, '*Hey, I had a troubled life, too. Morven must be the same as me!*''

Daniela shook her head at the sheer folly of human empathy. 'But you were mistaken,' she said.

Sara could think of no response. She gawped dumbly.

'You got the wrong end of the stick, that's all,' Daniela assured her. 'You are not like this girl in any way.'

Across the bridge, the police sirens had reached the car park. With one swift plunge, Daniela Atta thrust the knife into Joseph Bennett's neck. Bennett yelped, then gurgled. His severed vein jetted darkly and he dropped to the ground.

Sticky with his blood, Daniela stepped over Bennett's body and backed away. She took Morven's elbow, and the girl looked at her trustingly. Daniela shook her arm reassuringly, but kept her eyes on Sara.

She smiled. 'Know who you're like?' she asked, then shrugged. 'I think you can guess.'

Bowing cordially, Daniela Atta concluded, 'You, Dr Sara Jones, are just like me.'

EPILOGUE

Cara had grown used to answering questions. She'd been interviewed by the police and badgered by reporters. Of the two, the news people were worse. They had banged on the door non-stop, ever since she'd been allowed to return to The Retreat.

The day they found Mother's body, Surrey police had told Cara she'd need to leave the house for a while. The property was a crime scene, they'd explained, and their experts needed… Cara couldn't really remember what they'd said, but they needed to do whatever experts did. The bottom line was, she couldn't stay while they worked. The police had asked Cara if she had any relatives she could visit for a while. She'd said she had none.

What about friends?

She'd shrugged – no friends, either.

Someone got the idea that Cara should go back and live on the farm. Just as with The Retreat, they'd said, nothing would change there until the legal mess surrounding The Supplicants of Dusk was sorted out. The thought of being with Lorna again had made Cara cry so hard they never mentioned it again.

Finally, the police had just stuck her in a Weybridge hotel. Cara was allowed to pack a case, and she'd been sure to squirrel away her secret wad of banknotes. She didn't want anyone to find that. She no longer had the pay-as-you-go phone – when she'd admitted to calling Morven, she'd had to give it up.

Cara was unused to hotels and, at first, the anonymous sterility of the place was a tad unsettling. She had never seen soap that small. Really, Cara only came to enjoy being there after a couple of days. Once she had learned to go with the flow, she could see the attraction of hotel living. If she left her towels on the bathroom floor, the maids would give her fresh ones, even if they weren't dirty. It had been nice not being the maid for once. But just as she'd decided she could stay there happily for years, the police told her she was free to go back to The Retreat. Now she had to wash her own towels again.

The police left her alone these days, with the understanding she'd need to testify in court once Morven had been caught.

Reporters hadn't lost interest so quickly, though. At first, Cara would talk to them whenever they knocked, day or night. She'd found it scary and exhilarating at the same time. Going out to the newsagents had become an amazing thing – there, in actual tabloids, was her name and photo. She'd even been on television. But there were just so many news people in the world, and only one Cara. They knocked and rang the bell and shouted at the windows much too often, and they asked her things she didn't know about. They wanted to know what was going to happen to The Retreat, and who'd end up with all the money, and where Cara would go once the place had been sold.

Cara couldn't answer any of those questions – especially the ones about her future.

That was why, today, she hadn't answered the doorbell immediately. She did what she'd grown accustomed to doing, and tip-toed into the first-floor room Mother had used as an office. From that window, Cara could see who she was trying to avoid.

Down below stood a tall, dark-skinned woman with a big, blue-tipped afro. Next to her was… Cara had to stare for a minute, down at the black leather jacket and the stubbled head, to realise it was true – *it was Morven*! She'd released an ecstatic shriek and ran down the steps to the hallway so fast she almost stumbled.

She'd flung open one of the double doors and embraced Morven with an excited bear hug. Her friend had not resisted exactly, but she hadn't hugged back either. She simply stayed limp in Cara's arms.

When Cara released her, Morven looked at her earnestly and said, 'Hello. My friend here says I know you.'

'It's a bit hard to explain,' the woman with the blue afro said. 'Morven's been through some stuff. You know all about that.'

The woman took a drink from the glass of squash Cara had served. Mother had never let Cara buy squash, but now she was responsible for her own meals. The kitchen was newly filled with soft drinks and Oreo cookies and Lucky Charms cereal. The three women sat in the conservatory – once a place Cara had only been allowed in to clean.

'I don't remember much,' Morven said haltingly. She looked languidly through the conservatory's window, over the lawn, and to the Thames beyond. She showed no recognition. 'Daniela tells me it's for the best.'

‘It sure is,’ Daniela agreed. Quietly, she nodded in the direction of Morven’s gaze, adding, ‘And I’d appreciate it if you didn’t remind her of anything unpleasant.’

‘But how?’ Cara asked. ‘How did you…?’

‘Like I said, it’s complicated.’

Cara took a small sip of squash. She licked her lips in troubled thought. Finally, she said, ‘Did you… I mean, was it you who…?’

‘Took away Morven’s hurt?’

‘I guess so, yeah.’

‘No – not me,’ Daniela said, and then chuckled. ‘That stuff’s way beyond my pay grade.’

‘Then, how?’

Daniela waved a hand. ‘I know people.’

‘Daniela says we’re going away,’ Morven told Cara. ‘In a car. I’m going to help her do things.’

‘Help her do what?’ Cara asked.

Morven shrugged.

‘We’re going to have some big adventures,’ Daniela said. ‘There are lots of things that need doing out there. And some of us – I’m one of them – have the skills.’

Daniela reached over and rubbed Morven’s hair. It was starting to grow out. ‘Usually, people like me do these things alone,' she said. 'But then, I noticed this girl here, and knew she might be useful. I've seen with my own eyes that she's not bad in a crisis.'

The woman took another pull on her squash. 'And to top it all off, she needed me.'

Cara nodded, not really understanding.

'What about you?' Daniela asked. 'Are you good in a crisis?'

'I don't know,' Cara said sincerely.

Daniela grinned. 'I've got this hunch you could be.' She glanced around the glass-walled room. 'And they're not going to let you stay in this cult house a whole lot longer.' She drew in a deep breath that spoke of possibilities. 'Where else have you got to go?'

Cara snorted. 'Nowhere.'

'Then, that settles it,' Daniela said, setting down her glass. 'The car's not comfortable, but it's outside.'

She fixed the girl with a hypnotic stare. 'You want to come along?'

DEAD IN TIME

Terence Bailey

When successful London psychiatrist Sara Jones's relationship breaks down, she returns to the remote part of Wales she grew up in, keen to clear her head and start afresh.

But soon her former boyfriend, Metropolitan Police detective Jamie Harding, is back in her life – investigating a series of murders with links to the occult…